She wanted him to stay.

For the first time in her life she actually wanted a man to stay.

"Would you like some coffee?" she asked in a rush as he prepared to leave.

Hugh smiled, and she was struck by the warmth of that simple expression. "Thanks, but I drank four cups at Maude's. Tell you what. Promise to have lunch with me tomorrow and we'll call it even, okay?"

She couldn't say no. The word absolutely refused to come to her lips. "All right," she heard herself say.

"One o'clock?"

"That's fine."

Then he walked out into the night and left Anna alone with the realization that she had just made a date with a man.

She, Anna Fleming, had made the first date of her entire life.

D0424161

Dear Reader,

This is it, the final month of our wonderful three-month celebration of Intimate Moments' fifteenth anniversary. It's been quite a ride, but it's not over yet. For one thing, look who's leading off the month: Rachel Lee, with *Cowboy Comes Home,* the latest fabulous title in her irresistible CONARD COUNTY miniseries. This one has everything you could possibly want in a book, including all the deep emotion Rachel is known for. Don't miss it.

And the rest of the month lives up to that wonderful beginning, with books from both old favorites and new names sure to become favorites. Merline Lovelace's *Return to Sender* will have you longing to work at the post office (I'm not kidding!), while Marilyn Tracy returns to the wonderful (but fictional, darn it!) town of Almost, Texas, with *Almost Remembered.* Look for our TRY TO REMEMBER flash to guide you to Leann Harris's *Trusting a Texan,* a terrific amnesia book, and the EXPECTANTLY YOURS flash marking Raina Lynn's second book, *Partners in Parenthood.* And finally, don't miss *A Hard-Hearted Man,* by brand-new author Melanie Craft. *Your* heart will melt—guaranteed.

And that's not all. Because we're not stopping with the fifteen years behind us. There are that many—and more!—in our future, and I know you'll want to be here for every one. So come back next month, when the excitement and the passion continue, right here in Silhouette Intimate Moments.

Yours,

Leslie J. Wainger
Executive Senior Editor

Please address questions and book requests to:
Silhouette Reader Service
U.S.: 3010 Walden Ave., P.O. Box 1325, Buffalo, NY 14269
Canadian: P.O. Box 609, Fort Erie, Ont. L2A 5X3

RACHEL LEE

COWBOY COMES HOME

Silhouette®
INTIMATE™ MOMENTS®
Published by Silhouette Books
America's Publisher of Contemporary Romance

If you purchased this book without a cover you should be aware that this book is stolen property. It was reported as "unsold and destroyed" to the publisher, and neither the author nor the publisher has received any payment for this "stripped book."

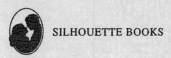

SILHOUETTE BOOKS

ISBN 0-373-07865-X

COWBOY COMES HOME

Copyright © 1998 by Susan Civil-Brown

All rights reserved. Except for use in any review, the reproduction or utilization of this work in whole or in part in any form by any electronic, mechanical or other means, now known or hereafter invented, including xerography, photocopying and recording, or in any information storage or retrieval system, is forbidden without the written permission of the editorial office, Silhouette Books, 300 East 42nd Street, New York, NY 10017 U.S.A.

All characters in this book have no existence outside the imagination of the author and have no relation whatsoever to anyone bearing the same name or names. They are not even distantly inspired by any individual known or unknown to the author, and all incidents are pure invention.

This edition published by arrangement with Harlequin Books S.A.

® and TM are trademarks of Harlequin Books S.A., used under license. Trademarks indicated with ® are registered in the United States Patent and Trademark Office, the Canadian Trade Marks Office and in other countries.

Printed in U.S.A.

Books by Rachel Lee

Silhouette Intimate Moments

An Officer and a Gentleman #370
Serious Risks #394
Defying Gravity #430
**Exile's End* #449
**Cherokee Thunder* #463
**Miss Emmaline and the Archangel* #482
**Ironheart* #494
**Lost Warriors* #535
**Point of No Return* #566
**A Question of Justice* #613
**Nighthawk* #781
**Cowboy Comes Home* #865

* Conard County

Silhouette Shadows

Imminent Thunder #10
**Thunder Mountain* #37

Silhouette Books

A Conard County Reckoning

Montana Mavericks
Cowboy Cop #12

Silhouette Shadows Short Story Collection 1994

"The Ancient One"

RACHEL LEE

wrote her first play in the third grade for a school assembly, and by the age of twelve she was hooked on writing. She's lived all over the United States, on both the East and West coasts, and now resides in Florida.

Having held jobs as a security officer, real estate agent and optician, she uses these experiences, as well as her natural flair for creativity, to write stories that are undeniably romantic. "After all, life is the biggest romantic adventure of all—and if you're open and aware, the most marvelous things are just waiting to be discovered."

For the little girls who taught me
that home is not always the safe place it should be.

May you all find a home that is.

Chapter 1

Anna Fleming was sure no one could see her.

She stood in the back of Good Shepherd Church in a dimly lit corner and watched the wedding ceremony. It was everything she had ever dreamed of for herself and the embodiment of all the dreams she had lost. A sad little sigh escaped her, but almost at once she lifted her chin and reminded herself not to wallow. It was always wiser to count one's blessings.

She was a mousy woman, small and bland looking in a shapeless brown dress and sensible shoes. Her dark hair was drawn back severely, and her wide brown eyes peered at the world from behind gold-rimmed glasses. Those glasses were the most flamboyant part of her apparel, but they were nothing out of the ordinary.

And that was how she liked it, she told herself as she watched Sheriff Tate's daughter marry the policeman from Los Angeles. No one noticed her, no one at all, and in her invisibility and anonymity, she found the only safety she had ever known.

Reverend Fromberg, a gentle man in his late forties, read the vows in a sonorous voice that reached the back of the church without difficulty. Anna listened to the words and wondered what it would be like to trust someone enough to make those promises. She couldn't imagine it. Trust, she had long ago learned, was more likely to be betrayed than fulfilled.

Stifling a weary sigh, she turned quietly and slipped out the side door into the vestibule, where she descended the stairs into the church basement. The room was brightly lighted and decorated for the reception and supper to follow the wedding. Anna walked swiftly around, checking to be sure that everything was in order. The caterers were putting last-minute touches on everything, and it wasn't really her responsibility, but she checked anyway. This was her church, and she was secretary to Reverend Fromberg, as well as leader of the youth group. She couldn't help but feel that whatever happened on church property reflected on her employer, and upon herself.

Satisfied, she darted back toward the stairway, planning to vanish back into the shadows in the church above, but found her way blocked by the looming bulk of the man known to everyone as Cowboy. He wasn't a large man, but he was solidly built, with dark hair and dark eyes, and a face that looked as if it had seen a great deal of hardship and sorrow. Anna was scared of him for no other reason than that she didn't know him, or anything about him, really.

Being caught by him like this, all alone—she completely forgot the caterers at the other end of the basement—startled and unnerved her. She jumped back and stumbled.

His arm shot out as swiftly as a striking snake and caught her elbow, steadying her.

Anna froze, looking up at him, uncertain what would happen next. Part of her realized he had just saved her from falling, but mostly she was aware that he was touching her. She hated to be touched. Suddenly, freed from her paralysis, she shook off his hand.

"Sorry," he said, his voice slow, deep and steady. "I didn't mean to startle you."

"I..." Suddenly embarrassed by her reaction to him, she felt she needed to say something. But what?

He gave her a half smile. "It's okay. I saw you come down

here and wondered if maybe you were sick or something. People don't usually run out in the middle of the wedding vows. I thought you might need help.'' He shrugged a shoulder. ''I didn't know all these other folks were down here.''

Before she could think of a single thing to say, Cowboy turned and climbed the stairs. Anna stared after him, her eyes full of unspoken fears and wishes.

Hugh Gallagher, known far and wide as Cowboy for some damn reason he'd never been able to figure out, took his place at the back of the church and watched Janet and Abel Pierce pose for photographs with the wedding party. A steady stream of guests began to make their way to the rear of the church, toward the stairs that led down to the church basement. There would be laughter and food and many more pictures taken before the day was over, but Cowboy turned toward the door, getting ready to leave.

He was invited to the reception—hell, the sheriff had invited damn near everyone in the county to one or another of the parties he was throwing to celebrate this event—but he wasn't a party person. Crowds still made him uneasy, and the basement itself was too confined a space to make him comfortable, even when it was empty.

He hesitated, though, thinking of mousy Miss Fleming, the church secretary, and how startled she'd been to run into him on the stairs. He didn't like it when people reacted to him that way. It reminded him of things better left forgotten.

If he made himself go down there, maybe he could talk to her a bit, get her over her fear. He didn't want her reacting that way when she saw him again. On the other hand, if he went down there he was going to have to deal with his damn claustrophobia and all the other phobias that he preferred to leave undisturbed as much as possible.

Hell.

He hesitated a few moments longer, then decided to head outside and smoke a cigarette. Forcing the issue wasn't going to make Anna Fleming any more comfortable with him. He would just have to bide his time until a better opportunity came along.

Outside, the October twilight was already fading into night. The air was chilly but still, not too uncomfortable. Besides, he was used to far worse after wintering in the mountains in lean-tos and tents. He stepped off the walk onto the grass and lit a cigarette, inhaling with real pleasure. He ought to quit, and knew he was going to have to if he ever got his dream of a youth ranch off the ground, but for now, he savored every puff.

He wasn't the only one who sneaked out for a smoke. A couple of minutes later the double doors opened to disgorge a group of laughing men. He recognized them all—with only five thousand people in this county, it was hard not to learn to recognize most of them—but he stepped around the corner so that he was out of sight. People tended to regard him uneasily, as if he were a time bomb, and while he didn't exactly blame them, he resented the hell out of it. Besides, he didn't much feel like being sociable. The only reason he was here was that he didn't want to offend the sheriff and his family. They'd been too good to him.

The group out front stayed where they were, and Hugh let the deepening night wrap comfortably around him. Unlike most people, he always felt safer at night. At night he could be invisible. At night he could vanish.

The basement was a madhouse. Everyone was drinking, laughing, talking. The noise level was almost deafening in the confined space, and the temperature was soaring, even with all the windows open to let in the fresh air.

Anna was beginning to feel claustrophobic, as well as far too hot in her wool dress. She had always hated large crowds and was able to tolerate Sunday worship only because everyone was so orderly. They were not at all orderly right now, and the champagne was making everyone a little bit raucous.

She was, she realized, afraid of being grabbed. It wasn't so much the crowding as the smell of champagne that was affecting her. The scent of alcohol had preceded some of the worst experiences of her life. As soon as she felt she decently could, she grabbed her jacket and slipped out the side door.

She was hurrying, not wanting to be stopped by anyone, and had her head bowed as usual. She didn't see Hugh Gallagher until she plowed right into him.

He reached out swiftly to keep her from falling to the cold, hard ground. She felt his arms close around her and heard him say laughingly, "We've got to stop meeting like this."

In an instant, panic flared in her. She flailed against his restraining arms, and as soon as he released her, she backed up quickly, nearly falling again in her haste to escape him. Some portion of her mind was screaming, "No! No!" even while another part was recognizing that he wasn't coming after her. That in fact he had stepped back, as if recognizing her terror and wanting to soothe it.

She stood there staring at him with huge eyes, breathing in helpless gulps, and sanity hit her as suddenly as panic had, filling her with miserable humiliation.

The man called Cowboy stared at her, his mouth opening as if he wanted to ask but thought better of it. Finally he stuffed his hands into the pockets of his nylon jacket and took another backward step. "I didn't mean to frighten you," he said.

"It's not you," she managed to say shakily but honestly. "Not you..." Her voice trailed away, a forlorn sound like the whisper of the wind on a frigid night. "I was just startled," she added, afraid that he might ask her what had scared her so.

After a moment, he nodded. "You're running away, too?"

Her heart slammed. How had he known? "Running away?"

"From the party. Stupid as it is, that basement gives me claustrophobia, and with all those people in there, I'd probably lose it." He shrugged as if it were an unimportant thing, but Anna felt something inside her respond to his honesty.

"I know what you mean," she managed to say, and wondered why she suddenly felt as if some little patch of ice inside her had thawed.

"You, too, huh?" He waited, but when she failed to respond he continued. "Are you leaving?"

"I thought I'd just go home. No one will miss me." The words admitted more than she wanted to, but it was too late to take them back.

He nodded as if he understood. "No one will miss me, either. I'll walk you to your car."

Another flare of panic. "I didn't bring a car."

"Then I'll walk you home." He hesitated. "You're safe with me, but with most of the sheriff's deputies at this shindig, I'm not sure you'd be safe on the streets."

She hadn't thought of that, and the night suddenly looked so big and empty. Frightening. Bad things happened at night. Weighing her options, she finally said, "Thank you."

They headed east down Front Street, past some of the town's most elegant homes. Anna's little house, rented from the church, was farther out, in a less prosperous neighborhood—although it was far better than some of the neighborhoods she had lived in.

"Do you always walk to the church?" Hugh asked her.

"When it's warm enough. It saves wear and tear on the car." She kept her head down, studying the sidewalk ahead of them. Some dried leaves stirred on a breath of breeze and for a moment danced ahead of them.

"I hear you," he said. "I walked myself."

"Oh. Where do you live?" She wished she hadn't asked. She didn't want to sound interested. But surely he would take it as a polite question.

"The other way, over toward Snider's Crossing."

Near the railroad tracks, she thought. One of the least pleasant neighborhoods in Conard City. But Sheriff Tate and Reverend Fromberg both liked this man, she reminded herself. They wouldn't feel that way if he was a bad person.

"Not a very good neighborhood," he said as if reading her mind. "But it's cheap. I'm saving every dime I can make to put into the ranch."

"The ranch?" She felt him glance down at her, but she

didn't look up. It had been a very long time since she had felt comfortable meeting a man's gaze.

"I bought a piece of land out by Conard Creek, up near the Morrison spread. It's not much for raising cattle for profit, but it's good for what I want."

"And what's that?"

"Well, I really haven't discussed it all that much with anybody except Nate and Dan." Nate and Dan being the sheriff and the minister respectively. "But I'm hoping to open a ranch for troubled kids. A place where they can get out of their lousy homes and neighborhoods and start getting it together."

"That would be really nice." She meant it sincerely. It was not at all what she would have expected from this rough-looking man with his uncertain background. "Did you grow up in a bad neighborhood?"

"Oh, yeah." He gave a little laugh. "I just moved from one war zone to another when I joined the army."

"I never thought of joining the army." Once again she had spoken without thinking, and wished she could snatch the words back. They revealed far too much.

"You, too, huh?" He let it go. "Well, with all the work you do with kids, you probably see how much trouble at home affects them."

"I certainly do."

"So...well, I kinda figure that if I can give them a place away from those problems and influences, most of 'em would straighten themselves out."

"A lot of them just need an opportunity."

"Exactly."

"Would you take only children from around here?"

"Maybe at first. At first I wouldn't expect to be able to take too many. I mean, there'd just be me, basically, and maybe a couple of other people. Gotta start slow."

Anna nodded, her gaze still firmly fixed on the sidewalk. "I know of a few who could sure use a place like that."

A car beeped cheerfully as it drove by, and they both looked, waving when they recognized Emma and Gage Dalton.

"They're leaving early, too," Hugh remarked.

"Gage's back is giving him fits lately," Anna explained. "He says it's the change in the weather."

"Most likely. And boy, did it change fast. Here we were having this incredible Indian summer, and now it almost feels like winter is coming."

"It is."

He laughed quietly. "That it is, Miss Anna. That it is."

She flushed a little, realizing she had stated the obvious in response to his jesting remark. The tendency came from dealing with children so much of the time. In addition to her work with the church youth groups, she tended the church nursery during services. After a while with children, you got to taking everything literally. "I'm sorry. I get so used to talking with children."

"Don't sweat it. You're just so all-fired serious, it's hard not to pull your leg."

She didn't know how to respond to that. She didn't think of herself as being serious, but she supposed she was. There wasn't a whole lot in life worth laughing at or getting overjoyed about. Life was a serious business.

"Anyway, the sheriff thinks the ranch is a good idea. I figure maybe we'd start with a half-dozen kids and see how it goes. I'd like to be able to take girls, too."

"Really?"

"Sure. Everybody gets so concerned about all the crime caused by boys that girls get overlooked. They don't commit as many crimes, but they have just as many problems at home and on the streets. Somebody needs to look out for them, too."

"But won't making it coeducational cause problems?"

"Not if I do it right."

They had reached Park Street and turned right, heading toward her house two blocks down. Most of the driveways were empty, since nearly everybody was partying.

Hugh spoke again. "I don't know how Nate is going to be able to afford to marry off so many daughters if he invites everybody in the county to the shindig."

"It's amazing, isn't it? But he knows everybody. And he's

not doing sit-down meals, so maybe it's not as bad as it could be."

"Maybe."

They reached her house at last, climbed the porch steps and stopped at her door.

"I'll just wait while you get inside, Miss Anna," he said. "You have a good evening, hear?"

She stepped inside, turned on the light and locked the door behind her. Then she ran into the darkened living room to look out the window to watch him walk away. He had a slow, easy stride, like a man who'd walked many miles and was in no hurry to get to his destination.

She envied him his calm confidence and steady determination. She wished that once, just once, she could feel as comfortable with herself as he seemed to feel. And it must be wonderful to be able to walk down a dark street and not feel a nagging need to look back over your shoulder.

She let the curtain fall over the window and turned on another light. She was home and she was lonely.

Nothing new. It was a fact of life. Loneliness kept her safe.

She had the nightmare again that night. It had been years since the last time, but it was still all too familiar when she woke up in a cold sweat, shaking with terror. The night-light she couldn't sleep without glowed softly in the wall socket, but suddenly it wasn't enough. Even the shadowy shapes of the furnishings refused to resolve into familiarity by its light.

Sitting up quickly, she reached for the switch on the bedside lamp. It came instantly to life, then, with a flash, burned out. Shaking, shivering, breathing raggedly, she desperately fought her way out from beneath the blankets and ran as fast as she dared into the kitchen. There, the flick of a wall switch cast immediate normalcy over the night.

The refrigerator hummed softly, as it always did. She could smell the very faint odor of gas from the range and realized the pilot must have gone out. Searching for matches gave her something to do, something ordinary and real. Something to drag her out of the consuming depths of her dream.

The matches were where she always kept them, but she dropped the box twice just trying to get it out of the drawer. She waited a moment, taking deep, steadying breaths, then lit the pilot light under the range cover. The match slipped from between her fingers into the drip pan, but she left it. It could stay until she was steadier.

She poured herself a glass of milk and tried to ignore the phone on the wall, but it was as if her eyes were attached to it by rubber bands. No matter how many times she jerked her gaze away, it snapped back.

He might be dead by now. The thought was seductive and wouldn't go away. It had been years since she had called, and he would have to be in his sixties now, wouldn't he? So maybe he was dead. God, she hoped he was dead.

But she didn't want to hear his voice. What if he answered the phone? Then she would know for sure he wasn't dead, that he was still out there. It was better not to know.

She sipped her milk and shivered again, this time from a chill. It was four in the morning, and while the house wasn't cold, her body thought it ought to be in bed under the covers. But she couldn't go back to sleep. Not now. She would only have the dream again. Once it came, it just kept coming back.

She wandered through the house, turning on lights as she went, refusing to worry about the cost. She sat in the big, overstuffed chair she had bought secondhand last winter and tried to read a paperback crime novel. She turned the pages four times before she realized she hadn't absorbed a single word.

Giving up, she tried to turn her thoughts back to the wedding. Back to how nice Hugh Gallagher had been to her. And he *had* been nice. As threatened as most men made her feel, it was really surprising that he had managed to make her feel safe enough to let him walk her home.

There was a gentleness in his manner, she realized. Something that had reassured her. The slow way he talked, the easy way he held himself, the quick consideration of her feelings had all combined to make her feel she could trust him at least that far. Only Nate Tate and Dan Fromberg had been able to get so far past her defenses.

Deep inside her, she was astonished to realize, was a barely born hope that she would see Cowboy again.

As soon as she recognized it, she felt panic begin to build in her. No. No, she told herself. No. It was too dangerous. There were too many secrets. Too many horrible things in her past. Even if she could trust him not to hurt her, she couldn't trust herself not to hurt *him.*

It wasn't just the fact that she was terrified of men that kept her away from them; she was terrified of what her past could do to her relationships, to her entire life, if anyone found out about it.

Solitude was her fortress, and she kept herself inside it of her own free will. She couldn't afford to lose sight of that.

But the phone kept beckoning her. He might be dead. It would be nice to know that he was.

The thought upset her, it seemed so evil, but the man had done evil things to her. She didn't exactly wish him dead, she assured herself. It was just that she knew she wouldn't be free of him until he was gone. Then she would have only the horrible things she'd done herself to be worried about. By comparison, her own deeds seemed paltry. She could handle that guilt.

She looked at the phone beside her chair and knew that she was going to call. She didn't want to. She couldn't stand the thought of hearing his voice again, but she had to know. Ever since she could remember, she had been doing things she didn't want to because of that man, and she longed to break his hold over her.

But she couldn't stop herself. As if watching from a distance, she saw her hand reach out for the receiver, watched her own fingers punch in a number she would never forget. Then, holding her breath, she waited while the phone rang. It was two hours later back there, and if he wasn't up already, he would be getting up soon.

On the sixth ring, a groggy male voice answered. "Hello?"

She slammed down the receiver immediately, disconnecting

the call. Her heart hammered wildly, and she could scarcely catch her breath.

He was still alive. Still sleeping in her mother's bed as if he'd never done anything wrong. She would bet *he* never had nightmares about what he'd done to her. Never. He probably slept like a baby.

And suddenly, unable to help herself, Anna burst into tears and cried until she couldn't cry anymore.

Chapter 2

"Anna, you have to rescue me."

Anna looked up from her desk as Reverend Daniel Fromberg stepped in from the brisk day outside. She made a point of always getting to the office ahead of him, and he had to insist in order to get her to leave before him.

Daniel Fromberg was a pleasant-looking man in his late forties. Just average in height, he had a slight build that sometimes made people underestimate his backbone. As Anna had learned during the past five years, Daniel Fromberg had a backbone of steel when it came to what was right.

"What's wrong?" she asked, feeling a smile curve the corners of her mouth. With two teenage children and a pair of unexpected two-year-old twins, Dan Fromberg was often in need of her help. It usually involved finding him a baby-sitter so he could save his wife's sanity.

"The dogs!" he said with an exaggerated groan as he dropped into the chair facing her desk. Eight weeks ago, the Frombergs' Irish setter had given birth to four adorable little pups. "They're driving me nuts. They're driving Cheryl nuts.

They're into everything! Piddling all over the place, making little piles behind the couch, the TV, the bed—you name it!"

"So get a gate and lock them into one small area of the house."

He shook his head. "I tried to. Clearly you do not know my children."

She laughed; she couldn't help it. "They let them out, huh?"

"All the time. The older ones finally got the message, but the twins...!" He shook his head. "They just love to release the catch. Cheryl tried using a twisty-tie to stop them, but Dan junior figured it out. Then we tried a padlock, but this morning Jolly—that's the momma dog—got fed up with being cooped up and knocked the darn thing down. I now have holes in the doorjamb and a broken gate. Cheryl's threatening to take the pups to the pound."

Anna felt a twinge of dismay. "You can't do that! Surely you can get someone to adopt them."

"That's what we thought. I mean, the whole reason we never got Jolly spayed was because the older kids wanted puppies, and Cheryl thought it would be a good experience for them. But now we've got too many puppies, and would you believe it? Nobody wants a dog, especially mongrels. Everybody already *has* a dog." He eyed her. "Except you."

"No, you can't do this to me."

"Do what to you? Give you a warm, furry little companion? Some soft-eyed little fuzzball that will curl up on your feet on cold winter evenings? A friend who will always be glad to see you and will lick your face when you get sad? How can that be construed as doing something to you?"

Anna felt herself weakening. It was true, she had been thinking about a pet, but she had thought a cat would be better suited to her sometimes long work hours. "It wouldn't be fair to a puppy to leave it alone all day."

"So bring it here," he said. "I'll even get you a pet carrier to keep it in. I'll pay for all the shots. I'll help you housebreak it."

"Well..."

"Just a minute." He dashed back outside and moments later returned carrying a small auburn-colored puppy in his arms. "I call her Jazz, but you can call her whatever you want," he said, and dumped the puppy in her arms.

Anna was lost. She felt the warm little body quiver fearfully in her arms and instinctively began to pet it and coo gently to it. Jazz's ears were huge, so long that Anna imagined they must touch the floor when the puppy stood. It had a plump little pink tummy just like a baby. "Dan..."

"Adorable, isn't she? And I'll pay to have her spayed, too, so you don't develop a puppy problem. Trust me, she'll brighten your life."

Anna looked down into soft brown eyes and felt a tiny pink tongue lick her chin tentatively. "You are so sweet," she heard herself say to the dog. "This is extortion, Dan. You know I can't let her go to the pound."

"Certainly not. She's yours."

Anna looked at Jazz and smiled. "Thank you."

"I'll get the carrier out of the car."

By the time Dan returned, Anna had already figured out a bunch of benefits to having a dog. She would be able to take walks on dark winter evenings without feeling quite as afraid or alone. She would have a dog to keep her company in the dead of night when she couldn't sleep. In short, Jazz would go a long way toward easing her loneliness without forcing her to take risks.

Then the puppy licked her chin again, and none of the rest of it mattered. She was in love.

Dan set the carrier down in the corner with a stack of newspapers. "I figured the least I could do is provide the first batch of cage liners."

"Thanks."

He sat down facing her again. "You look awful, Anna. Exhausted. Have you been having trouble sleeping again?"

"Just a little." She really didn't want to get into it in any depth. She had never told him what had happened to her and never intended to. Still, she sometimes thought he suspected. His expression was so kind that she had to stop herself from blurting out the whole story. The impulse terrified her, and her heart slammed.

Dan regarded her gently for a while, then said, "If you ever want to talk about it, I'm here. I think I'm a pretty good friend."

"I'm sure you are." But she didn't want to talk about it. She tried her best not to even think about it. "At least, you are when you don't have puppies to get rid of. What are you going to do with the rest of them?"

"Oh, I already found homes for them. Jazz was the only one left."

"You stinker!"

He rose, laughing. "Hey, all I did was convince you to take a friend for life!" Still grinning, he went into his office.

Anna sat for a while longer, holding Jazz until the puppy's eyelids began to droop. Then she put the dog in the carrier and locked the door. Poor little thing, she thought as she returned to her desk. It might be the natural way of things, but eight weeks seemed awfully young to be taken from your mother.

Not that her own mother had been worth much, she thought with a sudden burst of bitterness. The woman wasn't even fit for the title of mother. No question but that she herself would have been better off if she'd been taken away at eight weeks. At any time before she had turned twelve, in fact.

But she didn't want to think about that. With great effort, she forced her attention back to her work.

An hour later, Dan emerged from his office. "I have to go over to the hospital. Candy Burgess had a severe gall bladder attack last night, and they're doing surgery this morning. I promised to go by and sit with the family."

"All right. Are you taking your pager?"

He pointed to his belt. "Got it. Also, I asked a guy to come by and take a look at the church roof. Last winter we had some serious ice damming."

"I remember."

"I want to see if there's anything he can do to lessen it. He said he'd pop in when he had a minute and take a look, so if he gets here while I'm gone, will you show him where the damming was worst?''

''Sure.''

''Okay, then. You and Jazz have fun.'' He headed for the door.

''Say hi to Candy for me.''

He was halfway out the door as she spoke, but he leaned back in. ''If you want my opinion, it's all that dieting she does that caused this. Remember all those news stories a few years back about liquid diets causing gall bladder disease? I don't think it's liquid diets in particular. I think it's starving yourself that does it.''

''You might be right.''

His eyes twinkled suddenly. ''Of course. I'm always right. People should listen to me more often. Bottom line is, God made some of us small and some of us tall, some of us skinny and some of us heavy, but we're all beautiful in His eyes. And just for the record, I think all this weight consciousness is a conspiracy on the part of men to starve women into submission.''

She burst out laughing and heard his answering laugh as he hurried to his car. What a character! He was such a joy to work for—even if he *had* foisted a puppy on her.

Jazz was still soundly sleeping, and she found herself wondering how often she should walk the puppy. Probably every time it awoke, until she learned its schedule. And she'd have to stop off at the store on the way home to get some puppy food and a leash and collar. The prospect gave her something interesting to look forward to.

In fact, she decided, Dan couldn't have done a nicer thing for her than dropping that pup into her arms so she couldn't resist.

She was thinking about doggie dishes and leashes, and wondering if she could take care of the shopping on her lunch hour, when a battered pickup pulled up out front. She watched with a suddenly pounding heart as Hugh Gallagher climbed out and walked up to the door. Her mouth went dry, and try as she might to tell herself she was overreacting, she couldn't stop it. Had he come to see *her?*

He stepped through the door and gave her a wide, warm smile. "Miss Anna. How are you today?"

Before she could answer, Jazz, disturbed by the commotion, woke up and gave a squeaky bark. Hugh squatted immediately and looked into the cage. "Who's this little fella?"

"That's...um...that's Jazz. Reverend Fromberg gave her to me." Anna sounded as breathless as she felt, and hated herself for it. She wondered why Hugh was here, and was afraid to ask.

"Jazz? What a cute pup. Irish setter?"

"Partly."

"A mutt, huh? Well, that just means she'll be really smart, won't you, girl? Can I take her out?"

"I guess."

She watched as Hugh unlatched the cage and reached in with large, strong hands to lift the little pup gently. Jazz decided she liked him and started licking his chin at once. Anna felt a sharp stab of jealousy, then castigated herself for it.

Hugh rose and faced her, still holding the squirming puppy. "Dan asked me to come take a look at the church roof. Something about ice damming?"

"Oh, yes! He asked me to show you where the worst problems were."

"Well, get your jacket on and let's take a stroll. This little gal would probably love to get outside."

"I don't have a leash for her yet."

"Just wait a minute. I can rig something with the rope in my truck that'll do in a pinch."

She rose to pull her jacket off the coat tree and found herself fascinated again by the sight of Cowboy walking away from her. He had such a nice...sway was the only word she could think of. Something that riveted her eyes to his flat backside and long legs. She felt a twinge deep inside that she hadn't felt in a long, long time. Embarrassed color flooded her cheeks.

Uh-uh, she told herself. You know better than that, girl.

She pulled on the jacket and stepped outside, taking care to lock the office door after her.

It took only a minute for Hugh to fashion a slipknot leash for Jazz. The puppy was ecstatic to be outside and began to run this way and that, giving a squeaky bark of joy. Each time the loop around her neck started to tighten, she came to a swift halt.

"Smart little gal," Hugh said, giving Anna a smile. "She won't give you any trouble." He handed her the end of the rope. "Now, where exactly were the worst problems?"

They walked slowly around the church, with Anna pointing out the places where the ice had dammed the snow and caused leaking inside.

"It was terrible last year," she told him. "Reverend Fromberg went into the church one morning last winter, and he could hear water dripping everywhere. You couldn't see where it was dripping, but finally we noticed that it was running down the insides of the window frames."

"So it was coming down inside the walls."

"Apparently."

He nodded. "I'll have to go up on the roof and see if I can find out what's keeping the snow from sliding off. You'd think with that steep a pitch it wouldn't be a problem. I'll also want to get up under the eaves to try to see where the heat is escaping that's causing the ice to form. Can you leave the church open for a while?"

"Sure. Just let me know when you're done so I can lock it up again. I'll only open the side door, if that's okay."

He gave her a smile. "I only need one door."

Jazz had run off most of her energy and had squatted at four or five different points along the way, so Anna figured the puppy was ready to return to the cage for a nap. She unlocked the church's side door for Hugh, then hurried back to her office.

She loved this time of year, she found herself thinking as she and the puppy trotted along. The breeze was crisp, carrying a hint of the winter to come, and the light had a buttery color to it, the last golden glow of autumn. Any day now the snow would march down off the white-capped peaks to the west and sprinkle itself all over Conard City like powdered sugar.

Inside the office, she put Jazz in her cage, then hunted up a bowl and put some water in with the dog. The puppy lapped thirstily, then curled up into a little ball of fur and fell right to sleep.

Well, that wasn't too difficult, Anna thought as she settled back at her desk. She'd managed not to babble like a fool to Hugh Gallagher, she'd walked the dog successfully, remembered to give it a drink...hey, she was getting competent.

Chuckling at her own silliness, she reached for the next letter she needed to type, only to be interrupted by the phone.

"Anna, it's Dan. I'm going to be at the hospital a while. Candy had a bad reaction to the anesthetic, and we don't know what's going to happen. Say a prayer for her, will you? I don't know at this point if I'll be back to the office at all."

"I'll cancel your appointments."

"Thanks. Go ahead and take your lunch whenever you want. And close up early if you feel like it. You need some rest, my child."

Anna hung up the phone, wondering why she always felt like crying when Dan Fromberg got that gentle note in his voice and called her "my child." He called a lot of people "my child" when they were laid low by life and were calling on him in his ministerial capacity. Still, it affected her.

The phone rang again, just as she was getting ready to call and cancel the first appointment. This time it was Sheriff Nate Tate.

"Hi, sweet pea," he said in his deep, gravelly voice. For some reason he always called her sweet pea. "Is the boss around?"

"He's at the hospital and probably won't be back in again today."

"Somebody get hurt?"

"A bad reaction to anesthesia."

"Not good." But he knew better than to ask who was involved. "Well, I got a leetle bit of a problem here. Maybe you can help."

"Me?"

He chuckled warmly. "Yes, you, sweet pea. Everyone knows how well you get on with the kids in the youth group, and you're the closest thing we have around here to a youth counselor."

Anna felt a pleasant blush fill her cheeks. "Don't exaggerate, Sheriff."

"I'm not. Do you think you can come over here to the office? I've got me a little gal you know in a cell who shouldn't be in the cell. I really need somebody to talk to her and figure out what's going on. I'll tell you more when you get here."

"I'll be right over, but I have to make a couple of phone calls first."

"It's not that big a rush," he assured her. "This little lady is going to be sitting here a while."

It took Anna ten minutes to make the calls and reschedule the appointments for another day. Then she grabbed her jacket again, hesitating briefly about leaving Jazz alone. After a moment she decided that the puppy was as safe as could be in the cage. Outside, she found Hugh up on the ladder, looking at the church roof. "Mr. Gallagher?"

He looked down at her. "Hugh. Just call me Hugh. Or Cowboy."

"Hugh." She repeated his name, feeling flattered that he'd asked her to use it. "I have to run up to the sheriff's office. I don't know how long I'll be."

"No problem. I'll be a while here. Probably most of the afternoon. There's a lot that needs to be checked out."

"Well, if you need to leave, just make sure the church door is closed tightly. I'll lock it when I get back."

"You got it."

The wind seemed to have gotten sharper, and some low clouds were moving in, concealing the sun. She hunkered deeper into her jacket and wished she'd worn slacks today.

The sheriff's office was only a block away, in a corner

storefront overlooking the courthouse square. She'd come here often in the past when the youth group took tours of the office and the courthouse, and she knew most of the people who worked here from church, but she still felt uncomfortable walking into a place that was populated mostly by men. She stepped inside and hovered by the door for a few moments until Velma Jansen, the dispatcher, noticed her.

"Anna! Come on in. Sheriff's down the hall, first door on the left. He's expecting you."

Tate waved her in when she reached his office. He was a big man in his early fifties, with a rugged, permanently sunburned face.

"Come in, sweet pea," he said. "Close the door and grab a seat."

Closing the door proved difficult for her. Even after all this time, she couldn't be comfortable in a closed room with a man. But beside Nate's desk there was a window that overlooked the square, and the sight of people walking by eased her feeling of claustrophobia. She managed to take the chair facing him and folded her hands on her lap.

"What's up?" she asked.

"That's what I'm hoping you can find out. Lorna Lacey. You know her."

Anna nodded. "She's in the youth group. A dear, sweet girl."

"Right. That's what everyone says. In fact, when I checked her school record, I found out she's never been in any kind of trouble."

"I'd be surprised if it said anything different. She's a natural peacemaker. Active, outgoing, popular—I'd say she's what every girl her age would like to be."

"Mmm." Nate rubbed his chin and swiveled his chair so he could look out the window. "Well, something's wrong. This dear, sweet girl set a fire in an empty classroom this morning."

"Good heavens!"

He nodded and glanced over at her. "She set the fire and was still in the room. If a teacher hadn't happened along the hallway just when he did, the school and the girl would both be gone.''

Anna was appalled. She couldn't imagine anyone doing such a thing, but even less could she imagine Lorna Lacey doing it. That child was as close to an angel as a girl her age could be.

''You look chilled,'' Nate said abruptly. ''Let me get you some tea or coffee.''

''Tea. Please.'' Still stunned, she was hardly aware that he had left the office. Her gaze wandered out to the square, which looked bleak on this graying day. The flowers that usually filled the flower beds were gone, having died in the first frost nearly a month ago. Even the people who usually sat on the benches had vanished, driven away by the bitter wind.

Lorna Lacey. A petite girl of thirteen with soft blue eyes and long blond hair and an irregular face that saved her from being beautiful. But she was attractive, very attractive, because personality bubbled out of her, and she had an infectious smile. When Anna thought of Lorna, she thought of laughter.

But now she found herself remembering that Lorna hadn't been laughing as much lately and had missed quite a few youth group meetings in the past year. Anna had ascribed that to the changing interests of adolescence, but now she wondered.

What could be wrong? She hadn't heard stories of any kind of trouble either from Lorna or the other kids. The girl's parents, Bridget and Al Lacey, seemed like nice people. Bridget was a little restrained, but that didn't mean anything. Al greeted the whole world with a big smile, just like his daughter, and was well liked by everyone. He was active in the church, coaching youth soccer and basketball, and was always ready to lend a hand where it was needed.

Nate returned carrying a couple of mugs. He set the one with the tea bag in it in front of her, along with a couple of packets of sweetener and creamer, and a plastic stirrer. Anna reached for the mug gratefully and cupped her cold hands around it, soaking up the warmth.

''Thank you,'' she said.

''No problem.'' He sat back in his chair, holding his mug,

and resumed his study of the square. "Sleet tonight, I hear. Make sure you get home before it starts."

"I will." Neither of them, she guessed, really knew what to say about Lorna Lacey. "Are you sure Lorna started the fire?"

"She said she did. In fact, she seemed real eager to make sure we knew it."

Anna hardly knew what to say to that. "But why?"

Nate shrugged and looked at her. "That's why I want you to talk to her, Anna. I know people. You can't work with all kinds the way I do every day without getting an instinct. Now, most of the kids who get into trouble around here, I could pick 'em out by the time they were eight or nine. Sometimes even earlier. The troublemaking starts young. Some of 'em outgrow it. Those with rotten families are the ones least likely to outgrow it. But what I have never seen is a thoroughly good kid from a good home turn bad without a reason."

"Bad friends?"

He shook his head. "I'm a great believer in peer pressure, but most kids like Lorna, who are good through and through, withstand that kind of pressure and pick good friends. You know who she hangs out with. Any problems there?"

"I wouldn't have thought so."

"Me neither. So we got us a mystery, sweet pea. That child committed an act of arson, and all my warning bells are clanging that this isn't the act of a pain-in-the-butt kid. It's a cry for help."

Anna nodded, agreeing. It had to be. "But help from what?"

"God knows." Nate sighed and settled deeper into his chair. "I've gotta charge her with arson. No way around it. But what scares me more than arson is that I don't think she intended to leave that room even when the fire got really bad."

Anna gasped and nearly spilled her tea. She set it quickly on the desk. "Not Lorna!"

"That's the way it looks to me."

Even more appalled now, Anna looked blindly out the window. "She hasn't been coming to youth group meetings as often."

"No? Then maybe whatever this is wasn't sudden. Maybe something's been building for a long time. She could be depressed. That's not uncommon at her age, but maybe she doesn't know how to ask for help. Maybe she doesn't even guess what's wrong with her. Or maybe she got involved in drugs somehow. Or somebody just slipped her a mickey this morning and she's on a bad trip. I don't know."

He sipped his coffee, then turned to face her fully. "What I know is, I got a kid in one of my cells who shouldn't be there. It's not like the handwriting has been on the wall for years. And I'm not gonna be happy until we find the root of this little problem. I don't want that child to become an ugly statistic because we couldn't figure out how to help her."

"Certainly not!"

"So you'll talk to her?"

"Of course I will!"

He smiled. "I figured you would, sweet pea. I figured you would."

"Have you talked to her parents yet? Do they have any idea?"

"No idea at all."

"They're not going to leave her in jail overnight."

"They may not have any choice. Judge Williams has set a bond hearing at five o'clock to try to avoid that, but Lorna said she's just going to tell the judge she'll do it again if she gets out."

Anna drew a long breath. "I'll talk to her."

"Please. At the very least maybe you can find out why she thinks it's better to be in jail than out. I got my own ideas, and they ain't pretty."

Nor were the possibilities that were occurring to Anna, but she didn't want to give voice to them. At least, not until she knew what was going on.

"Anyway," Nate said, putting his mug down, "you've got a definite way with kids this age, especially the girls. I've noticed it. Hell, everybody's noticed it. The kids you work with trust and respect you. That gives you a big advantage from square one over some psychologist I might drag in from somewhere else. At least we can skip over the part about developing trust.''

''Just don't forget that I'm *not* a psychologist. And speaking of psychologists, the school has one.''

''But he's never dealt with Lorna before. How long do you think it would take him to get her to open up compared with you?''

''I can't venture a guess.'' And if Lorna had a guy problem of some kind, she might *never* open up to a man.

''I don't think we have that kind of time, whatever it is. I've known that girl since she was in diapers, and she won't talk to me. But I don't think I know her anywhere near as well as you do. So go talk to her, sweet pea. Find out what's wrong.''

''If I can.''

A few minutes later she climbed the stairs to the jail. Nate had buzzed the jail guard from his office, and she was taken directly to a consultation room. Lorna was brought in just a few minutes later.

''Hi, Lorna.''

The girl didn't answer. She sat down at the table and kept her eyes averted.

Anna hesitated, trying to feel her way through this. ''We've missed you at youth group. Don't you want to come anymore?''

Lorna gave a quick, negative shake of her head without looking at Anna.

''That's a shame. Everyone there likes you so much.''

Lorna hunched her shoulders but didn't say anything.

Anna decided to take the bull by the horns. ''Sheriff Tate tells me you set fire to a classroom at school this morning. He didn't want to put you in jail, but he had to.''

Again no response.

''You've never done anything like this before, Lorna. Not even the little stuff that most kids do. So it seems to me that if you felt you had to start a fire, something must be hurting you terribly. If you tell me what's wrong, we'll do whatever we can to fix it."

Lorna looked up at her then, her gaze bleak, almost hollow. "Nobody can fix it."

"Nobody can fix what?"

But the girl didn't answer. She lowered her head again.

Anna wanted to reach out and touch her, but she wasn't sure that would be the right thing to do. Lorna had isolated herself emotionally, that much was apparent, and a touch might be truly unwelcome.

"When I was your age," she said finally, "something horrible was happening to me, and I couldn't figure out how to stop it. Finally I ran away from home for good, but that really didn't fix much. In fact, it made some things worse." She realized she had Lorna's attention now, so she continued. "Looking back at it now, I realized I should have trusted some of the adults in my life. I should have told them what was happening, because any one of them could have helped me. But I didn't. And that was a big mistake."

Lorna glanced at her, then looked quickly away without saying anything.

"Just give us a chance, Lorna. The sheriff and I both really want to help you."

"You can't. Nobody can."

"You can't know that until you let us try."

Lorna stood up so suddenly that her chair fell over backward. "I want to die! All I want to do is die! Nobody can help me. Nobody at all! Go away. Go away before you get hurt!"

Anna hesitated, but Lorna turned suddenly to the door and started beating on it, screaming, "Get me out of here! Get me out of here now!"

Shaken, Anna watched helplessly as the deputy took Lorna back to her cell. When she felt she could trust her legs to hold her, she went downstairs to Nate's office.

"Well?" he said when he saw her.

She shook her head. "She won't talk to me. But she said

something very strange. She told me to go away before I get hurt."

"Was she threatening you?"

Anna shook her head. "Can I sit down a minute? My legs are still shaking."

"Help yourself. So she wasn't threatening you?"

"I didn't get that feeling." She sank gratefully into the chair. "But something is terribly, terribly wrong, and I got the distinct feeling that someone has threatened *her*."

He nodded, compressing his lips grimly. "Yup. That's about the only reason I can figure that she'd want to stay in a jail cell. Now we have to find out who and why. Damn!" He passed his hand over his eyes, then drummed his fingers on the desktop.

"I'll talk to her friends," Anna offered. "The kids she always hung out with in the youth group. Maybe they can shed some light on this."

"You do that. I'd talk to 'em myself, but I don't want 'em to clam up for fear of getting Lorna into more trouble." He gave her a crooked smile. "That's the disadvantage of this uniform."

"I'll let you know if I find out anything. And will you let me know how the bail hearing goes? Maybe she won't make good on her threat."

"If she does, it's going to be a long night for her. God, I can't see leaving a young girl like that in a cell. We don't even have proper facilities for it. What if my men have to bring in some drunk tonight to sleep it off? Or worse?" He shook his head. "Hell, if it comes to that, I'll take her home with *me*. In custody. Maybe Marge and the girls can get to the root of it."

Anna nodded. "That might be a good idea. But no matter what, Nate, I wouldn't send her home."

He arched a brow at her and nodded slowly. "That's what I was thinking. I got a feeling there's something very wrong there. But I have to have something to go on, Anna. I can't just stick my snoot in without something."

"I know." Nor could she. But she could certainly call Lorna's friends.

A few minutes later she headed back to the church. The wind had grown cruel, and she had no trouble believing there would be sleet later on. The sky was leaden now, with no hint of the autumn sun left anywhere, and the last of the dead leaves were sailing across sidewalks and lawns. The town already looked deserted, as if it had settled down for its long winter sleep.

Dan Fromberg had returned, and greeted her the instant she stepped in the door. "Candy's okay," he told her, coming to stand in the doorway of his office.

"Wonderful!" She hung her jacket on the rack and rubbed her hands briskly together.

"I made fresh tea," he told her, pointing to the drip coffeemaker they used for brewing tea. "You look like you need to warm up."

"It's gotten really bitter out there. Oh, I forgot! I need to go lock the church door. I left it open for Hugh."

Dan shook his head. "He checked with me a minute ago, and I locked it."

Anna felt disappointed to realize she'd missed him. She immediately scolded herself for the feeling. "What did he say?"

"It looks like we're going to need some major work done. He says we need to replace the insulation in quite a few places, so escaping heat under the eaves doesn't cause the snow to melt, then turn into ice. He also pointed out some spots where the roof is concave, and it's trapping the snow rather than letting it slide off."

"That does sound expensive."

He grimaced. "I'm going to have to dip very deep into the building fund, but at least we can afford it now." Last spring, when they really should have had the work done, the fund had been nearly empty, having been used for repairs to the foundation. Good Shepherd Church was aging. "But first I'm going to get another estimate to compare."

Anna poured her tea and cradled the cup gratefully. "Did he mind?"

Dan shook his head. "He suggested it, actually. He's a very honest guy, you know."

She nodded and sank gratefully into her chair.

"So you went up to the sheriff's office? What happened?"

She outlined matters as briefly as she could and watched as his mouth drew into a thin line.

"This doesn't sound good," he said when she concluded.

"I'm going to call some of her friends tonight and see if any of them have any idea what might be wrong."

"Good idea."

Jazz whimpered just then, and Dan squatted down to take her out of her cage. "Hey, little one," he said softly. "How're you doing? Did you piddle on your paper?" He looked over his shoulder at Anna. "I can't believe anything's wrong at home," he said. "Bridget and Al are both the nicest people."

She nodded, and Dan looked down at the puppy he held.

"On the other hand," he said, "none of us ever really knows another person." Straightening, he turned to her. "So, have you had lunch?"

"No."

"Me neither. I'll go out and get us something from Maude's diner. In the meantime, why don't you see if any of Lorna's friends are home from school yet?"

He handed her the puppy and put fresh newspaper in Jazz's box before he left.

The pup seemed content to curl up on her lap while she sipped tea and dug out the roster for the youth group. One by one, she started calling the girls who seemed closest to Lorna. Only one of them was at home yet, and she said she hadn't really talked to Lorna in a while.

"She's gotten kind of quiet, Miss Anna, but I don't know why. She doesn't hang out like she used to. But I can't believe she actually started that fire at school. Everybody's talking about it. It just isn't like Lorna."

"So she hasn't found a different crowd of friends?"

"No. She doesn't have many friends at all anymore. I mean...well, we all still like her, but she doesn't want much to do with us. We ask her to go places with us, and she always says no. I always have a pajama party for my birthday, and Lorna always comes. Not this last time, though. She was the only one who didn't. When I asked her why not—I mean, I felt really hurt—she said she just didn't feel like it."

"So there's nobody at all she's close to anymore?"

"I don't think so. Debbie said she thinks Lorna's just getting snobby because her dad's a dentist. Mary Jo argued with her about that and said Lorna just isn't feeling good lately."

"Did Mary Jo say why?"

"No. And that's all I know, really. You want me to talk to the others?"

"Thank you, but I'll do that. If you think of anything, let me know?"

After she hung up, Anna found herself looking down at the puppy in her lap, thinking about how trusting young animals were, and how easy it was to shatter that trust. Something had shattered Lorna's trust.

Dan came through the door on a gust of cold wind, carrying a big brown bag from Maude's. "Steak sandwiches," he said. "I don't think either of us will want dinner. Which is okay with me, because Cheryl took the kids to Cheyenne this morning to visit their grandparents."

"So you're baching it?"

"Fine by me." He set the containers down on her desk and took his coat off. "I love those kids to death, but every once in a blue moon, it's nice to watch what *I* want on TV."

He pulled the chair closer to her desk while she cleared papers to one side, then set out containers full of food. Not only had he gotten the steak sandwiches, but he'd brought a salad, and brownies for dessert.

"Did you find out anything?" he asked while they ate.

"Nothing really useful. Apparently Lorna's even withdrawn from her friends."

He paused in the process of taking a bite of his sandwich. "Now that's really not good."

"That's what I think." She found she didn't feel hungry at all, but in order not to appear ungrateful, she nibbled at the salad.

"You know," Dan said presently, "I can think of a lot of things short of mental illness that could have caused this change in the child, and none of them are pretty."

"I know." That killed the last of her appetite. She absolutely didn't want to think about those things, but she couldn't avoid it. Experience had taught her that the bad things could happen to people you knew, including yourself. For Anna, they weren't just newspaper stories.

"Anna?" Dan was looking at her with concern. "Would you like to quit early today and go home? You look really strung out."

"I'm okay. Just worried about Lorna. I think I'll go to her bond hearing at five."

"It's at five? I'll go, too. Maybe I can get something out of her parents."

"I hope you have better luck than Nate did."

"Nothing, huh?"

She shook her head. "And frankly, I don't expect anyone will get anything out of them."

"You seem awfully certain about that."

"I have my reasons." And more than that she would not say.

Chapter 3

Cowboy was disappointed when he finished inspecting the church roof and Anna still hadn't come back. Not that he had any business being disappointed. Anna Fleming was two or three cuts above the women who usually consented to spend time with him. And since deciding to clean up his act and get on with life, he was avoiding the women who didn't avoid him.

He was kind of ashamed of himself anyway, ashamed of the way he'd fallen apart. He knew as well as anybody that post-traumatic stress disorder wasn't something you opted to have, but he still felt weak for having had it. Nothing had happened to him in his life that didn't happen to a whole lot of people, but he'd come apart at the seams anyway, after the Gulf War. It had been one straw too many, so to speak.

Not that he was excusing himself. He never excused himself. And it wasn't that he felt he'd done anything wrong. He'd been a soldier doing a soldier's job. But nightmare images eventually gave rise to nightmares.

Still, he wasn't particularly interested in wandering down the paths of his own memory lane. Learning to look forward was one of the biggest hurdles he'd had to clear on his road to recovery, and he wasn't going to allow himself to backslide.

After he gave Dan Fromberg the roofing estimate, he made his way back to his one-room apartment on the second floor of a hotel that was almost as old as Conard City. Not that that was so godawful old, he supposed, but the building bordered on ancient.

It must have been a grand old hotel in its day, he often thought, near enough the train terminal to be convenient, but not so close that its patrons would have been breathing coal smoke and the aroma of cattle in the stockyard awaiting shipment. In fact, it was just about midway between the courthouse and the terminal. The way people were apt to lay things out in the days when your own two feet were the favored form of transportation.

What a person mainly noticed about the place now, though, was that the halls were dark and musty, the stairs and floors creaked, and it looked like a firetrap.

His apartment was different, though. In the old days, they'd believed in building rooms big. He had a huge living room, an alcove for his bed, a tacked-on kitchenette and a bathroom with a claw-footed tub. His tall windows overlooked the street and faced south, so that sunlight poured in all winter long. All of this for less than anything else he could have rented in town.

If he hadn't been so fixed on his plan for a youth ranch, he could have turned this place into something spectacular.

But this afternoon, with the sky so leaden and a sleet storm getting ready to move in, he was finding it just a bit difficult to remember the potential he'd seen here. The hallway and stairs were as dark as if it had been night, and his apartment wasn't much better. He turned on a couple of lamps, but it didn't help much. The early-winter night would be falling soon, and all of a sudden he didn't want to be sitting here alone.

He decided his budget could handle dinner at Maude's, so he pulled on a warmer jacket and drove back up the street toward the church and Maude's place, which was right across the street from Good Shepherd. By the time he reached the diner, night had fallen.

Maude's was brightly lit but nearly empty. He slipped into a booth that let him look out the front window, and as he scanned the menu, he saw Anna and Dan leave the church together and get in their cars.

Anna's was an old vehicle, one that had seen all its better days long before it had come into her possession. It was big, built like a tank, and she backed up cautiously before pulling out of the parking lot and heading up the street. He realized she hadn't brought the dog, and he wondered if she was going to leave it in the office all night. That didn't seem right.

But then he noticed that she wasn't heading toward her home. Instead she turned up to the courthouse square. So did the reverend.

Shrugging, he went back to the menu. Maybe they had a meeting to go to.

"What'll it be, Cowboy?" Maude asked in her usual belligerent fashion as she slapped a mug of coffee down in front of him. She was a plump, older woman with grizzled gray hair and a no-nonsense face. "Eat hearty. They say it's gonna get damn cold tonight."

"Sleet's in the forecast."

"Yup. And don't skip the pie, neither. We got an elderberry pie that'll knock your socks off."

"Save a piece for me, then." He gave her a smile, but she didn't return it. He wondered if anyone had ever seen Maude smile. "Two bacon cheeseburgers with extra fries and a bowl of spinach, please."

"Spinach?" She looked surprised.

"If you have it."

"Oh, I have it, but most folks want salad."

"I like spinach." He shrugged.

"Why don't you have a side of onion rings instead of them extra fries? We got a shipment of some really good sweet onions."

"Sounds good." He'd never eaten here when Maude hadn't

changed his order somehow. On the other hand, he'd never regretted following her suggestions.

She stomped away, leaving him to sip his coffee and stare out into the night. It was warm in here, he found himself thinking. Warm. Despite the threatening weather, people would come and go. He figured he might stay here a while.

He was certainly in no hurry to go back to his empty apartment.

The five-o'clock bail hearing for Lorna Lacey was a special session called for the child's benefit. The court's earlier business was finished, and no other prisoners stood in the dock.

The girl herself, hands handcuffed before her, sat with her head down at the defense table. Beside her sat an attorney Anna didn't recognize, apparently someone the Lacey family had brought in from another town. Sam Haversham, the prosecutor, was standing at his table skimming through a thin file. Probably Lorna's file, Anna thought. It was amazing how quickly you could develop a file when you got in trouble with the law.

Apart from herself and Dan, the only other observers were Bridget and Al Lacey, both of whom were sitting with Dan in the front row. Anna sat farther back, preferring to be unobtrusive. Besides, she hated courtrooms. They gave her the willies.

At the front of the room, the court clerk sat at her desk beside the judge's bench, and in front of the witness box sat a stenographer, feeding the leading edge of a fresh stack of fan-folded paper into her machine. Two bailiffs stood to the side, chatting quietly with Nate Tate.

The door to the judge's chamber opened, and one of the bailiffs called out, "All rise" as Judge Francine Williams walked to the bench. Lorna, Anna noticed, had to be encouraged to stand by a gentle tug on her elbow. When the judge sat, everyone followed suit.

Judge Williams sat and spent a moment glancing over some papers in front of her. "Good afternoon." She devoted a few minutes to reciting the case number and charges for the record, and having the attorneys identify themselves.

"Now," she continued, "let's get right to the point, shall we? We all know why we're here, and I'm willing to dispense with the usual formalities, if no one has any objection?"

"No objection, Your Honor," both lawyers answered immediately.

"Good. I'm sure everyone wants to get home for dinner. We have an unusual case here, unusual at least for Conard County. We have no facilities suitable for the keeping of a thirteen-year-old girl. Our limited juvenile facilities are set up only to handle boys, and I really don't want to see this child in the county jail overnight, so I'm going to ask the prosecutor to be reasonable in requesting bail. Mr. Haversham?"

"We're fully prepared to be reasonable, Your Honor. In fact, considering that Lorna Lacey has never been in trouble before, we were prepared to agree to have her released on her own recognizance. However, another fact has come to light, which I need to bring to the court's attention."

"And that is?"

"Miss Lacey told Sheriff Tate that if she is released on bond she will start another fire."

Anna's hands clenched in her lap.

Judge Williams looked at Nate. "Is that true, Sheriff?"

"Yes, ma'am."

She turned her attention to Lorna's attorney. "Mr. Carlisle, what's going on here?"

The lawyer cleared his throat as he rose to his feet. "A moment to confer with my client, Judge?"

"By all means," the judge said. "Be advised that if your client made such a threat, I won't be able to release her from custody. Would you like to straighten that out for me?"

"Certainly, Judge."

The lawyer sat back down and had a hurried, hushed conversation with Lorna. Anna found she was holding her breath, and her nails were digging in to her palms. Her heart squeezed when the man stood back up to speak.

"My client…is aware of the consequences of her statement," he said.

"Does that mean she's not taking it back?"

"I...for ethical reasons, Judge, I...ah..."

A sound passed through the courtroom then, a sound of muted dismay. Bridget Lacey looked as if she might cry.

Judge Williams sat back, a perplexed frown on her face. "You leave me no choice, young lady."

Sam Haversham stepped forward. "Your Honor, we have an alternative to propose. Sheriff Tate has offered to take Miss Lacey home to his family in custody so that she won't need to spend the night in jail."

"That's highly irregular." Francine Williams tapped a pencil on the bench, frowning down at the girl. Finally, she sat forward. "Off the record here."

The court reporter's hands dropped to her lap.

"Mr. Haversham, I'd like you to consider a grant of immunity here."

Anna leaned forward, holding her breath. What was happening?

Sam stepped forward. "I think I know what you have in mind, Your Honor. I'll offer immunity."

Williams looked over at the young girl. "Miss Lacey, you've been offered immunity for any answer you give to the questions I'm about to ask. That means whatever you say is off the record and can't be used against you in any legal proceeding. Do you understand that?"

Lorna's attorney added a quick, whispered explanation. Lorna nodded.

"Good," Judge Williams said. "Now, Miss Lacey, are you telling me you want to stay in jail?"

"Yes."

"But why?"

Lorna lifted her head then, looking straight at the judge, and the anguish in her voice caused Anna's heart to break. "Because I'm bad! I do bad things! And I'll keep on doing bad things! I tried to burn down the school! If you give me a chance, I'll try to burn it down again!"

When Lorna finished, she dropped her head to the table and sobbed.

The judge let out a heavy sigh. "I'd like to see counsel in

chambers, please? Miss Lacey, I'd like you to come, too. And, Sheriff Tate, I think you're going to need to hear this, as well, if the defense has no objections?''

Mr. Carlisle hastened once again to his feet. ''No objection, Judge. That's fine.''

''And, counsel, I imagine her family hired you?''

''Yes, Judge.''

''You know where your ethical duties lie here, right?''

The attorney put his hand on Lorna's shoulder. ''*She's* my client, Judge. I made that clear to the family.''

''Make sure you remember that. Let's go talk this over.''

Anna had the feeling everyone in the courtroom knew what was coming. The type of thing you didn't say out loud, in public. The type of thing no one wanted to hear about someone they knew. The kind of thing Anna knew all too well.

As soon as the group had disappeared into the judge's chambers, Al Lacey rose and walked from the courtroom. He looked at no one as he left. Anna felt her stomach turn over in revulsion as she watched him go. Bridget followed a few moments later, her face set like stone.

Dan came to sit with Anna. ''I'm praying I'm wrong, but the handwriting is about six feet high on the wall, isn't it?''

She nodded, battling a storm tide of emotions that all of this was raising in her. ''That poor child,'' she managed to say finally. ''That poor, poor child.'' Long-buried anger simmered in her stomach, making it hurt.

''It could be something else.''

Anna didn't even bother to reply. She'd given up on vain hopes a long time ago. ''Why didn't somebody keep him from leaving?''

''Al? I don't think they can detain him without some kind of proof. That's probably why Judge Williams took Nate into chambers with them. If Lorna says anything about what's going on, Nate will take action.''

Anna folded her hands tightly together. ''I hope she tells the judge. Oh, God, I hope she tells.''

Dan reached out and gently touched her shoulder. ''She

might not, Anna. There are an awful lot of people in that room, some of them strangers to her."

"I know." And she did, only too well. Some things just couldn't be spoken of, no matter how they tore you apart. There were some things just too awful to tell strangers. "If she doesn't tell them, Dan, I'm going to do everything in my power to find some proof, some evidence. We have to help her!"

"We could be wrong in our supposition," he reminded her gently. "The problem might not be her parents at all."

She looked him straight in the eye. "You don't really believe that."

He compressed his lips. "No, I don't. But I'm praying as hard as I can that this will be just a juvenile overreaction to something that isn't so terrible after all. God have mercy on that child if it isn't."

Twenty minutes later everyone traipsed back into the courtroom. The judge settled at the bench and spoke to the court reporter.

"On the record again, Mrs. Jubilo. All right. I'm denying bond. Lorna Lacey will remain in the custody of the sheriff's department until trial. Mr. Carlisle, what I said before holds. If Miss Lacey wishes to withdraw her threat at any time, or wishes to confide in you or anyone else the cause for her behavior, the matter of bail will be immediately reopened."

"Yes, Judge."

"I'm also recommending that Miss Lacey undergo psychological counseling. I realize we don't have psychologists growing on trees around here. In fact, I believe the only one we have is the school psychologist, and I'm not sure he'd be able to handle this situation. However, Sheriff Tate has kindly agreed to arrange for counseling in Laramie, and for a deputy to take Miss Lacey to appointments once a week. Any objections?"

None were voiced.

"Now," Judge Williams continued, "while it is highly irregular, I'm going to put Miss Lacey in the personal custody of Sheriff Tate. By that I mean that she will spend her days in jail and her nights at the sheriff's home with his family. This release will be contingent upon Miss Lacey promising to behave while in the sheriff's custody. No fires, no running away, no nonsense of any kind. Miss Lacey, will you give this court your promise?"

"Yes, ma'am."

Anna heaved a huge sigh of relief. She couldn't think of anything better for Lorna than to be in the custody of a man who had raised six healthy, happy daughters, three of whom were still living at home.

"Now," the judge continued, leaning forward, "I'm going to take one more extraordinary step here. From now until this matter is settled, or until Miss Lacey explains her actions to my satisfaction, all of her contacts with any member of her family must and will be supervised by a member of this court or a member of the sheriff's department. Is that clear?"

Both lawyers answered that it was, but the judge was more interested in Lorna's reaction. "Miss Lacey, do you understand what I've said? You can't see your family without someone from the court or the sheriff's department there. How do you feel about that?"

Lorna lifted her head and looked right at the judge. "Good," she said. "Except my sister. Can I see my sister?"

"How old is she?"

"Four."

The judge hesitated. "Not immediately," she finally said. "Let's see how it goes this way first. We wouldn't want to put your sister in a difficult situation, would we?"

To Anna's horror, Lorna's face drained of color.

"No," the girl said hoarsely. "No. I don't want to see her at all."

Francine Williams nodded slowly. "That might be best for a little while. Just one other thing, Miss Lacey. Every one of us in this courtroom wants to help you. Find one of us you can trust and give us the information we need to do just that. You are not alone."

Five minutes later, Anna was back in her car. She had left Jazz in her cage at the office so she wouldn't have to be left all alone in a cold car. It was, she decided, the perfect time to go get puppy chow and a collar and leash. Then she could pick up Jazz and take her straight home to a warm house.

But while she was thinking of Jazz, most of her attention was focused on what had just happened in court. Old wounds of her own had been torn open as she sat there, and she felt as if she were bleeding inside. Once upon a time, a judge had looked down from his bench at her and said almost exactly the same thing. He'd said, "We want to help you, but you have to trust us first." Finally she had.

And somehow she had to get Lorna to do the same thing: trust someone. The sheriff. Reverend Fromberg. The judge. Herself. It didn't matter so much who, as long as it was someone who was willing to go to bat for her.

Distracted as she was by worry and seething emotions from her own past, she spent more than was wise at the grocery, buying Jazz the fanciest blue collar and leash, a big bag of puppy chow, a box of puppy treats, a small bone and several squeaky toys. She picked up some carpet cleaner that was guaranteed to remove pet stains, but talked herself out of a flea collar. At this time of year, it would be a wasted expense. She also picked up a few groceries.

When she stepped back outside, the first spit of sleet was falling, fine, icy crystals that stung her cheeks. The pavement was wet, still warm enough to melt the sleet. That wouldn't last long. Hurrying, she emptied the shopping cart into her car and drove swiftly back to the office.

As soon as she opened the door, Jazz started barking, a high-pitched puppy yelp. Looking into the cage, she saw that the dog had had an accident. She cleaned it up swiftly and replaced the soiled paper with fresh newspaper. Then she put Jazz back into the cage and carried her out to the car.

The cage wouldn't fit into her car, though. Finally giving up, she put it in the trunk, then took the puppy into the passenger compartment with her. Jazz insisted on curling up on her lap, but she didn't think that would cause much trouble.

Then she tried to start the car. And tried again. The starter whined, but the engine wouldn't catch. What now? Sleet crystals were rattling against the windows of her car, warning her that the streets would soon be dangerous. Forcing herself to wait in case she had flooded the engine somehow, she counted seconds in the tick of ice on her windows.

The night was dark and empty. Funny, she thought as she drummed her fingers on the steering wheel, there had been a time when she had believed being out alone at night would protect her. Then she had discovered otherwise. The night was a time when predators stalked the young and weak. It was full of threat. At night she wanted to be safely within the walls of her snug little house.

She shivered as the night's chill began to find its way into her jacket. Jazz whimpered softly, suggesting that she was getting hungry. Anna patted her gently and tried to start the car again. And once again the engine refused to turn over.

A tap on her window startled her, and she gasped, turning her head swiftly. Hugh Gallagher stood there, bent over to look in her window. "Car trouble?" he asked through the glass.

She rolled her window down an inch. "It won't start."

"I heard. The engine's not catching. Let me lift the hood and see if the choke's stuck, okay?"

"Thank you."

Her gaze followed him as he walked around to the front of the car. Then the hood lifted with a protesting groan and he vanished from view.

He was a nice man, she told herself. He'd proved that already. She didn't have to be afraid to be in his debt.

He rattled around under the hood for a few minutes, then slammed it closed and came back to her window. "It's not the choke, Miss Anna, and I can't see well enough to check anything else out. How about I drive you home and take a look at it in the morning?"

She hesitated. It wasn't that she really had any option, but she hesitated anyway. It had been a long time since she had been comfortable getting into a car with a man. Any man.

Even after all these years, she was still uneasy. But common sense won.

"If you wouldn't mind. I have the dog and all these groceries...."

"No problem. My truck's right across the street. Just let me bring it over."

A couple of minutes later, he had her groceries and the dog cage loaded in the back, and Anna and the puppy in the front seat with him.

"I'm glad I happened to be having dinner at Maude's," Hugh said as he pulled out onto the street.

"So am I. I really didn't want to call a tow truck. I can't afford that expense right now." Especially not now that she was going to have to get her car fixed. "I hope you didn't interrupt your dinner to help me."

"Naw. I was just finishing a piece of Maude's elderberry pie. You ever have any?"

Anna never ate out; her budget wouldn't allow it. "No, I'm afraid not."

"Well, let me take you over there for lunch tomorrow, before she runs out of elderberries."

Anna didn't know how to answer that, because she wasn't exactly sure what he intended by the invitation. Before she could think of anything to say, he went on.

"Did you hear about the fire at school today? They say the Lacey kid set it. Now, I don't know folks in the county as well as people who've lived here all their lives, but I did see that girl a lot around the church, and she always seemed like a good kid to me."

"She is. One of the best."

"Well, I just can't figure it. Now, if it'd been Bobby Reilly, I would have thought it was just what you oughtta expect, but not that girl."

"I know." She felt her heart accelerating as they edged near a topic she didn't want to discuss with him—or with anyone, for that matter. She didn't want to have to tell anyone what she suspected Lorna's problem was—at least, not unless she got some proof of it.

"You ask me," he said, "there's something wrong there, and it isn't that girl."

They eased to a careful stop at the corner, then turned onto Anna's street.

"Gettin' slippery," Hugh remarked. "Guess I oughtta put the chains on after I drop you off."

"That might be wise." God, how she hated this stilted conversation. How she hated being so uncomfortable with men that she couldn't think of anything to say to keep the ball rolling. How she hated being the prisoner of hurts that were so old they ought to be almost forgotten.

He turned into her driveway, and she felt the tires slip and spin on the icy pavement as he braked to a halt and switched off the ignition.

"You stay right where you are," he said. "I'll come around and help you out. Those shoes you're wearing don't look like they'll give much traction."

They wouldn't, she thought. They were a pair of cheap pumps she'd bought just because she had to keep up appearances at work.

Hugh climbed out and came around to her side. He opened the door and reached for her elbow to steady her. "It's like a skating rink. Hang on to me."

Even with all her caution, her feet slipped anyway, and he caught her around the waist. All of a sudden there was nothing between them but a squirming puppy and the layers of their clothing.

He smelled good, Anna realized with astonishment. He smelled really good, like freshly cut wood and soap. His arm around her felt powerful, but the way it held her was not at all frightening. She ought to feel trapped and terrified, but instead she felt…strange. As if the world had stopped between two heartbeats.

Then he backed off a little, giving her space but keeping his arm around her waist. "Let's get you onto the porch. I'll bring your groceries in."

A few moments later she was safely inside her snug little house, watching Hugh Gallagher carry her groceries and the puppy cage inside. It took him two trips, and he insisted on putting everything in the kitchen while she stood there like a dolt, silent, clutching the puppy to her breast as if the poor little thing was a lifeline.

She ought to do something, say something. Make some gracious gesture to thank him. Instead she was feeling shell-shocked by today's events, and by the realization that she didn't want Hugh to go. She wanted him to stay. For the first time in her life, she actually wanted a man to stay. Was she losing her mind?

"Would you...would you like some coffee?" she asked in a rush as he prepared to leave.

He smiled, and she was struck by the warmth of that simple expression. "Thanks, but I drank four cups at Maude's. Tell you what. Promise to have lunch with me tomorrow. I'll bore you to death with my plans for the youth ranch, and we'll call it even, okay?"

She couldn't say no. The word absolutely refused to come to her lips. "All right," she heard herself say.

"One o'clock?"

"That's fine."

Then he walked out into the night and left Anna alone with the realization that she had just made a date with a man.

She, Anna Fleming, had made the first date of her entire life. She should have been exhilarated, but instead she wondered if she'd just made another one of her gargantuan mistakes.

Jazz appeared to be pleased with her new environment. As soon as Anna set out bowls of water and food, the puppy dug in, in her eagerness making a minor mess that made Anna smile.

But she couldn't smile for long. It was as if the shadows in the corners of the room were whispering to her, trying to call her back into the nightmares of her past. It was because of Lorna, she decided. She was watching her own nightmare unfold again through the child.

Remembering the roster she had put in her purse, she left

Jazz eagerly eating and went to get it. She had to call the other girls from the youth group, to see if any of them had a hint of what was wrong in Lorna's life. If she could find a key, any key, she might get the girl to open up to her.

The first two girls had nothing new to offer, but then she got through to Mary Jo Weeks.

"It's awful, Miss Anna," Mary Jo said. "I've been crying on and off all day. I knew something was wrong, but I didn't know how bad it was."

"What do you mean?"

"I mean, bad enough that she would set a fire. I heard one of the teachers say he thought Lorna meant to stay in the room until the fire killed her. It's terrible!"

Anna hesitated, aching for Mary Jo, but not wanting to give the girl empty platitudes. Finally she said, "We can't know that, Mary Jo. That's just somebody's speculation."

"But what's going to happen to her now? Is she going to jail?"

Jail, Anna thought, could be better than some things, but not many. She couldn't say that to Mary Jo, though. "At present she's going to be staying with Sheriff Tate's family, until we find out what's going on."

"That's not so bad, then. But what do you think is wrong?"

"I don't know, not for sure. But I need you to help me, Mary Jo. I need every little thing you can remember that might give me a clue to what's wrong here."

"You're trying to help her?"

"Of course! There are a lot of people who want to help her. I don't know anyone who wants to see her go to jail. But unless we find out what the problem is, she may have to."

"Oh, no! I don't want that to happen to her—ever!" Mary Jo started crying again, and Anna waited patiently, making soothing sounds. There was never just one victim, she thought bitterly. There were always others.

When the young woman had her tears under control, Anna asked her if she remembered anything, anything at all, that seemed unusual.

"Well, I thought it was weird when her dad wouldn't let

her come over to spend the night anymore. I mean, we'd always been best friends, and at least once a month I'd sleep at her place or she'd sleep at mine."

"When did that stop?"

"About a year ago, I guess. But what was so weird was that he'd let me come over there, but he wouldn't let her come to my house. I asked Lorna why, but she just shrugged and said nobody could explain parents. My mom and dad started to feel insulted by it and didn't want me to go over there anymore after a while."

"I can understand that."

"Well, it made me mad, so a couple of times I made 'em let me go anyway."

"Did anything strike you as unusual?"

"Not really."

Anna felt something brush against her leg and discovered the puppy had joined her and was looking up at her with hopeful eyes. Bending, she scooped Jazz onto her lap. "This is a harder question, Mary Jo, and I want you to think very carefully about it. When you spent the night with Lorna, did anything happen that made you feel uneasy? Did anything seem not quite right? Anything at all?"

"Hmm..." Mary Jo was silent for a bit. "Well...it sounds silly, but her dad made us get ready for bed at eight o'clock. I mean, we always used to stay dressed until we went to bed, but the last few times he insisted we get ready before we watched TV. I thought that was kind of weird, but parents can be crazy sometimes, you know?"

"I know."

"Anyway, that just seemed stupid to me, but..." She hesitated. "This sounds awful, Miss Anna, and I don't want you to think poorly of me."

"I won't. I promise."

"Well..." Mary Jo drew a long breath. "I don't have a sick mind or anything, but it just made me uncomfortable to see Lorna running around in front of her dad in those baby doll pajamas. She didn't put on a robe or anything. My dad would have a fit if I sat around in the living room dressed like that.''

It was now Anna's turn to draw a deep breath. Her heart accelerated. ''But he didn't say anything or do anything?''

''Not about her running around like that. But then she was acting funny. I couldn't figure it out. It was like she didn't want to be dressed that way, either. She kept her arms all folded up and scrunched herself into a corner of the couch, like she wanted to hide. And she didn't say much after that. Her dad got on her about being so gloomy. She just kind of ignored him, and then he tried to tickle her out of it. Tried to tickle me, too, but not much. I figured that was because I wasn't one of his kids and he didn't think it would be right. But he tried to tickle her, and she said the weirdest thing.''

''What was that?''

''She said, 'Don't touch me.' And then she looked at him like she was gonna kill him. It sort of scared me. I didn't know she hated her dad that much.''

Anna drew a shaky breath. ''Thanks, Mary Jo. You've been a great help.''

''Really? I hope so. Oh! I just remembered one other thing. The last time I was over there, she had this big old pipe wrench under her bed. I asked her what it was doing there, and she told me she was afraid of burglars coming through the window. Did you ever hear anything so crazy?''

Anna had. Under her own bed she had kept a hammer. It required a lot of effort for her to find her voice. ''Thanks, Mary Jo. This is what I needed.''

''Good. If I think of anything else, I'll call you. But you know, Miss Anna, I haven't been over there since. When my dad heard that Mr. Lacey had tried to tickle me, he flat put his foot down about me ever going there again.''

''Your dad is right, Mary Jo. Absolutely right. Don't go over there again.''

When she hung up the phone, her hands were shaking. She looked down at the little puppy curled contentedly on her lap and tried to drag herself back to the present. But it was so difficult. Memories long buried were beating on the doors of her mind, demanding recognition.

Sleet rattled sharply against the window, and the wind moaned sorrowfully. A draft snaked across the floor and wrapped around her ankles, causing her to shiver. She needed to change. She needed to get into something warm and comfortable, and make herself some dinner. She needed to get busy so she could take control again and push the memories away. And she needed to figure out what she was going to do about Lorna.

It was going to be a long night.

Chapter 4

In the morning, the world was covered with a clear, sparkling glaze of ice. Anna looked out her window and wondered how she was going to get to work or to the sheriff's office. Not only did she not have a car, but it looked too treacherous even to walk.

She'd spent a disturbed night, sleeping fitfully, almost as if she were a child again, afraid that the bedroom door might open at any moment. Afraid that another night of fear and humiliation was about to begin.

She wondered if Lorna had slept any better at the sheriff's house. She hoped so.

Jazz was startled by the ice out back, slipping and sliding and looking at Anna with confused dismay. She finally managed to find purchase on some blades of grass that were poking up, and made a little puddle and a little pile. Anna praised her extravagantly, causing the puppy's tail to wag like a racing metronome.

While Jazz ate breakfast, Anna made herself some coffee and poached an egg. She was just getting ready to sit down when the phone rang.

"Anna? It's Dan. Listen, the roads are really bad this morning, so don't even try to come to work, okay? If it melts off later, we'll talk about whether it's worth going in, but for now, just stay put."

"You won't get any argument from me."

"Enjoy the break," he added. "I intend to. I've got this new computer game I've been dying to try. Talk to you later."

Anna ate her egg and a piece of whole wheat toast and wondered how she would fill her day, since she couldn't go anywhere. Plus there was the problem of Lorna, and she was really reluctant to let matters ride another day. What the child needed more than anything in the world right now was to know that someone was on her side and would protect her. She didn't need to spend even one more day alone in hell.

Making up her mind at last how she was going to handle the matter, she called the sheriff's office and was put straight through to Nate Tate.

"Lovely day, isn't it, sweet pea?" he asked in his deep, gravelly voice. "We've had a three-car pileup on the state highway, reports of cars in ditches all over the county, and half my men can't get to work. Velma managed to make it in, though, and she's teaching Lorna how to work the dispatch desk."

The image of wizened, chain-smoking, blunt-talking Velma Jansen working with a soft-spoken thirteen-year-old made Anna feel like smiling for the first time that day. "What's Lorna think of that?"

"Unless I miss my guess, she's thrilled. So what's up? Are you stuck in a ditch, too?"

"No, but probably only because my car died at the church last night."

"How'd you get home? Did you call a deputy?"

"Hugh Gallagher took me."

"Well, that's the next best thing. He's one fine man."

Anna knew she should come to the point, but she seized on Hugh as an excuse to avoid it just a little longer. "Is he?"

"You bet. He's a bona fide war hero, you know. Everybody knows he had some head problems after the Gulf War and hid up in the mountains with those vets for a few years, but that isn't the whole story. Anyway, for all that, he's got his head screwed on straight. But I don't gossip, so you'll just have to find out the rest for yourself."

Anna had to chuckle at that.

"Now, what's up, sweet pea? Not that I want to rush you or anything, but you never know when there might be another pileup on the state highway. Some of those damn truckers are pushing through like that pavement is dry."

"Well, it's about Lorna." She drew a deep breath and squeezed her eyes shut, reminding herself to keep her own feelings out of this. She had to speak to save the girl. "I'm convinced her father is sexually molesting her."

"So are all of us who were at that hearing yesterday. But there's not a whole lot I can do without proof. If she won't talk, my hands are tied."

"I talked to one of her friends last night, Nate. And she said some things...well, I think if I tell her what I know, I might be able to persuade her to confide in me."

He was silent for a moment. She could almost hear him ruminating. "All right. It's worth a stab. At least if she talks to you, I'll have something to start with. Okay, sweet pea, get into your outdoor gear. I'll have a deputy at your door in ten minutes."

"I'll be ready."

"Damn county's going to hell in a handbasket," he muttered. "See you in a few minutes, Anna."

Anna put Jazz in her cage, then dressed with trembling hands. She was about to do something she hadn't done in fifteen years: expose her past to another person. She didn't kid herself that she was going to get anywhere with Lorna if she didn't. God, she hoped she had the strength to go through with it.

The deputy took longer than ten minutes to get there. More like twenty, actually. Anna was just grateful that Nate had sent a woman. Sara Ironheart apologized profusely for the delay, but said she'd had to stop at an intersection to help get a car out of the way.

"Don't you live all the way out at the west end of the county?" Anna asked her. "How did you manage to get in this morning?"

Sara flashed her a smile. "I never got home last night. I've been on duty since three o'clock yesterday afternoon."

"You must be exhausted!"

Sara shrugged. "I caught a couple of catnaps at the office."

"Well, I hope the roads clear soon, so you can go home."

"I don't think that's going to happen. It looks like snow is moving in, and unless some of the other guys manage to find their way in, Nate's going to need every one of us still here to stick it out."

"It's been a long time since I've seen an ice storm like this."

"I don't recall us ever having one here. Usually it's just snow. Funny weather yesterday. Really funny."

The chains on the tires of the Blazer clanked loudly as they drove down the ice-coated streets. The trees looked like something out of a fairy tale, encased in ice and icicles. If the sun had been out, the world would have glittered and sparkled, but overhead, leaden clouds dulled the day.

"How's Joey doing?" Anna asked, referring to Sara's eighteen-year-old brother. When she had first moved here, Joey had been in the youth group and going through some hard times.

"Glad to be away at college, I think. I'm so glad my husband was able to talk him into at least trying it. I'd sure hate to see him miss the opportunity."

"Gideon seemed to have a good influence on him."

"He's been a good influence on all of us," Sara said. "And he's sure taken the load off my grandfather's shoulders."

"You board horses for people at your ranch, don't you?"

"Board some and raise some. Gideon's a wonder with those ponies." She shook her head and smiled. "The man is magic with horses. You ought to come up sometime and watch him work with them. It's well worth seeing."

"Some day I'd like to ride a horse."

Sara smiled at her. "We can arrange that, too. We have

some really gentle ponies that are good for getting started on. Gideon's thinking about giving lessons to town kids who don't get the chance to ride like the ranch kids. I'm sure he'd love to practice on you."

"I'll think about it." But Gideon Ironheart, pleasant as he was, intimidated her. He was so big and muscular, and so exotic looking with his long black hair. She didn't think she would ever feel comfortable enough to take riding lessons from him.

They pulled up at last in front of the sheriff's office, and nervousness washed over Anna. It was no worse than stage fright, she told herself. Just do it. Just walk through it and do what needs doing.

Lorna was still sitting at the dispatcher's desk, working with Velma. When she looked up and saw Anna, she broke into a wide smile that nearly broke Anna's heart. This child looked so different today from yesterday. So much more alive and hopeful.

"Hi, Miss Anna!" Lorna said cheerfully. "Did you get stuck, too?"

"No, I just wanted to see you, so Sheriff Tate had Deputy Ironheart pick me up. Have you tried walking out there? You need ice skates!"

Lorna laughed and tossed her long blond hair. "I fell on my bottom this morning at the sheriff's house when I was helping put down salt on the driveway. And now it's going to snow. I hope it snows so deep that nobody can go anywhere." She looked suddenly wistful, and Anna identified with the feeling. How many times had she hoped her stepfather wouldn't be able to make it home from work?

"This child," said Velma, through a cloud of cigarette smoke, "just wants to be stuck here at this desk forever. Can you believe it? She actually likes talking to all these deputies and answering the phones. Next thing you know, they'll be retiring me and giving her my job."

Lorna grinned at her. "You shouldn't give them such a hard time."

"Child," said Velma, "giving deputies a hard time is my stock-in-trade. Somebody's got to keep them in line."

Nate Tate came down the hallway and greeted Anna. Then he turned to Velma. "Let Lorna go visit for a while with Miss Anna. We can't have you working the girl too hard. We'll run afoul of the child labor laws."

"Working her?" Velma snorted. "Boss, this child is having fun. Now scoot, Lorna, and go visit with Miss Anna."

Nate led Anna and Lorna to an empty office and left them alone with the door closed. Anna sat on a creaky office chair, while Lorna went to the window to look out.

"Did you have a good time at Sheriff Tate's last night?"

Lorna nodded. "He has a nice family. He didn't even make me wear handcuffs like I thought he would. I just had to promise I wouldn't run away from him, so I did."

"That was a wise promise to make. And he does have a lovely family."

"They're all so happy," Lorna said wistfully. She kept on looking out the window. "We made popcorn after dinner and watched some funny movies. It was really fun." She paused. "I bet his daughters don't think about running away."

Anna drew a long breath to steady herself. "Do you think about running away?"

"All the time."

"Why?"

Lorna didn't answer.

Anna hesitated, wondering whether to keep beating around the bush or to just charge right in. For the first time in her life, she wished she had some formal training in psychology. At last she said, "I used to think about running away when I was your age. Finally I did."

Lorna turned from the window, looking at her with evident interest. "Did you make it?"

"That depends on what you mean by making it. I got away. But I paid a terrible price for it. There isn't much a fourteen-year-old girl can do on the streets. Nobody will hire you. I wound up having to do things I'm too ashamed to talk about."

Lorna came closer and sat, facing her. "I won't tell anybody. I promise."

Anna shook her head. "I don't like to talk about it. But running away is never an answer, Lorna. I found that out the hard way."

The girl nodded. "I kind of figured that out myself. Did they catch you and make you go home?"

"They caught me. But no, they didn't make me go home."

"How come?"

"Because I finally told them the truth about what was going on. After that, they made sure I didn't have to go home."

Lorna caught her breath but still didn't say anything. Her look was one of painful yearning in the instant before she averted her face. Silence reigned for several minutes.

Finally Anna spoke. "I talked to Mary Jo last night. She's worried sick about you."

Lorna nodded but didn't reply.

"Killing yourself isn't the answer, either, Lorna. Honey, you've got to trust one of us enough to tell us what's wrong. We can't help you if you don't tell us."

"I can't. I *can't.*"

"Of course you can. Don't you see? Nobody can hurt you anymore if you just tell us what's wrong. I'll protect you. Sheriff Tate and the judge will protect you. Nobody will ever lay another finger on you."

"You don't know. You can't promise that."

"Yes, I can. And I'm promising it right now. But we can't do anything unless we know what's going on."

Lorna kept her head down and didn't answer.

Anna rose and went to the window, searching for the courage to bare her soul. The words didn't want to come. They lodged in her throat, stuck like glue. She dug her nails into her palms, then forced the words out past lips that felt like wood.

"Mary Jo said you sleep with a plumber's wrench under your bed."

"So?"

"I used to sleep with a hammer under mine."

She heard Lorna gasp, and part of her wanted to go to the girl and wrap her up in a tight hug. But she couldn't move. She kept staring out at the alley and the gray day. A solitary snowflake drifted down and vanished on the ice below.

"I know what's going on, Lorna. But I need you to tell me yourself. Nobody can do anything if you don't tell us yourself."

The girl sounded breathless. "You...you could be wrong."

"I'm not wrong. I slept with a hammer under my bed for too long to be wrong. I ran away from home and lived on the streets. I've been there, Lorna. I'm not wrong."

"You...you promise...you won't tell anybody?"

Anna hesitated. She needed Lorna to tell the sheriff or the judge about this. On the other hand, the first and most difficult step was getting Lorna to speak about it at all. One step at a time.

"I promise," she said, and turned to look at the girl. "I won't tell unless you say it's okay. But you'd better tell somebody fast, before that man leaves town and takes your sister with him."

Tears were running down Lorna's face now, huge drops, and she wrapped her arms around herself as if she were trying to hold in a pain too great to bear. "He said...he said he'd hurt Mindy if I told."

Anna crossed the room swiftly and stood before Lorna, taking the girl's shoulders gently in her hands. "Honey...honey, look at me. He can't hurt you *or* Mindy if you tell us. Don't you see? He wouldn't dare, because we'll know about it."

The sobs came then, huge racking sobs that shook the child's entire body. Anna drew her up, gathered her close and rocked her gently, murmuring softly as she stroked Lorna's hair. Her heart ached, and her throat was so tight she could barely force the reassuring murmurs out. Tears burned in her own eyes, and she felt the kindling of an old, old rage, a rage she thought she had buried.

Anna had no idea how much time passed before Lorna finally fell silent and grew still from exhaustion. Her back and neck ached from the way she was folded around the girl, but she hardly noticed.

"What will they do to me?" Lorna finally asked.

Anna stood back and gently dried the girl's eyes and face with the sleeve of her sweater. "Do to you?"

"If I tell."

"They'll make sure you never have to go home again. They'll find you a good foster home."

"And Mindy?"

Anna felt a sharp pang. "Has he hurt Mindy, too?"

Lorna shook her head and sniffled. "No."

"But he threatened to."

"He said—" Her voice caught and broke. "He said he'd do the same thing to her if I ever told anyone."

"They'll protect her, Lorna. But I can't tell you exactly what will happen, since he hasn't hurt her yet. I honestly don't know. But I think they're going to be all over him like white on rice, you know? They won't give him a chance to hurt her."

Lorna nodded and sighed shakily. "Will he go to jail?"

"I don't know. My stepfather got five years' probation, and he wasn't allowed to be around children anymore."

Lorna looked down at her hands, and a big tear squeezed from beneath her eyelid. "It's not fair."

"No, honey. It's not fair. It's the most unfair thing on the planet."

"What if nobody believes me?"

Anna touched the girl's cheek gently. "There was a courtroom full of people last night who figured out what was going on. Couldn't you tell? All of us are ready to believe you, honey."

"Do I have to tell the sheriff?"

Anna hesitated. "I don't know. Would you feel more comfortable telling Judge Williams? Because she's a woman?"

"Can she stop him?"

Anna felt a small smile curve her lips despite all the anguish she was feeling for this child. "Sweetie, Judge Williams is a powerful woman. I have a feeling she can do even more than Sheriff Tate about this."

Lorna sniffled again and looked down at her hands. They were knotted tightly together, so tightly that her knuckles were white. "Will you stay with me?"

"You can bet on it. Do you want to wait and just tell this to Judge Williams first?"

Lorna nodded slowly. "I guess so." She gave Anna a brave smile. "Once is enough."

"I agree."

"Did you have to tell more than once?"

"Unfortunately, yes. I told the lady at the runaway shelter the cops took me to, because she was trying to make me go home. Then I had to tell the cops. And then I had to tell a judge. Maybe we can cut a few steps out of it for you. Is that what you want?"

"I guess so." Another tear rolled down her cheek. "I don't know if I can talk about it, Miss Anna. I really don't."

"We'll all help you, honey. Believe me, we all know how hard it's going to be."

Nate called the judge and had a message taken to her in court. She asked him to bring Lorna and Anna to her chambers at twelve-thirty. When they arrived in the spacious room with a long conference table, a court reporter was there, setting up her equipment. For a minute Anna thought Lorna was going to bolt, but she touched the girl's shoulder reassuringly and guided her to a chair.

A few minutes later, the judge joined them. She'd cast off her black robe and sat at the head of the table in blue jeans and a sweater. She was an attractive woman of forty, with a trim figure, a brilliant smile and a no-nonsense reputation in the courtroom.

"Boy, isn't it cold today?" Francine Williams asked with a smile for Lorna. "All right, Miss Lacey. I realize this is going to be very difficult for you, but I need the court reporter here to take your sworn statement. It will save you having to go through this again unless there's a trial."

"Trial?" Lorna paled. "I don't think..."

"That's a long way down the road, if it even comes to that," the judge hastened to assure her. "And I'm going to do my darnedest to see that it doesn't. Okay?"

Lorna nodded hesitantly.

"So it's okay with you if Mrs. Jubilo stays?" the judge asked her.

Again Lorna nodded.

"From now on," the judge admonished her, "I'll need to hear you say yes or no in answer to my questions, so Mrs. Jubilo can record your answer, all right?"

"Yes, ma'am."

Mrs. Jubilo administered the oath. Then the judge spent a few minutes questioning her about whether she understood the oath and what it meant to lie under oath. Lorna was very clear on that.

"So now, Lorna," the judge said, "why don't you tell us why you set fire to the schoolroom yesterday?"

Lorna bit her lip and looked down. "I wanted to die." Her voice quavered, then steadied.

"Why did you want to die, Lorna?"

The story tumbled out then, spilling forth like water through a ruptured dam. She stumbled at times, cried at times, and at times was nearly incoherent, but the words just kept coming as she told them of the hell she had been living for the past year.

She told them how her father came to her room at night, after her mother went to sleep. She said that at first she wasn't even sure he was doing anything wrong but just knew she didn't like it. She spoke of the horrible, disgusting ways he touched her and made her touch him, of how he had told her he had a right to do anything he wanted with her, because she was his property. How, when she finally threatened to tell, he told her that he would hurt her little sister. That was when she realized for sure he was doing something wrong.

"He liked to make me cry," she said in a small, thin voice. "He liked me to fight him. So I stopped fighting."

And then she told them how she had decided to kill him.

How she had put the plumber's wrench under her bed and was going to bash his brains out the very next time he came to her room. She told them how he found it and laughed at her, and told her that if she didn't do what he wanted from then on, he was going to hurt her sister. How he was going to do the same things to her little sister.

How she had finally decided that the only way out was to kill herself.

When the torrent finally stopped, Lorna put her head down on the table and wept. No one said a word. Anna put her arm around the girl's shoulders and blinked back her own tears. Dear God, she wondered, how could anyone do such things to a child?

Francine Williams waited until Lorna was calm again before asking, "Does your mother know about this?"

"No."

"Are you sure?"

Lorna shrugged. "I don't think so. I didn't tell her, because I was afraid he'd hurt Mindy."

"Would you like to live with your mother if we get your father out of the way?"

Lorna's answer was surprisingly swift in coming. "No. No! She didn't help me...she didn't *help* me...."

It made perfect emotional sense to Anna. Of course, in her case, her mother had refused to believe her.

But Judge Williams seemed to understand, too. "All right, then. I'd like to release you from custody on your own recognizance if you promise not to try to hurt yourself again, but for now I guess I can't do that. I'll have to look into a temporary foster home...."

"I'll take her," Anna said, closing her eyes against the difficulty of what she was about to admit. "I know I'm not a registered foster parent, but...well...I've been through it, too, Your Honor. My stepfather molested me when I was Lorna's age. At least I know some of the things she's feeling and experiencing. At least for now..." She opened her eyes and found Francine Williams regarding her kindly.

The judge nodded. "That might be a very good idea, at

least temporarily. You realize I can't make you a permanent foster parent until you're approved, but as a temporary measure—well, you have an excellent reputation in this community, Miss Fleming, and everyone is aware of your wonderful work with the children in the Good Shepherd youth group. Lorna, how would you feel about living with Miss Fleming until we get this sorted out?''

Lorna lifted her tearstained face. ''I'd like to stay with Miss Anna.''

''All right, we'll do that, then. I'm granting Miss Fleming guardianship of Lorna Lacey until such time as this court chooses to make other arrangements. I'll have the order prepared by the end of the day, Miss Fleming. Until then, Lorna will remain in the sheriff's custody.''

Then she leaned forward, looking at Lorna. ''With regard to your father, Lorna, I'm going to issue a warrant for his immediate arrest. And I'm going to have the child protection people look into the matter of your sister. Trust me, I'm not going to let anyone hurt her. Or you. Ever again.''

By one o'clock, the pavement in the downtown area of Conard City had cleared of ice. Sanding crews had been out, and the gradual increase of traffic had taken care of the rest.

Hugh Gallagher drove to Good Shepherd Church to pick up Anna for lunch. He figured they would have a nice meal together, and then he would take another look at her car. He hoped he could fix the problem for her, because he had a strong suspicion she couldn't really afford a repair bill.

He had mixed feelings about this lunch date, though. It had been a long time since he'd taken a woman out for any reason, even something as innocuous as lunch. He had an ulterior motive here in hoping that he could persuade Miss Anna to help him with his youth ranch, but he was also uncomfortably aware that he was drawn to her. Something about her appealed to him, and that made him uneasy, primarily because it might mess up any business relationship he hoped to have with her.

Not that it probably mattered. Any way you sliced the pie, he figured she wouldn't reciprocate his attraction. There was no reason on earth why any woman would be attracted to a man like him. Any sensible woman would avoid an involvement with him like the plague, and Miss Anna struck him as a very sensible woman.

Which made him even more uncomfortable with his attraction to her. It could never be comfortable to be attracted to someone who wouldn't reciprocate.

But hell, he told himself, he was a grown man, and he could handle these things. So he would buy her lunch, talk about his youth ranch and see if he couldn't entice her into helping him.

He was acutely aware that his past, particularly the years he'd spent living in the mountains with the other vets who couldn't handle the world, was likely to make him a doubtful candidate for the trust of the people who would have to refer children to him. Sheriff Tate and Reverend Fromberg kept telling him not to worry about it, that they would stand beside him, but that didn't do much to reassure him. He'd gone out of his gourd up there in those hills, and the fact that he hadn't gone nuts in a long time now was no guarantee he would never do it again. Folks who looked into such things were apt to have serious doubts about him.

So he saw Anna, with her sterling reputation in Conard County and her much-lauded work with the youth group, as the perfect counter to his period of unsteadiness. He needed a woman, anyway, if he was to help out girls as well as boys, and Anna, with all her experience, looked like the perfect choice to be codirector of the ranch with him. He couldn't think of anybody in the county who would be better.

But first he had to get her to trust him and believe in him. That would be a whole lot easier if he didn't start panting after her.

But she was a cute little package, he thought anyway, as he drove to the church. He liked her bright brown eyes and her classically oval face. Her delicacy, as if her bones were not just small but tiny, made him feel protective. With all that, she had a cute little figure, too, to judge by what he could make out under those shapeless dresses and suits she preferred.

She hid all her assets as best she could behind glasses and

ugly dresses, and kept her hair tightly bound, but he'd learned long ago to look past the superficial. That woman, he thought, would be beautiful if she ever relaxed.

He pulled in to the church parking lot and walked over to the office. Dan Fromberg was there, but no Anna.

"What can I do for you, Hugh?" Dan asked.

"I came to take Miss Anna to lunch."

Dan looked him up and down, and then a twinkle came to his eye. "Really? This is an interesting development."

Hugh opened his mouth to say it was purely business, then stopped himself. He didn't know what Anna thought it was, and he didn't want to embarrass her. "Yeah," he said, letting the unspoken question remain unanswered.

"Yes, indeed." Dan's twinkle faded. "Unfortunately Anna isn't here. I gave her the morning off, for the weather, and said to play it by ear this afternoon. Her car was here when I came in, but I haven't seen her. There's no answer at her house, either. If she doesn't turn up soon, I'm going to call the sheriff."

"She left her car here last night," Hugh said. "It wouldn't start, and I drove her home."

"Then maybe I'd better call the sheriff right now. Grab a seat."

Hugh perched on the couch, resting his elbows on his thighs and letting his hands dangle between his knees. They were large, work-roughened hands, scarred from mishaps here and there, like the white line between his thumb and index finger where a saw had slipped. He tried to imagine a delicate little thing like Anna Fleming wanting those hands on her, and he just couldn't. Her hands were soft and white, graceful as birds. His thumb and forefinger would probably close easily around her tiny wrists. Naw. These weren't a lover's hands.

And he had to stop thinking of that, anyway. He had more important fish to fry when it came to Miss Anna Fleming.

Dan came out of his office. "Anna's in court. Something came up with the Lacey girl, and nobody seems to know when they'll be done."

Hugh nodded. He'd been stood up before. Rising, he

reached to zip his jacket. "I'll just go on out and take a look at her car, then. I promised her I would."

He felt Dan's eyes on him as he turned toward the door. It was a whole lot easier to be stood up when nobody knew about it, he thought.

"Hugh?"

He paused and looked back at the minister.

"Do you think you can get the important work done on the roof before we get buried in snow?"

Hugh gave him a half smile. "You mean before tonight?"

Dan laughed. "It's only supposed to be a couple of inches. I know, it would have been easier over the summer, but we didn't have the money then, because of the flood problem. So what are our chances now?"

"I can get right to work on the insulation under the eaves. That'll help stop the melting and refreezing that's causing a lot of the ice damming. The rest of the roof...well, if we get us a patch of good weather after this storm moves through, we might be able to get the whole job done."

Dan nodded. "Do what you can, then. After you see to Anna's car. The job is yours."

Hugh stepped outside, half convinced he'd gotten the job because Dan Fromberg wanted him to be around Anna more. He thought about it, then shrugged. Not likely.

There was enough light for him to see his way around Anna's engine now. It was a 1976 Chevy, from the age when they still made cars a man could work on in his own driveway, back before all those computerized parts that needed special diagnostic equipment. Back when a man could still get his hands in there to work, before everything got shrunk to the point you had to drop the engine to do anything at all.

It didn't take him long to discover that the problem was in the distributor. The cap was cracked pretty badly, and some water must have gotten up in there last night when she was driving through the sleet. Easy and cheap to fix. She also had some bad-looking spark plug wires. Might as well take care of them and the plugs, too, while he was at it.

He hopped into his truck and headed for the auto parts store. It wasn't often that life gave you a simple fix.

It was two-thirty when Anna got out of the sheriff's car in front of the church. The day had warmed up a little, and water was dripping from the church roof. The sky was still dark gray, however, and occasional snowflakes drifted gently to the ground.

The first thing she noticed was that someone was bent over the engine of her car, presenting a rather nice view of a hard rump clad in denim. For all that she had sworn off men a long time ago, she still wasn't immune to such things. And there was definitely something about the male posterior and legs encased in well-worn denim that caught her eye every time.

Her reaction embarrassed her even as she had it, bringing a helpless bloom of color to her cheeks. She was just punchy from all the emotions of the past few hours, she told herself. Sharing Lorna's anguish had been as difficult as anything she had ever done.

But then she realized that the man bent over her engine was Hugh Gallagher, and that she had had a lunch date with him. Embarrassment swamped her. Never in her life had she missed an appointment, and this man had been kind enough to help her out. She wanted to sink.

He straightened and turned to look at her, a wrench in one hand. His hands were covered with black smudges, and there was even a smear on his cheek.

He smiled. "It's almost fixed, Miss Anna."

"L-lunch," she said, stammering. "I'm so sorry!"

He shrugged. "Some things are more important. Dan told me you were at the courthouse with the Lacey girl. It's okay. Can we do dinner instead?"

"Um...I'm getting guardianship of Lorna this afternoon at five. I really don't want to leave her alone her first night with me."

He nodded, and something in his face gentled. "You're a good woman, Miss Anna. Well, I'll take both of you out to

Maude's for dinner. You just ask Lorna if that's okay with her and give me a call by six, all right?"

"I...thank you," she said. "Thank you very much. And thank you for fixing my car."

"Wasn't anything at all." He shrugged. "That's what neighbors are for. Now go on inside before you get chilled."

"You'll let me pay you, won't you?"

He looked at her standing there in her slacks and jacket and seemed to reach some kind of conclusion. "Parts only," he said finally. "You can pay for the parts."

"Thank you." Feeling oddly flustered, she hurried inside and found Dan seated at her desk, talking on the telephone. He waved and indicated he would be out of her seat in just a minute.

Anna used the time to hang up her jacket and slip her over-the-shoe boots off. When she turned around, Dan was hanging up.

"What happened?" he asked, standing. "Did Lorna talk to the judge?"

Anna nodded. "She told her everything. I'm getting temporary guardianship of her at five o'clock today."

"That's good. That's really good. I was up most of the night praying for that child."

So had Anna been, in her own way. "Nate is going to try to collect her things from home, but he doesn't know how much luck he'll have. He's also going to arrest Al."

"Good."

It was one of the few times Anna had ever seen Dan's face grow hard. She watched as he looked down at the floor, rocking gently back and forth on his heels. When he looked at her again, his expression was still hard.

"You know, Anna, I believe in forgiveness, but I'm going to find this awfully hard to forgive. And you're going to need some financial help with that child. Let me give you a sum so you can buy her some things to wear and some extra food. Take it from me, they eat an incredible amount at that age. The church will help you out."

Then he turned and went into his office, leaving Anna to

wonder if she'd made the right decision when she had offered to take Lorna. She might once have walked in the girl's shoes, but that didn't mean she was a fit guardian for her.

In fact, she was probably the most unfit person on the face of the earth.

Chapter 5

Anna picked up Lorna from the sheriff's office at five-fifteen, just ten minutes after she'd received the call from Nate that all the paperwork had been received. When she arrived, he drew her into his office for a few quick words away from Lorna.

"I picked up Al Lacey," he told her, keeping his voice low so they couldn't be overheard. "You need to be aware of what's going on. Al will probably make bail in the next day or two. I can't see any legitimate reason for the judge to refuse it. So he may try to see Lorna, even though the judge is going to order him to keep clear of her."

Anna nodded. This was a complication she hadn't considered, and it made her distinctly uneasy.

"I don't think he'll try anything else," Nate went on, "but he sure is going to try to find some way to get Lorna to recant her story."

"I won't let her talk to him." Brave words. The thought of standing up to Al Lacey scared her to death. He was a man just like her stepfather, a child molester, and she was still terrified of her stepfather. Why else did she sometimes lie awake at night, feeling that she would never be safe until that man was dead? But for Lorna's sake, she was somehow going to have to find the courage to do what was necessary.

"Well, it gets worse yet," Nate said. "Bridget Lacey doesn't believe Al hurt the girl. She is absolutely convinced Lorna's lying. And what's more, she's being downright nasty about it. Some of the things she said weren't fit for my ears, let alone the ears of a girl that age." He gave Anna a wry smile. "I hope you don't have to hear that crap, but you probably will. Are you still sure you want to do this?"

Anna nodded, even as she felt nervous tension knot all her muscles and awaken butterflies in her stomach. "Somebody has to do it, Nate. And honestly, I don't think Lorna needs to live in a house with a man right now."

"I couldn't agree more. Lorna needs to sleep at night without wondering when the bedroom door is going to open. But, sweet pea, if you need anything, anything at all, I'm just a phone call away. I can be there in five minutes, any time, night or day."

"Thanks, Nate." She looked up at him, feeling a rush of warmth for this man who had never done anything except make her feel as safe and as welcome as possible in his county. Why couldn't there be more Nate Tates in the world? Why couldn't she have had a father like him? Life could just be so damned unfair at times.

Lorna was eager to go, smiling and cheerful, acting as if she'd just come out of a long nightmare and was sure there were only good things ahead. Anna hoped with all her heart that Lorna wouldn't be disappointed.

But she also feared that when the exhilaration wore off, Lorna was going to crash. Right now she was riding high on the relief of having escaped her demon, but sooner or later she was going to realize what that escape had cost her: her mother and her sister. Her family.

But for now, Lorna was focused on something of more immediate importance. As they drove toward Anna's house, she asked, "Miss Anna? Do you really want me to come live with you?"

"I certainly do. But I'd better warn you, I don't live in as nice a house as your family. Secretaries don't make as much money as dentists."

"That's okay." Lorna was silent for a moment before saying sadly, "Money isn't worth a whole lot if you're not happy."

"No, I guess it isn't." Anna hesitated, wondering if she should say any more or just let Lorna talk in her own way at her own pace. Better not to force a discussion of what had happened, she decided.

"My dad was always buying me pretty things," Lorna said after a moment. "I think maybe he felt bad."

Anna thought it far more likely that Al Lacey was trying to buy his daughter's silence, but she didn't say so. If Lorna wanted to believe the man was capable of shame and guilt, she couldn't see any reason to say otherwise. At least, not yet.

"I feel so bad for not making him stop."

Anna's hands jerked on the wheel, and she had to straighten the car out. "Lorna…Lorna, you're not responsible for what happened. And you weren't responsible for making him stop. There was nothing you could do to stop him, not when he was threatening your sister. The only thing you could have done was exactly what you did. You told people who could help you."

"I should have told you sooner."

"Maybe. But how were you to know we'd believe you? Or that we'd do anything about it? And I can certainly understand you being afraid for your sister."

"I guess."

Lorna's euphoria was wearing off, Anna realized. She sought for a safe change of subject. "I'm afraid I don't have a bed for you yet, but we'll get one tomorrow." Dan had certainly given her enough to help with Lorna's expenses. "For tonight, we'll toss a coin to see who gets the sofa bed."

Lorna shook her head. "That's okay. I'll sleep on the sofa bed. You shouldn't give up your bed for me, Miss Anna. You're doing enough."

Anna reached out and gently touched the girl's shoulder.

"You're a sweetheart, Lorna. Hey, I have a puppy now, you know."

"Really?" Lorna's expression brightened, and she turned to look at Anna. "When did you get it?"

"Yesterday. Her name is Jazz, and I'm sure she's going to love you to death."

"I always wanted a puppy, but Mom's allergic."

Anna glanced at her as she stopped at a stop sign, and saw something dark pass over the child's face, but it was gone so quickly she wasn't sure what she had seen.

"I can cook," Lorna said. "And I can help with the cleaning."

"That's wonderful!" She felt touched by the offer. "Hey, I'm getting the better end of this deal, you know. Someone to help with the cooking and cleaning. I hate cooking and cleaning."

"I think it's fun."

"Don't tell me that. I might take advantage of you."

Lorna laughed, and the shadows seemed to pass—for now.

Anna turned the car into her driveway and switched off the ignition before she turned to look at Lorna. "Do you know Hugh Gallagher?"

"The guy everybody calls Cowboy? Sure. He helped coach the girls' soccer team at church last year."

"Well, he wants to take us both out to dinner at Maude's tonight. Would you like to do that?"

"Sounds like fun."

There was not the least hesitation in the response, and Anna was both relieved and envious. Apparently Lorna hadn't translated her experience with her father into a reflection on all men. Anna unfortunately had...although, to be fair to herself, she had had some really nasty experiences with men when she was living on the streets.

What she knew for sure was that she wished she could regard this coming evening with Lorna's equanimity.

The instant Anna and Lorna stepped into the diner, Maude descended on them. Maude's usually annoyed expression melted into one of tenderness when she set eyes on Lorna. She stomped across the dining room to sweep the girl into a motherly embrace and tell her that she could have anything she wanted for dessert, on the house.

Lorna, far from being pleased by this announcement, appeared dismayed. Anna saw her look quickly around, as if she was wondering how many other faces in the room concealed knowledge of her dirty secret. Much to Anna's relief, no one else seemed particularly interested in them.

As soon as Maude moved away, returning to the business of running the diner, Lorna leaned close to Anna's ear and whispered, "She knows. Does everyone know about it?"

"By the time all of this is over, everybody's going to know about it," Anna told her truthfully. "But you don't have anything to be ashamed of, honey. Not one thing."

But Lorna looked at her sadly. "Yes, I do, Miss Anna."

"No, you most positively don't. But if you want to leave..." Now that they were here, Anna was reluctant to let Lorna change her mind. If the child started hiding out because people knew what had happened to her, she might well wind up an isolated recluse. On the other hand, Lorna might simply be feeling too raw to face it all right now—something Anna could certainly identify with. So if Lorna really wanted to leave, she would take her. This time.

But Lorna had already spied Cowboy sitting at a table near the back. He had risen and was waving to them, and Lorna smiled and returned his wave, heading back toward him without hesitation.

Lorna had guts, thought Anna. More guts than *she* had ever had. She'd spent her entire life trying to keep people from knowing about her past.

Hugh held out their chairs for them, treating both Lorna and Anna with equal gallantry. What struck Anna most, though, was that he had exchanged his usual work shirt and jeans for a nicely pressed pair of gray slacks and a white shirt, and had gotten a haircut. He looked so nice that Anna found herself tempted to stare.

His attention, though, was for Lorna. He told her he was

glad she had decided to come, then engaged her in conversation about last year's soccer team and his hopes for this year's. Anna, who knew nothing about soccer, didn't have to do anything except sit back, read the menu and pretend to listen.

After they ordered, Hugh began to steer the conversation back to areas that included Anna—the work on the church, how her car was running and finally to the youth ranch he wanted to open.

As soon as the subject came around to that, Anna tensed. She had a strong feeling that he wanted more from her than a few suggestions from time to time. But she couldn't give him any more than that. Any deeper involvement with such a project might well open her past to scrutiny. It was bound to be more involved than being granted temporary guardianship of Lorna.

Her work with the church youth group was different. She had fallen into that gradually since she had started working for Reverend Fromberg. Dan was her reference, the only reference she needed to work with the children of Good Shepherd Church. She was not the only youth counselor at the church, although she volunteered considerably more time than anyone else. But even so, no one had ever thought to investigate her background.

It would be different with the kind of thing Hugh was proposing. He would be inspected by the state and probably the county, and all his counselors and helpers would be, too. Otherwise the state and county couldn't order children to be put in his care.

Anna's past couldn't stand up to that, she believed. She would be a detriment to his hopes and plans. But she didn't know how to tell him that, especially since so far he hadn't asked anything particular of her.

Watching him eat and talk with Lorna, she found herself wishing that just for once her life could be uncomplicated. That just for once she could sit with a man and not think about anything except how attractive she found him to be.

And she did find Hugh very attractive. It would have been

nice, just once in her life, to look at a man with yearning and feel free to yearn. She'd missed all the normal stuff a teenage girl was supposed to go through. She'd never had a crush, and she'd never had a normal date.

And it didn't do any good to think about it, Anna reminded herself sternly. What was past was past, and all that mattered was the kind of person she was *now.*

Much to her relief, Hugh avoided putting her on the spot about the ranch. He kept the conversation general, talking about the horses he hoped to have, and how he believed that having a job to do and animals to care for could help build self-esteem and responsibility in kids. It was clear to Anna that he honestly believed environment was responsible for a lot of the trouble kids got into.

"Now, I'm not saying there's no such thing as a sociopath or a psychopath," he told Anna. "God knows I've seen 'em. But I think the majority of kids who get into trouble do so because they have too much freedom, not enough self-respect and no real rewards for being good. That's all environmental. And those are the kids I want to help."

"You don't think anything can be done for sociopaths?" Anna asked.

Hugh shook his head. "They either mature out of it eventually, or they wind up in jail for life. Those are people with a serious screw missing in their characters, Anna. And I don't think any head doctor can put it back in there. I'll be the first to say that you can't always tell the sociopaths from the troubled kids at these early ages, and I'm willing to give 'em all a chance—but I don't expect the sociopaths are going to improve much."

"I don't like to think that some people are just inherently bad."

"Neither do I. But a small percentage of people simply aren't interested in anything except their personal gratification. God knows why."

"Like my dad," Lorna said suddenly. "He doesn't care about anything except what he wants."

Both Anna and Hugh looked at her, but neither of them seemed to know how to answer that bald statement.

"My dad knew what he was doing was wrong," Lorna continued flatly. "He knew. That's why he told me not to tell anyone. So what does it make you when you do something you know is wrong? Is that a sociopath?"

Anna and Hugh exchanged looks. "Not always," Anna said finally. "We all sometimes do things we know we shouldn't. Sometimes we just do bad things."

"Yeah." Lorna put down her fork and pushed her plate aside. She looked at neither Hugh nor Anna. "I did some bad things."

Anna leaned toward her, feeling an ache of sympathy. "That doesn't mean you're a sociopath, Lorna. In fact, I'm sure you're not."

"So am I," Hugh said gently. "Sometimes we have to do bad things to survive. I know I did."

Lorna looked swiftly at him, her eyes full of hope.

"It's true," Hugh said. "I did some pretty awful things to survive. I didn't have a choice at the time. But now that I have a choice, I'll never do those things again. Never."

"Neither will I," Lorna said.

"Well, then—" Hugh smiled "—you're not a sociopath. You're not even a bad person. You're someone who had to do some bad things to survive. It's what you do now that counts."

Anna watched as Lorna absorbed what he had said. Little by little the youngster's face lightened and relaxed. When Anna turned to Hugh, she found him watching the child, his face full of concern and genuine caring.

Hugh Gallagher, she decided, was a remarkable man. No two ways about it. She was actually sorry when dinner was over and they went their separate ways.

In the morning, Anna drove Lorna to school. While Lorna went to her classroom, Anna went to see the principal with the guardianship papers.

John Kreusi invited her to be seated and scanned the papers

at some length. When he finally looked up, the expression on his face was guarded. "I'll need to make a copy of these papers before you leave."

"Certainly."

"According to this, Lorna isn't allowed to see or talk to either of her parents."

"That's correct."

"That's a rather extreme, rather unusual order. Can you explain it to me?"

It seemed, Anna thought, that life was going to make her deal with this subject no matter how hard she tried not to. "Lorna was being sexually molested by her father. He's in jail right now, as a matter of fact, but he'll probably make bail shortly. For obvious reasons, Lorna isn't allowed to see him."

"And her mother? Why not her mother?"

"Bridget Lacey apparently doesn't believe her daughter's story."

"I see." John Kreusi looked out the window, as if the gray day held great fascination for him. "I'll have to decide what to do about the child."

"What to do?"

"Yes." He faced Anna again. "Two days ago, Lorna attempted to burn down this school building. Our usual reaction in these cases is to put the child on suspension."

"Suspension!" Anna could hardly believe her ears. "Didn't you hear what I just told you? For the last year this child has been sexually abused by her father! The last thing she needs now is to be suspended from school."

"I have to consider the other children here."

"The whole reason she tried to burn the school down was because she couldn't escape her father. She's away from him now. There's no reason on earth to think she might try anything like that again."

"I have only your word for it—"

"And Lorna's word! You weren't there. You didn't hear her tell her story. If you had, there wouldn't be a doubt in your mind!"

"But I wasn't there. And from what you tell me, her own

mother doesn't believe her. Yet you're asking me to risk the lives of other children because Lorna Lacey has made an unsubstantiated claim against her father.''

Anna couldn't stand it. Rising to her feet, she let her anger come bubbling to the fore. ''This kind of claim is almost always unsubstantiated, Mr. Kreusi. But the judge heard her, and I heard her, and we both know how hard it was to get her to tell us what was going on. You'll just have to take my word for it, and the judge's.''

''I'll have to follow the court order, to be sure, but I can't be forced to keep this child in school where she may be a danger to the other children.''

''She's not a danger! She's promised not to do anything like that again.''

''And I'm supposed to believe that? Girls this age get hysterical. They exaggerate things—''

''Exaggerate!'' Anna glared furiously at him. ''Mr. Kreusi, it is people like you who make it possible for fathers to do these things to their daughters!''

''I resent that! I know Al Lacey—''

''We all know Al Lacey. But not one of us except him and Lorna knows what he did to her in the middle of the night. And what about you and all your educators here? Where were you when the child became steadily more withdrawn? Didn't any of you ever think to investigate what might be upsetting her? For the love of God, you saw her every single day!''

''Children this age—''

''I don't want to hear about children this age. You will not treat this girl like a criminal! Enough harm has been done to her!''

''I have to consider the other children—''

''Fine, then I'll take Lorna home with me. You can discuss this matter with the judge.''

Turning, Anna strode out of his office to the front desk. ''I want Lorna Lacey now,'' she told the woman at the counter. ''I'm taking her home immediately.''

It was only later that she realized that for the first time in her life, she had stood up to a man and given him a piece of her mind.

She took Lorna with her to the office and left her sitting in the front room while she went back to Dan's office to explain what was going on. Dan looked as upset as she felt.

"Have Lorna come in here," he said. "I've got some books she can read while you call the judge. No point in her hearing that discussion."

But the judge was in court, and the judicial assistant could only promise to have her call. Still furious, and all the more so because she couldn't get immediate action, Anna called Nate and told him what had happened.

"For the love of Pete," he said disgustedly. "That girl needs somebody to bend over backward for her right now. I thought for sure the school would do it. Hell. All right, sweet pea, you sit tight while I see if I can't talk some sense into the man. Had to do it a few times with my girls. They were always up to some hijinks or other, seems like. Meantime, you wait for the judge to call. I got a feeling Francine Williams isn't going to like this, either."

Anna sat at her desk for a few more minutes, staring out the window and fighting an urge to smash something. It had been a long time since she had felt this angry, and to be honest, she wasn't sure that all her anger had to do with John Kreusi's treatment of Lorna. No, some of it had to do with the way her own mother had refused to believe her when she had tried to tell her what was happening. Some of it had to do with the doubting responses from the cops in her own case, and the reluctance of the judge to give her stepfather anything stronger than probation.

Times were changing, but apparently they still hadn't changed enough.

But it *was* different for Lorna, she reminded herself. Lorna had the sheriff and a judge on her side. There *were* people who were prepared to believe a child when she told them that her father was molesting her. And that was an improvement.

And, to be fair to John Kreusi, he did have reason to wonder if he could trust Lorna. She *had* started the fire, after all. But his comments had gone beyond that, far beyond that. And that was what was making Anna so angry.

There was so little a child could do for herself. She couldn't leave home, move to another town and build a new life. A child had nothing and no one to depend on except her family and the authorities who were charged with protecting the welfare of children. If the people who could help didn't believe a child's complaints, the child was left absolutely helpless.

Anna, better than many people, could understand what it did to a child when the people she depended on either hurt her or didn't believe her. She understood the depth of those wounds, and the way they gutted a person's ability to trust. If she could do anything at all for Lorna, it would be to shield her from attitudes like John Kreusi's. If Lorna couldn't trust her own parents, the people she ought to be able to trust more than anyone else in the world, she at least ought to be able to trust the other authority figures in her life. And Anna was determined to see that she could.

Marge Tate, Nate Tate's wife, dropped in around two o'clock that afternoon. The judge still hadn't called, and Lorna was occupying herself reading a book from Dan Fromberg's bottomless library.

Marge was a beautiful woman in her late forties, with hair that was still a bright red, and dancing, laughing green eyes.

"I came to kidnap Lorna," she told Anna. "I'm going shopping and thought she might like to come along." She turned to Lorna. "If it's okay with Miss Anna, would you like to?"

"Oh, yes!" Lorna closed the book hurriedly and sent a pleading look to Anna. "Is it all right?"

"Of course." Anna couldn't imagine saying no to the child. In fact, she was going to have to figure out what Lorna could do with her time until this school issue was settled. The girl couldn't just spend her days sitting in this office reading books. Maybe she would have to look into home schooling.

For an instant Anna felt overwhelmed. She'd acted on impulse by offering to take Lorna, an impulse born of a strong protective feeling. But it was beginning to look as if she'd also taken on a whole bunch of complications she hadn't previously imagined.

Lorna was already pulling on her jacket.

"I think—if it's all right," Marge said, "I'll just take Lorna home to have dinner with us? The girls asked if she could come over again. I promise to have her home by eight."

"That would be fine," Anna replied with a smile, seeing the hopeful look on Lorna's face. "She had a great time when she stayed with you the other night."

"So did we." Marge smiled at Lorna. "Nothing fancy tonight, I'm afraid. Tonight's our night to eat chili dogs in front of a science fiction movie. You can help me pick out the film at the video store."

Then Marge turned back to Anna. "You're welcome, too, of course."

"Thank you, but I need to see about getting a bed for Lorna before the stores close."

"Oh! Well, I can help with that. We have a daybed the girls don't use anymore and all the linens for it. Come to think of it, we also have a dresser and a desk stored in the basement. I can have Nate bring them over later, if you like."

Anna had lived in this town for five years, but the generosity of her neighbors could still surprise her. She felt a trickle of warmth begin to thaw her anger. "That would be wonderful."

"Good. I'll talk to Nate about it when he gets home. Sure you don't want to come for dinner? I make a mean chili dog."

Anna had to laugh. "Really, thanks, but there are a bunch of things I need to do."

"Another time, then. Come on, Lorna. The stores are waiting."

Anna watched from the window as the two of them walked to Marge's car, a cherry red Fiero. There wasn't a doubt in her mind that Nate had asked his wife to come on this mission of mercy, to counteract the impression Lorna must have gotten from being yanked out of school this morning. The Tates were good people. But then, so were most of the folks in Conard

County. She couldn't allow John Kreusi and the Laceys to blind her to that fact.

She managed to keep a positive view until she realized it was five-thirty and apparently the judge wasn't going to call her back. Of course, thinking about it, she wondered why she had ever thought the judge would want to get involved. Kreusi's decision about Lorna was a school administrative decision, not something a judge could get involved in.

So what now? What the hell was she supposed to do? But no answers came to her. None at all.

Chapter 6

Anna hadn't been using the room she was giving to Lorna for a bedroom, so she hadn't hung any curtains. As soon as she left the office, she went home to measure the windows. She wished she knew what color the linens for the daybed would be so she could coordinate. She thought about calling Marge Tate, then decided the easiest and safest thing to do would be to get white curtains. After all, she didn't know how long Lorna would be staying with her.

Night had fallen, and the streets were nearly empty. Freitag's was open until eight-thirty, but there were only two other cars parked in front of the store when Anna pulled up. The continuing threat of the season's first snowfall was apparently keeping people at home. Probably a good thing, since at the beginning of every winter everyone seemed to need to learn all over again how to drive on slushy roads.

Though it was just two days past Halloween, Freitag's was already sporting Christmas decorations. Thanksgiving somehow almost got forgotten in the extended Christmas shopping season, even here in this little town. At least they weren't playing Christmas carols on the piped-in music.

Freitag's was in a century-old building where the wood floors creaked beneath the patrons' feet and many of the display tables and racks were still built out of solid oak. Housewares was on the third floor, and Anna took an aging elevator up. There she found two bored, middle-aged sales clerks eager to help her choose curtains.

She settled finally on plain white ones with foam-insulated backs to keep down the drafts over the winter. They seemed so sterile to her, however, that she began to wander around and look for other things that might please Lorna. Nothing much, she warned herself, mindful of her limited budget and the church's charity. Just some little things.

She picked out some ceramic knickknacks to grace Lorna's dresser, and a lamp that was prettier than it was practical. She promised herself she would go downstairs and get a better desk lamp from the office supplies department, and once she made that decision, she bought a little fiberboard table and a white table skirt, figuring she could put the pretty lamp on it beside the bed. Later, if Lorna wanted, they could dye the skirt. She also picked out a big, fluffy white rug to put beside the bed.

Downstairs she purchased the desk lamp, but halted herself before she also bought a white blotter set with a delicate gold design on it. Lorna would want to pick out some of these things herself.

But Anna felt good, really good, about what she had done. She found herself smiling and humming, and feeling that in some small way she had been given a chance to right a terrible wrong. Lorna had been severely hurt, and she needed to know that someone cared about her enough to pay attention to the little things.

A boy of high school age helped her get everything into her car, then went back inside the store. Snowflakes were falling now, and before getting into her car Anna paused to watch them twinkle in the streetlights as they spiraled downward. The year's first snowfall always made her feel different somehow, as if the coming hush of winter entered into her with its promise of white magic and Christmas just ahead. Later she would get as tired as anyone of needing to shovel her driveway and of having to plan outings around the weather, but right now, as the first snowflakes kissed the ground, she felt full of hushed awe.

"She's lying, you know."

The harsh voice brought Anna whirling around to find herself face-to-face with Bridget Lacey.

"That girl of mine is lying," Bridget said flatly, her face twisted in anger. "The little bitch is a liar and always has been. Her father didn't do a damn thing to her!"

Anna had no idea how to respond. All she knew was that she was frightened by the way the other woman was looking at her.

"Do you know why she tried to burn down the school?" Bridget demanded. "Because her father wouldn't let her go to Cheyenne to stay with her cousin. She got some wild notion in her head that she had to go there to live, and there was no talking her out of it. So finally Al flat-out told her no, and this is how she gets even!"

"Mrs. Lacey—"

"Shut up. I don't want to hear anything you have to say, Miss Goody Two-Shoes. You don't know what you're messing in. You and the judge and the sheriff—all holier than thou. Taking a thirteen-year-old girl's word over the word of a man who's been a pillar of this community for fifteen years! Al is a good man. A *good* man! He's never hurt a soul in his entire life!"

The woman pointed a finger at her. "It'll all come home to roost, just you watch. The little slut just wants the freedom to run around with boys, and her dad wouldn't let her do it. Well, she's your headache now. See how you like it when she doesn't come home till all hours of the night! See how you like it when she insists on dressing like a whore. But I tell you, Al is going to be vindicated, and when he is, both you and that girl are going to rue the day you started this mess!"

"I didn't start—"

"I know you and your kind, bitch. You think I don't know who it was planted all these evil ideas in Lorna's head? You go around pretending to be all perfect and then mix yourself up in things that are no concern of yours!"

By this point Anna was backed up against her car door, and there was no place to go to get away from Bridget Lacey. She was beginning to feel a little afraid, wondering what this woman might be capable of, but she couldn't think how in the world to defuse this problem. She stared up at Bridget, who was far larger, and wondered wildly if the woman was going to hit her.

But Bridget didn't hit her. Not yet. She just leaned closer and growled, "I'm going to get you, Miss Butter-won't-melt-in-your-mouth. I'm going to make you pay."

A male voice cut across Bridget's threat, and never had Anna heard a sound more welcome. "Is there a problem here, Miss Anna?"

Anna turned her head and nearly collapsed in relief when she saw Hugh Gallagher standing on the sidewalk. His posture was relaxed, his expression pleasant—except for his eyes. Those eyes held the promise of hell as they looked at Bridget Lacey.

The woman apparently got the message. She took one look at him and hurried away. Anna sagged against her car.

"You couldn't look any paler if you'd just been talking to a vampire," Hugh said gently. He slipped an arm around her and steadied her. "Are you okay?"

"I just need a minute...." Reaction was hitting her in a cresting wave of weakness that left her shaking. She found herself filled with the worst urge to just bury her face in Hugh's shoulder and burrow into his arms until she felt safe from the whole world.

"It's all right," he told her gently. "It's okay." With tender fingers, he brushed her cheek softly and tucked a strand of escaping hair back behind her ear.

"I heard what she said," he continued. "It sure wasn't pleasant. I'll be damned if I can understand how a woman could feel that way about her own child."

"It's not unusual," Anna said shakily. "She doesn't want to believe her husband cheated on her. She can't stand the thought that he might actually have done it with her daughter. Her whole life is falling apart, and it's just too much for her."

"It's still a poor excuse to dump all that vitriol on the child and you. You're a kind woman, Miss Anna. Not many folks would make excuses for someone who had just treated them like that."

Anna shook her head. "I'm not being kind, and I'm not making excuses for her. There aren't any excuses." She'd spent the better part of her life trying to find some forgiveness and understanding in her heart for her mother, and she'd managed to find some understanding. But understanding was a long way from forgiving or excusing.

She shivered again, feeling the cold that had seeped through her jacket while they stood there. Hugh at once loosened his hold on her. "Are you okay?" he asked.

"I'm fine. Really."

"Ready to drive home?"

She couldn't help smiling at his concern. "I'm *fine*."

"Okay, I'll follow you—just to be sure no one else does."

It had never occurred to Anna that Bridget Lacey might try to follow her home. She thought Hugh was being a little too apprehensive, but she had to admit she liked his concern.

The snow was falling thickly now, whirling into eddies on the wind as it whipped along the streets and around corners. As she drove forward, huge flakes flew at her windshield, almost giving her the feeling she was free-falling through stars.

Her tires skidded a little, then grabbed, as she turned into her driveway. Hugh pulled in right behind her and got out of his truck, coming to steady her as she stepped out of hers.

"Let me carry your packages in," he told her. "You just go inside and get warm."

Lorna had left a note saying that she had fed and walked Jazz, so Anna started a pot of coffee brewing while Hugh carried her purchases to the spare room. When he'd brought everything in, he paused in the doorway of the kitchen. "Where's Lorna?" he asked.

"She went over to the Tates' for dinner. She'll be back around eight."

"Well, you're going to need some help hanging those curtain rods and curtains. I've got the tools in my truck. Why don't you let me help?"

She hesitated, reluctant to accept any more help from this man. It was nothing about him personally, but it seemed he had done entirely too much for her in just a few days—fixing her car, taking her and Lorna out to dinner, seeing her safely home, rescuing her from Bridget Lacey. She was reluctant to be beholden to anyone, and it was beginning to feel as if every time she turned around, Hugh Gallagher was doing something else for her.

"It'll only take a minute," he said, as if he sensed her reluctance. "And it's a whole lot easier if you have the right tools—which I do." The grin he gave her was engaging enough to ease her qualms. "Besides," he said, "I'm angling for a cup of that coffee. It sure does smell good."

She had to laugh and agree. He hadn't left her any other choice—and for once she didn't mind.

He went out to his truck to get the tools, while Anna put her other purchases in the closet so they'd be out of the way if Nate brought the furniture tonight, when he returned Lorna.

Watching Hugh hang the curtain rods was an experience in itself. He shucked his jacket, giving her a wonderful view of a work-hardened male body clad in denim and flannel as he stretched to measure, and climbed up and down a short stepladder.

Anna found herself leaning back against the wall and simply staring, letting her eyes look at a man the way she had steadfastly refused to for so long. What, she wondered, would it be like to want a man the way men seemed to want women? What would it be like to actually want to touch a man in love, rather than being forced to touch him in fear?

"There, that was easy," Hugh said, stepping down from the ladder. Both curtain rods were in place above the windows, more level than Anna would have made them. "Now, where are the curtains? We might as well get 'em up while we have the ladder."

She dug the bags out of the closet, and together they put the hooks on the curtains and hung them on the rods.

"Looks good," Hugh said when Anna stepped back to survey the effect.

"Yes, it does. But unfortunately, now I can tell how badly the walls need painting."

He laughed. "It's always that way, isn't it? Do one little thing, and you suddenly find a couple more that need doing that you'd never have noticed otherwise." He ran his hand over the wall. "Actually, I think you've got wallpaper under this coat of paint. You might want to think about stripping it before you try painting again."

"Not tonight," she said wryly. "Painting and stripping the walls will just have to wait."

He cracked another laugh and looked at her in a way that made her breath suddenly lock in her throat. He didn't move any closer, but she felt as if he were suddenly surrounding her. A combination of panic and excitement filled her, rooting her to the spot. For the first time in her life, she experienced the exhilaration of danger.

But then he looked away, releasing her, leaving her feeling somehow disappointed. He was going to leave, she realized, and she very much wanted him to stay.

"I was just about to make a quick supper," she heard herself say, her voice a bit unsteady and breathless. "Would you like to join me?"

His gaze came back to her, a little more cautious than a minute ago. "If it's not too much trouble."

"It's no trouble at all." He was afraid, too, she realized. Whatever she had felt a few moments ago, he had felt it, too, and it had made him uneasy. Somehow it was easier for her to handle, knowing that it had disturbed him, too.

Hugh offered to help with dinner, but there really wasn't anything to do. "I cook large batches of things on weekends and then freeze individual servings. All I need to do is heat up some of the lasagna and toss a salad."

She gave him a fresh cup of coffee and pointed him to the table. He took his dismissal with smiling good grace and watched her as she bustled around. At first she felt nervous under his scrutiny, but she rapidly relaxed.

"What did you do before you came to Conard City?" he asked her.

She felt the uneasy quickening of her heart that always came whenever anyone questioned her about her past. But of course, he didn't know the whole story. He couldn't know it. "I worked as a secretary for a marketing firm in upstate New York."

"Why'd you ever come to a little out-of-the-way place like this? It must seem dull after the city."

She shook her head. "I didn't live in New York City." Except for a brief time as a kid on the streets. "The town I worked in was bigger than this, but not gigantic. Besides, it's the people who make a place, and the people here are nice and friendly. I got tired of cities, anyway. They're so crowded." So crowded with memories, she thought, hoping he wouldn't press further. She couldn't imagine that she would ever want to share her memories with anyone. Or that anyone would ever understand how she felt any time she saw a New York cop or a streetwalker on the corner, or heard certain street names.

"How about you?" she asked. "What made you come here?"

"Well, now, that's a long story. I left the army on a disability and wound up back home in Chicago. Trouble was, I couldn't hold a job for long because..." He hesitated. "Well, I just wasn't doing too well, you know? Some little thing would happen, and I'd suddenly feel like I was somewhere else. I don't know if you know much about post-traumatic stress disorder?"

"Just a little. I've heard about it." And sometimes have it, but she didn't want to confide that to anyone.

"Well, some woman would speak Farsi to her kid, or I'd hear a particular shout—well, all of a sudden I was back in Iraq. Or wherever. Makes it kind of tough to hold a job."

Anna nodded, turning to look at him as he spoke. She forgot

about the tomato she was holding in her left hand and the knife in her right.

"Eventually I wound up living on the streets."

She nodded again, feeling herself lean toward him, identifying intensely with what he was saying, needing him to continue.

"Life on the streets is hard," he said after a moment.

"Oh, I know!" She was hardly aware that she spoke, and her words were barely more than a tense whisper. He heard them, though. She could tell by the way his gaze suddenly fixed on her. For a moment she feared he would question her, but he didn't. He just gave her a nod and went on.

"Anyway, it wasn't any kind of improvement over living in a fleabag hotel, or in an apartment. I still wasn't getting away from the things that were setting me off, and I was getting rousted from every warm place I could find to sleep. After a bit I started hearing about this place out west where some vets had a nice little community going in the mountains and the locals left them alone." He shrugged. "I hitchhiked out here, and I've been here ever since."

The oven timer dinged, jerking Anna sharply back into the here and now. She realized her hand was aching from gripping the knife so tightly, and it was a wonder she hadn't squashed the tomato.

Turning quickly, she sliced the tomato into the salad bowl, then dried her hands and pulled the casserole containing the lasagna from the oven. She wanted to know more about Hugh but found herself strangely reluctant to ask. It was almost as if she felt that hearing about his past would awaken memories of her own. Part of her wanted to have it all out in the open, and part of her shuddered at the very thought. She'd already let Hugh know too much, she told herself. If word of her past got around this little town, she would be out of a job and looking for somewhere else to live. People would never consider her fit for the role of church secretary and youth counselor. Never.

Hugh praised her lasagna generously and dug in to the salad like a man starved for vegetables. Anna found herself enjoying a rare bit of pride and pleasure in being able to give another person so much enjoyment. She couldn't remember the last time she had received a compliment that wasn't directly related to her work.

She even managed to get up enough nerve to ask Hugh a question. "Did living in the mountains help?"

"Yeah. It did." He gave her a smile with a little side-to-side movement of his head, as if to say, *It did and it didn't.* "It removed the stimuli that were most likely to set me off. I guess the best way I can explain it is that living in the city was like a constant rasping on my nerves. When I got to the mountains, the rasping was gone. Finally the flashbacks stopped entirely."

"And now that you're living in town again...?"

"It's still pretty much okay. I was one of the lucky ones, I guess. My problems started almost right away after Iraq, so I got over it quicker. The ones who have a delayed reaction go through it a lot worse and a lot longer."

He forked a tomato into his mouth and chewed it. "You're a damn fine cook, Miss Anna."

"Thank you. And just call me Anna, please."

He gave her a warm look. "Anyway, to finish a long and boring story, I stayed up in the mountains a lot longer than I really needed to, mainly because I felt some of the guys up there needed me. I still go up there from time to time to check on 'em, and Billy Joe Yuma and I take blankets and food up there whenever we can. But I don't need to hide out anymore. I need to do something useful with my life."

"I can sure understand that." It was the primary reason she had chosen to take a job with a church. It gave her something positive to contribute, to make up for all the negative things she had done with her life.

"And I guess that's why I need to do this youth ranch thing. I know what it's like to be out of control. I know what it's like to need help to get a handle on life before it steamrolls you. Kids are at an even bigger disadvantage than adults. A far bigger disadvantage. They don't have the emotional or intellectual maturity to deal with the tough stuff on their own."

"That's so very true." She looked down at her plate, thinking how different her life would have been if she had known at fourteen what she knew now. She would have made some very different decisions, with a very different outcome. "There's a tendency at that early age to take extreme measures."

"There sure is." Hugh looked down at his plate, then gave her a surprisingly shy smile. "You understand children very well."

She felt her cheeks warm. "Thank you."

"I was hoping you could help me with the ranch."

As rapidly as it had come, the color drained from her face. No! The denial was like a thunderclap in her head. She felt herself start to tremble.

"Did I say something wrong?" he asked.

"I can't do it," she said shakily. "I mean...I'll be glad to make suggestions, but I can't actually be part of it. I *can't!*"

He looked as if he wanted to ask why, but after a moment he nodded and smiled. "I'll be grateful for your suggestions, Miss Anna. I really will. Thanks."

And as easily as that, the dangerous moment was gone. She didn't have to explain. The butterflies in her stomach didn't subside quite so easily, but then he changed the subject, letting her off the hot seat.

"About Lorna setting fire to the school." He pushed his plate aside and reached for his coffee cup. "Word is that the school isn't going to let her come back."

Anna looked up, distressed. "How did you hear that?"

"From somebody who knows somebody. You know how gossip goes. Apparently one of the school secretaries said something about it."

Anna shook her head and pushed her own plate away, losing her appetite. "I don't think that's settled yet. I know Nate was going to look into it. I called Judge Williams, but she hasn't called back. I guess that's because it's not really a legal matter. It probably *is* up to the school. But I don't want them to treat her like a criminal. She doesn't deserve it."

"Maybe not."

"Most certainly not!"

He smiled faintly. "Lorna's lucky to have you on her side, Anna. But consider this—don't get mad at me, just consider this possibility. The child did something very wrong. Admittedly, she had a lot of provocation. But maybe it wouldn't hurt her to realize there's a right way and a wrong way to deal with things. Burning down buildings isn't the right way."

Anna looked at him. "Are you saying she *should* be punished?"

"She may well be, by the courts. She *did* commit a crime. They may decide to give her detention, a suspended sentence, community control, or just community service. But I think it's very unlikely the case is just going to go away. She's been charged and arraigned, and she's only out on bail."

Anna looked down at the table, wishing she could argue with what he was saying but knowing he was right.

"I realize the child had extraordinary provocation, Anna. And the court, as near as I can tell, has been bending over backward to help her. But she committed a crime."

"But she doesn't need to be treated like a criminal! She's been through enough!"

"I agree with you. To a point. But one thing society can't allow people to do is break the law with impunity. Even if she gets a not-guilty verdict because she was suffering from abuse syndrome, or whatever they call it, society is still going to exact its pound of flesh. And that's not necessarily a bad thing for Lorna. She made a choice, a poor choice, and there are consequences to that. It won't hurt her to realize that. The important thing is that we don't compound her problems by reacting in the wrong way to this. My guess is she's going to get some community service hours."

"And the school? Should they be allowed to just throw her out?"

"For a few days, at least. Think about it. What would you want them to do if some other student had tried to burn down the building, and you had a child in that school?"

Anna couldn't argue with the justice of what he said, much as she wished she could. "Lorna's a special case."

"I think everyone will agree on that. But there's no reason to think she should get off entirely scot-free. It wouldn't be good for her."

"Maybe not. Maybe not."

Hugh reached out and covered her hand with his. "I know you feel very protective of her. Just like a mother should. But one of the lessons we all need to learn in life if we're ever to be responsible adults is that actions have consequences. The important thing here is to make sure that she understands that any punishment she receives is related directly to her decision to try to burn the school down, not to anything her father did. And she needs to be persuaded to accept the consequences as being just. It's an invaluable life lesson."

Anna sighed and nodded, and wondered why it didn't bother her that he was touching her. She usually hated to be touched by men, even briefly, and the way his hand was resting on hers was neither brief nor impersonal. But she liked it anyway. It was comforting, somehow, and reassuring.

And she was sorry when he drew his hand away.

"I'm not telling you what to do," he said. "It's not my place. Lorna's your responsibility now, and you should do what you think best."

"No, I see your point. It just seems unfair that on top of everything else she should be punished for crying out for help in the only way she could figure out."

"I hear you." With that, he rose and carried dishes to the sink. "Where's the soap?"

"Oh, just leave the dishes. Really. It's only a few things, and I can wash them up later without any trouble."

"You cooked. The least I can do is wash the dishes."

They wound up washing them together—he scrubbed, and she dried. And it was easy, she found herself thinking with something akin to wonder, to share the task with him. He didn't make her feel intimidated or uncomfortable.

Nate arrived with Lorna just as they were finishing up, and he had brought all the promised furniture with him in the van. Lorna was really excited about it, just thrilled with the white daybed and matching furnishings.

"You should see, Miss Anna," she said excitedly. "Everything matches!"

"How nice!" Although she couldn't help wondering why the child of a wealthy dentist hadn't had matching furniture all along.

"Lorna seems happy enough with it," Nate said. "Where do you want me to put it?"

They all helped move the furniture into the spare room. Lorna was thrilled by the curtains, thrilled by the white wicker furnishings given her by Nate, thrilled by everything. Anna couldn't imagine that she hadn't had things just as nice or nicer at home and wondered if Lorna's gratitude was more for being away from her dad than anything else.

Not that it really mattered. Lorna's gratitude clearly pleased Nate, and it certainly made Anna feel good about her purchases. After the bed was assembled and the royal blue dust ruffle was in place, they left Lorna to arrange her room as she saw fit.

Nate and Hugh both accepted an offer of coffee and joined Anna at the table in the kitchen.

"That child is a joy to have around," Nate said. "She tries so damn hard to please. You wouldn't believe she's the same girl I arrested just a couple of days ago."

"I hope it lasts," Anna remarked. She didn't expect it would.

Nate's look was at once wise and kind. "She'll be bound to crash sooner or later. By the way, it's been arranged for her to see a psychologist in Laramie every Friday afternoon. Sara Ironheart has been detailed to drive her up and back."

Anna felt a flicker of concern. "You're sure this psychologist can deal with these particular problems?"

"Her whole career is devoted to dealing with incest survivors, especially children. If anyone is suitable, she is. And she comes highly recommended."

"Okay, then. I don't mean to sound suspicious, but—well, Lorna's very vulnerable right now, and I wouldn't want somebody to make a mess of her."

Nate smiled at her. "I didn't take offense. You're the girl's guardian, after all."

"Temporarily. Just temporarily." Why did it upset her so to admit that? She let the pang go, however, because she didn't have time to analyze it just then. Later, she told herself. She would think about herself and Lorna later.

"Anyway," Nate said, "she'll be missing school on Friday afternoons until the judge decides otherwise."

"Speaking of school..." Anna looked at him.

"I talked to John Kreusi. He's thinking about it."

"The judge never called me back."

"I'll talk to her in the morning, then, but I don't think there's anything she can do. I think this one falls under the school regulations."

Anna nodded. "I was wondering about that."

"However, the girl needs schooling, and you sure can't do it yourself, sweet pea. You have a job. I'm sure I can get John to come to his senses, but it might take a day or two."

"A day or two out of school won't hurt her that much. I suppose I ought to see about getting her assignments from her teachers so she can at least make a stab at keeping up."

"That'd be a good idea. And now," Nate said, rising, "I've got to be getting back to my family. They think I'm a stranger who occasionally pretends to be one of them."

Anna had to laugh, but she didn't believe it for one minute. On many occasions she had seen how clearly Nate doted on his family.

"I guess I'd better be going, too," Hugh said. "Gotta get some serious work done on the church tomorrow."

It was still snowing when Anna said good-night to them at the front door. Snow was accumulating everywhere now, not quite enough yet to fully bury the grass, but she had a feeling that by morning the world would be a uniform white.

She closed the door on the chill and went to check on Lorna.

Chapter 7

Anna Fleming was becoming a nuisance, Hugh Gallagher decided a week later. Wearing nothing but the black briefs he'd slept in last night, he stood at the tall windows of his living room and looked down at the snow-covered streets through the white whirl of a blizzard.

A blizzard. An unexpected, unpredicted blizzard. What had been forecast as an inch or two was turning into one of those wild Wyoming storms for which he felt a great deal of respect. On a day like this, away from the security of town, you could get lost in the whiteout and not be found until spring. When he'd been living in the mountains, days like this had been life-threatening.

According to the weather report, once the snow cleared out, the temperatures were going to fall to twenty below zero. Dangerous cold after a dangerous storm.

He ought to be feeling pretty good. He ought to be standing here grateful that he had to go out in this only to work on the insulation at the church, something he could do from the inside of the building.

Instead he was wondering why Anna Fleming was messing with his mind.

Not that she was actually *doing* anything to mess with his mind. Her mere existence seemed to be enough to do that. He'd dreamed of her last night, then first thing this morning. When he saw all that snow, all he could think about doing was heading over to her place to shovel her out.

Except there was no point in shoveling her out until the wind settled down some. The way it was right now, the damn stuff would blow right back as fast as he could move it.

Sighing, realizing he wasn't going to be able to put her from his mind, he went to the telephone and called the church. Nobody answered. Well, he couldn't very well work on the insulation if nobody was there to let him into the building.

He called Dan Fromberg's home next, and Cheryl answered. In the background he could hear the toddlers squealing and squawling. "Dan's not going in at all today," Cheryl said. "The schools are closed, and I'll kill him if he bails out on me." She laughed as she said it. "Besides, there's a huge drift across the foot of our driveway, and I don't want him giving himself a heart attack trying to move it."

"The streets don't look any too good here in town, either," Hugh told her. "I can tell the plows came through earlier, but everything's buried all over again."

"So it's a free holiday," Cheryl said, then added wryly, "at least for people who don't have kids."

"Are you sure you don't want me to come dig you out?"

She laughed. "Only if you can magically open up the schools! No, really, Hugh, this is a great chance for us just to be together. We don't get many of those opportunities."

After he hung up, he went to look out the window again. He could spend the day reading, something he hadn't been able to do enough of lately. Most folks liked to settle in with the TV to relax, but he never had. Since coming down from the mountains, he'd begun to build a paperback library for himself, and right now there were a couple of thrillers just sitting there on the bookcase, crying out for his attention. It had been a long time since he'd last taken an entire day to do nothing but read.

Except that Anna Fleming was driving him nuts. He kept thinking of her and that girl snowed in—admittedly, she was snowed in not twenty feet from the neighboring house, but snowed in nonetheless. Maybe she needed food or milk or something. Somebody ought to check up on her.

All he had to do was pick up the phone and call her. Except that he knew she wouldn't tell him the truth. If he called her, she would say everything was fine and not to worry. He'd noticed that stubborn streak in her. It was a mile wide, and only a blind fool would miss it.

But that was one of the things he liked about her. She had a stubborn independence to rival his own, and he suspected that she had things in her past every bit as dark as the things in his. There was no mistaking that look she got sometimes, as if she'd seen the worst and wasn't shocked by it anymore.

Except that she could still be shocked by people like Kreusi, who didn't put kindness before everything else. That was a quirk in Anna that really interested him. How could she know so much and be so unsurprised by the evil things people did, and then be so shocked by a simple act of unkindness?

Maybe he ought to ask her sometime. Maybe she would tell him it was really simple: that she expected ordinary, decent folk to be kind until they proved they weren't ordinary, decent folk. Maybe she had somehow managed to keep right on expecting the best when she had seen the worst.

She intrigued him, that little lady with her soft, frightened brown eyes. He noticed how jumpy she got around him, and initially there had been no mistaking how afraid of him she was. But that fear seemed to have settled down, and it made him feel good, somehow, that she was coming to trust him.

And he knew damn well that as soon as this blizzard let up he was going over to shovel her out, because he wouldn't be able to stop thinking about it until he did.

Boy, he was getting it bad.

The thought amused him. For years now he'd been pretty much immune to women on an emotional level. Even before he got sent to the Persian Gulf, he'd felt a distance between himself and other people that he couldn't quite bridge. It was a common feeling among special forces types who had actually seen action. You had to feel different when you knew exactly what you were capable of and you'd actually done it. Most people only suspected.

But after the Gulf War…well, something had been broken. He'd gone surreptitiously into Iraq, hiding out for weeks until it was time to do his job. He'd moved among the people, he'd talked to them and he'd seen what he'd done to them. They'd thought he was one of them, but he wasn't.

And that had ripped him up in some essential way. He still couldn't really deal with it. Oh, he knew he'd been a soldier on a soldier's mission, but it hadn't felt like it.

And then, when it had been time to pull out, he'd moved through that wasteland of burning oil wells and had felt sure he'd died and gone to hell for his sins.

Which he surely deserved to do.

Oh, hell, forget it! In disgust, he turned from the window and went to shower and dress. War made for intolerable moral dilemmas, and he knew it. Moaning about it wouldn't change anything. He'd done his duty, and now he damn well had to live with it. And someone sure as hell had to be willing to do the tough stuff, so why not him?

But he felt, in a very deep and important way, that his soul had been stained beyond redemption. And that meant he wasn't good enough for a woman like Anna Fleming.

So why the hell couldn't he keep her out of his head?

By noon the wind seemed to be letting up, so Hugh pulled on his winter gear and went down to his truck. It was parked in the alley beside the building, and he had to dig it out from the drift that had built up over it. It started right up, though, and soon he was grinding his way down the drifted streets on tire chains.

The plows were back out, he saw, working their way up the side streets toward Front and Main. The sheriff had evidently cleared out the area around the front of his office with the plow blades he mounted on the front of all his vehicles every October. The snow was still falling, but in the hiatus from the wind, signs of life were beginning to show everywhere. Shopkeepers were shoveling the walks in front of their stores. Kids were playing in the drifts in front of homes. More than one person was trying to clear his driveway. The whine of snowblowers could be heard from every direction.

He skidded as he rounded the corner onto Anna's street, but the chains caught quickly, and he straightened out. The plow had already been through here, leaving mounds two and three feet high on either side of the street.

Anna and Lorna were already out shoveling the driveway. He parked in the street and climbed out, pulling his shovel from the back of the truck.

"Figured you might need a little help," he called to Anna. The smile she gave him made him glad he'd come. And for once she didn't try to talk him out of helping.

He dug in on the street side of the huge mound and began to sling the snow off to the side. The plow had packed it pretty well, making it heavy and hard to lift, but the strain on his back and shoulders felt good. He hadn't been getting enough hard physical labor lately, and his body, once tuned to the peak of physical conditioning, really missed it.

By the time he'd cleared away the mess left by the plow, Anna and Lorna had finished the rest of the driveway. They started together on the sidewalk, but that was easy by comparison, a very light six inches of snow that hadn't been compacted yet.

Then Lorna, apparently feeling both her oats and her youth, made a snowball and threw it at Hugh.

"You can't expect me to ignore that," he said, and reached for a handful of snow.

"Leave me out of this," Anna said hastily. Neither Lorna nor Hugh was willing to do that. They both threw snowballs at her. She ducked and twisted and got caught in the back.

"Now you're in for it," she said, and grabbed a handful of snow.

For a couple of minutes they lobbed snowballs at one another, laughing and running until they were breathless. But it was the sound of Anna's laughter that really grabbed Hugh. He'd heard her laugh softly before, always a quiet, restrained sound. But never before had he heard her laugh with complete abandon. The sound struck him somehow, working its way into the quiet places of his heart.

It also caused him to be inattentive, which left him wide open for a snowball Lorna threw at him. It caught him on the side of the head and jarred him back to reality.

"I'm sorry," Lorna said, breathless and laughing. She backed away and held up her hands defensively. "Honest, I thought you were going to duck! I really didn't mean to hit you in the head."

He took a menacing step toward her, which caused her to shriek with laughter, but he didn't go any farther. He kind of felt as if he was walking on eggshells here, and the last thing he wanted to do was something that might upset either Lorna or Anna. Given his own background, he was all too well aware of how some innocent thing could trigger a reaction to a bad memory.

He brushed the snow off the side of his head, but some of it melted anyway, and icy water trickled down inside the collar of his jacket and shirt.

"Let's go inside," Anna said, still smiling. "It's time for hot chocolate and cookies."

"Cookies?" Hugh was definitely interested.

"Homemade," Lorna said. "Anna and I made dozens of chocolate chip cookies to take to the youth group meeting tomorrow night."

They went in through the side door, leaving their boots on some spread-out newspaper. Anna gave Hugh a towel to dry the side of his head, while Lorna ran to her room to change into dry clothes. Anna did the same, returning a few minutes later wearing a soft green sweater and matching corduroy slacks.

Sitting at the table with the towel around his neck and Jazz in his lap, Hugh watched Anna bustle about and found himself aching to go to her and wrap his arms around her. Stupid. It was really, really stupid to feel this way. It could only screw up his plans for getting her to help with the ranch. But he wanted to hug her anyway. He couldn't remember ever having felt that way about a woman before, and he didn't like it. Wanting sex was something he was familiar with and could deal with. But wanting a hug?

"Is Lorna back in school?" he asked, trying to distract himself.

"Tomorrow. John Kreusi settled on a one-week suspension. I thought about fighting it, but I remembered what you said...." She looked over her shoulder at him and smiled, giving him a little shrug. "I guess it doesn't hurt to learn that actions have consequences."

"No, it sure doesn't."

"She's been keeping up with her work, though, and I know she misses her friends. I also think she's a little nervous about going back."

"Hardly surprising. The whole damn town is talking about her and her dad, and taking sides like you wouldn't believe."

"I'd believe it, all right. I've been hearing some of it. You wouldn't believe how many times I've been flat-out asked if Lorna's telling the truth." Anna shook her head and put mugs of steaming cocoa on the table. "Marshmallows?"

"Absolutely. It wouldn't be cocoa without them."

She brought a bag of marshmallows from the cupboard and handed it to him. "Help yourself." Then she went to get cookies from a big plastic container on the counter.

Hugh popped one of the big marshmallows into his mug and watched it start to melt. "It's hard to believe that someone you know and like could be guilty of something so awful."

Anna put a plate of cookies on the table. "Child molesters aren't monsters with scaly skin and rotten breath. They're ordinary, likable people. More likable than most, in my experience."

He looked up at her. "How many have you known?"

Her hesitation was visible, and it got his radar going. What was she hiding?

"A few," she said after a beat. "I've known a few. And

take it from me, everyone who knows them likes them and thinks they're incapable of such awful things.''

They both heard Lorna coming down the hall, and exchanged looks. By the time the girl entered the kitchen, the conversation had moved on to the upcoming holidays.

''I love Christmas,'' Anna was saying. ''It's always been my favorite time of year. Still, I think the stores are starting the displays too early. I'm really not ready to think about it yet.''

''We have to have Thanksgiving first,'' Lorna added. ''Are we going to have a turkey, Anna?''

''I...guess so. Usually I just do the Thanksgiving dinner at the church.''

''Me, too,'' said Hugh.

''Well, then, we ought to have our own here,'' Lorna said. ''And Mr. Hugh can come, too, right?''

Anna and Hugh exchanged glances. He realized that Lorna was trying to construct a surrogate family for herself for the holidays, and he guessed Anna realized it, too.

''Sounds fine to me,'' Anna said.

''Sure does,'' Hugh agreed. He figured there would be plenty of time later for Anna to rearrange things to suit herself, and he intended to let her know that he wouldn't be wounded if she decided she didn't want to include him.

Although, truth to tell, he probably *would* be wounded, he realized wryly. Because he really liked the idea of having Thanksgiving with a surrogate family rather than the large crowd at the church.

''Do you have parents, Mr. Hugh?'' Lorna asked.

''They died a while back.''

''That's too bad. No brothers or sisters, either?''

''Oh, I have a brother out in Arizona. Don't see him much anymore.''

''Why not?''

''Lorna...'' Anna said warningly. The girl flushed.

''Sorry,'' she said. ''I guess that was a rude question.''

Hugh sipped his cocoa, trying to decide how to handle it. ''It was a natural question,'' he said finally. ''It's just difficult for me to answer. We...just sort of drifted apart while I was in the army. I was always a long way away, you know? I stopped in once or twice, but we just didn't seem to have anything in common anymore.'' He shrugged. ''People grow apart sometimes.''

''I don't want to grow apart from my sister,'' Lorna said.

Hugh looked at Anna, but she didn't look as if she had any better idea how to handle that than he did. Just when he thought the silence had gotten so long that the child would probably burst into tears, Lorna shrugged and reached for another cookie.

''I guess we'll just have to see,'' she said.

For a moment Anna looked as if she might cry.

After finishing her cocoa, Lorna went to her room to finish her schoolwork. As soon as the bedroom door closed behind her, they could hear the radio come on, blasting some kind of cacophonous rock music.

Hugh sipped more cocoa and wondered if this was a good time for him to leave, but he felt reluctant to do so. Here he was sitting, across from this lady with mysteries in her eyes, and he found himself wanting to use the time to get to know her better. Problem was, he didn't know where to begin.

''Have you heard any more from Lorna's mother?'' he asked her finally.

''Only indirectly.'' She gave him a humorless smile. ''She's apparently talking all over town about what a lying slut Lorna is.''

He shook his head, feeling anger grip him. ''That woman's not fit to be anybody's mother. I heard what you said last week about her not being able to believe this. But whether she believes it or not, she shouldn't be going all over town talking about her daughter that way.''

''I couldn't agree more.''

''I think she knows exactly what she's doing. I think she figures if she can poison everyone's mind against the girl, they'll never get a jury to convict Al.''

''It won't be easy anyway,'' Anna said. ''It's her word against his, and people are surprisingly reluctant to convict with nothing more than that. They'll probably reach some kind of plea bargain, and a jury will never come into it."

Hugh looked at her. "You seem to know an awful lot about this stuff. Do you know somebody else who was molested by a parent?"

Anna looked away, drawing a deep shaky breath. And suddenly Hugh knew who had been molested. "God, Anna. I'm sorry. I didn't mean to pry...."

Not knowing what else to do, he pushed his way back from the table and reached for her, drawing her up from her seat. He felt her instant resistance and thought she was going to fight him like a cat. But just as he was about to let go of her, she sagged against him and burrowed her face into his shoulder as if she wanted to hide forever from everyone and everything.

He guessed he could understand that.

Holding her gently for fear of scaring her, he stroked her back softly and felt the quiver and quake of her slender form as she fought with whatever demons he'd just unleashed with his thoughtless question. Not that he felt particularly guilty. How was he supposed to know? And molestation *had* been the topic of conversation.

Damn, this all must be such a nightmare for her. He felt a strong surge of admiration at what it must have cost her to step in and help Lorna. This was definitely the kind of woman he wanted to help him with his ranch. This was exactly the kind of person he needed to make this thing go.

But he felt guilty for even thinking of that right now. Anna was hurting, and he wanted to console her—except that he didn't have a notion in hell how you could console somebody with a problem like this. It was almost too big to contemplate.

"I'm sorry," Anna said presently, her voice wispy. She stepped back a little and lifted her head from his shoulder. He didn't quite let go of her, and she didn't especially seem to want him to. "I keep it pretty well buried most of the time, but the last couple of weeks, what with all this about Lorna—well, it's gotten very close to the surface. I feel like my emotions are as fragile as glass."

"I can understand that." He wanted to squeeze her close and rock her like a child, telling her everything was going to be all right. But he couldn't tell her that. Nobody could. And he had a feeling she wasn't ready to be squeezed and rocked by anybody. "Was it your father?"

"My stepfather." She gave a little gasp that sounded like a bitter laugh. "Every now and then I call him to see if he's still alive."

As if she was shocked to have admitted so much, she spun away from him and went to the sink, where she could stare out the window. The snow was blowing again, undoing all their earlier shoveling, but Hugh hardly noticed. He was as intensely focused on her as he had ever been on anything in his life.

"I won't feel safe until he's dead."

Hugh wasn't shocked. Not even hearing those words from Anna, whom he'd found to be unfailingly kind and gentle. "That's hardly surprising," he heard himself say.

She turned then, looking straight at him, and her eyes were wells of pain. "You don't think I'm despicable?"

"Of course not. Hell, Anna, I've killed men with my own bare hands. How could I be shocked that you feel that way about someone who hurt you worse than I can even imagine? If I were in your shoes, I would've killed the son of a bitch."

She almost smiled. It was a pale little expression, lifting just one corner of her mouth, and it didn't quite make it to her pained brown eyes. "I used to dream about it. I used to hope he'd get killed in a car accident, or shot by a mugger, or swept away on a tidal wave. It didn't matter, as long as he just didn't come home."

"But you got away finally, didn't you?"

"I *ran* away."

"Sounds wise to me." He hesitated, forcing himself to stay where he was for fear that if he touched her, he would terrify her. He was angry. He was so angry that he felt as if his blood were seething, but he didn't want his anger to frighten her.

She shrugged one shoulder but didn't reply directly to his comment. He wondered what had happened to her when she ran away, but he didn't ask. Instead he waited, giving her time to decide whether to trust him further.

She spoke. "When I saw what was happening to Lorna, I could hardly turn away."

He nodded.

Anna leaned back against the counter and wrapped her arms around herself, as if she were holding herself together. "I've spent a lot of time trying to forget all this, Hugh. But life seems determined to remind me."

"It goes that way sometimes." He hesitated, unsure whether to inject himself into this conversation. Then he decided that he might as well offer a piece of himself in exchange for the pieces of herself. "I felt that way after I left the army. I was determined I was going to forget everything that had happened, but I couldn't get through a single damn day without something reminding me. It was like I was just gonna keep reliving it until something snapped. Sometimes I felt if I could just let it run its course, the snap would come and set me free from all of it. It never did."

Her expression gentled. "Are you free from it now?"

"Mostly. But not completely. I'd be lying to you if I said I was all done with it. But these days it pretty much limits itself to my dreams. Or to odd moments. You know..." He hesitated, cocking his head to one side. "It's hard to describe. I'll get this little flash from a distance, something inside my head. It's kind of like an echo, or something you almost see from the corner of your eye."

She nodded encouragingly. "It's not really there."

"Yeah, sort of. It's not like the flashbacks used to be. I mean, man, those things were *real.* I was really there, doing it all over again, you know? This is more like...oh, I don't know. When you hear a snatch of a tune but can't quite place it, and you're not really sure you didn't just imagine it. It brings you feelings, maybe even memories, but it's not really there."

"That happens to me, too. I never had flashbacks, though. Thank God. But I have all these little phobias now." She flushed faintly. "Like the way I reacted to you at the church."

"I didn't think that was so out of line, Anna. Women have plenty of reasons to be uneasy when they run unexpectedly into a strange man."

"You're not exactly a stranger. I've seen you around a lot. I know a lot of people have a high opinion of you."

It was his turn to feel uncomfortable. "I'm nobody special," he said finally.

"Sure you are. And a lot of people think so."

Something in her had apparently relaxed, because she stopped hugging herself so tightly and turned to point out the window. "Our efforts have been wasted."

"Apparently." The world outside was once again a white swirl. "This sure isn't what they predicted."

"No, but it's actually kind of nice. I always love days like this. It's so cozy, and so nice not to be able to go anywhere or do anything. Would you like some more hot chocolate?"

He hesitated. On the one hand, he felt it would be surprisingly easy to burrow in here for the day and play family. It had been the devil of a long time since he'd had a family of any sort, and Anna made it really attractive to just sit here and while away the time. On the other hand, it could be a real mistake to take her up on the offer and outstay his welcome. He didn't want her to feel as if he was moving in on her.

"You really don't want to go out in this if you don't have to," Anna said. "Why don't you just stay a little longer and see if it lets up?"

It was an offer he couldn't refuse. "Thanks. Just a little longer. But then I've really got to get to the store. I always wait until I don't have a darn thing left in the fridge before I go to the grocery, but this time I guess I waited one day too long."

She smiled at that. "So eat some cookies while I make some more cocoa. Or would you like a ham sandwich? Lorna and I baked a ham last night. A really *good* ham."

"Are you trying to tempt me?"

"Am I doing a good job?"

He had to laugh. "You know you are. A ham sandwich would be wonderful. Can I help make it?"

She shook her head and pointed to the chair. "Just sit and let me do it."

First she went to ask Lorna if she wanted a sandwich. When she returned, she looked thoughtful. "She's not hungry."

"Is that a problem?"

"She looked—oh, I don't know. A little down. I keep waiting for the crash. It's been a week now, and sooner or later all of this is bound to hit her. But maybe I'm just being a worrywart."

Hugh shook his head. "Probably not. There's a whole bunch of stuff here she's going to have to deal with sooner or later. Did she see the counselor Friday?"

Anna nodded. "She didn't want to talk about it, though."

"That's probably understandable. Talking about some of this stuff just once has got to be hard enough."

Anna pulled the ham out of the fridge and a loaf of rye bread from the breadbox and began to make sandwiches. "Mustard, mayonnaise, lettuce?"

"All of the above."

The phone rang just as she finished slicing the ham. She wiped her hands on the towel and went to answer it. Hugh's gaze followed her, and he was suddenly uncomfortably aware that he liked looking at her. It was the strangest thing, and he couldn't remember ever having felt this way before, as if it was somehow enough just to look at somebody. Not even the long stemmed beauties of his past had ever made him feel this way. He was like a kid with a crush.

But all thought of long-stemmed lovelies and adorable little brown-eyed ladies fled when Anna suddenly turned pale and slammed the phone down.

"Anna?" He was on his feet in an instant, prepared for anything. "Anna, what's wrong?"

She was hugging herself again, and this time the gesture actually frightened him.

"Anna?"

She turned her pale face toward him. "It was Al Lacey. I'm sure of it."

"Did he say so?"

She shook her head, and two spots of color appeared on her cheeks as she began to get angry. "No. No, he's too damn smart to do any such thing!"

"What did he say?"

"He said I was going to be sorry I ever persuaded Lorna to lie."

Chapter 8

When Hugh left Anna's house late that afternoon, he headed straight for the sheriff's office. Anna had flatly refused to call Nate about the phone call, feeling—perhaps justifiably—that Nate wouldn't be able to do anything about an anonymous call. But Hugh still felt it would be wise to let Nate know about it. And maybe he would have some suggestions about what to do.

For his own part, he was ready to camp on Anna's front lawn to make sure she was safe. The threat had been unspecific enough that it would be easy to dismiss, but he wasn't in a mood to dismiss it. Not when it came to Anna and Lorna. He felt a very strong surge of protectiveness for them, the kind of protectiveness he had once felt for his buddies in his squad. The kind of protectiveness you feel for people who depend on you completely.

Of course, neither Anna nor Lorna depended on him that way, but it didn't change what he felt.

Unfortunately, camping on her lawn would probably only make her miserable and embarrassed and make him damn cold. Not that he couldn't handle the cold. It sure didn't hold any terrors for him. But he couldn't follow her everywhere like a bodyguard, nor was he even certain it was necessary. Was Al Lacey the kind to take physical action on a threat like that?

Hugh doubted it. For God's sake, the man was a child molester, a cowardly son of a bitch who had apparently terrified Lorna into submission by threatening her baby sister. That kind of coward couldn't stand up to anybody who might fight back. It just wasn't in them.

The streets were calf-deep in snow again. He had no idea whether it was the same stuff that had fallen earlier that had just been blown all over again by the wind, or whether fresh stuff was still falling. Nor did it really matter. The driving was treacherous, and even his chains and the sandbags in the back end of his truck weren't keeping him from skidding every now and then.

When he reached the sheriff's office, he slid into a parking place and came to a jolting halt when his front tires hit the curb. The courthouse square looked as if it was inside one of those little glass globes that people liked to shake up to make the snow fall, except it was darn near invisible in the darkening afternoon. Wouldn't be long before night settled over the world, he thought, as he climbed out.

The wind snatched at him, snaking inside his jacket and nipping at his ears. He bent into it and walked around to the front door of the office. When he stepped inside, the warmth hit him like a blast. The wind grabbed at the door as he closed it, and it shut with a bang.

Velma was sitting at the dispatcher's desk, smoking a cigarette and looking for all the world like a wrinkled lady of leisure.

"No business, Velma?" he asked her.

She waved her cigarette. "Wouldn't make a damn bit of difference if there was, Cowboy. Ain't nobody going nowhere in this crud. At least, nobody intelligent. So what are you doing out?"

"I wanted to talk to Nate for a minute, if he's here."

"He's in his office. Go on back. He's been sitting around here all day wishing something would happen."

"Quit slandering me, Velma," Nate called from his office. "I've been praying all day that there won't be even one car accident. Seems pointless to risk a deputy's neck because some jerk didn't have the sense to stay home." He poked his head out and grinned at Hugh. "Present company excepted, of course. Grab a cup of coffee and come on back."

Hugh filled a ceramic mug from the coffeepot on a table near Velma's desk and went back to Nate's office.

"Pull up a chair, son. Take a load off."

Hugh sat, crossing his legs loosely and gesturing with his mug to the blizzard outside Nate's window. "Kind of early for this, isn't it?"

"I got a feeling deep in my bones that this is going to be one hell of a winter. We get one, every now and again. I can't help thinking of all the ranchers and all their cattle. This is going to hit 'em hard."

Hugh nodded. "I'm thinking about the guys up in the mountains. I don't think they were ready for this."

"Soon as it clears up a little, Billy Joe and I are going to take up some blankets and provisions. Want to come along?"

"Sure. I'd like that."

Nate swiveled his chair around and faced Hugh directly. "So what's up, son? You ought to be snug in your apartment right now."

"I still have to hit the supermarket."

"I think they're closed. You need something to get by until tomorrow?"

Hugh thought about it. "Nah. I guess I can make it. I've got a box of cereal and some milk. But I sure wasn't ready for this, either."

"None of us were. The weather service blew this forecast."

Hugh had to smile. "To say the least." He sipped his coffee and searched for a way to begin. "I was over at Miss Anna's a little while ago. I went over to help shovel her out during that lull we had earlier."

Nate chuckled. "Waste of time, wasn't it? A whole lot of

people are looking out their windows right now at a whole lot of wasted effort."

"Actually, I think we made it worse. The wind's blowing the snow even deeper between the mounds we made. Anna's driveway is going to be a mess come morning."

"Mine, too. So what happened?"

"Well, she invited me in for a hot drink and a sandwich, and while I was there, somebody called her. She thinks it was Al Lacey."

"Damn it." Nate slapped his palm on the desk. "I was afraid he might try something."

"Well, he didn't identify himself, so it could be almost anybody, I reckon. A lot of folks in this town seem to think the girl is lying."

"I've heard." Nate frowned, shaking his head. "I guess it's understandable. Al Lacey has been practicing dentistry here for fifteen years. People feel like they know him. And Bridget grew up here. They don't want to believe Al could be capable of such a thing, and they don't want to believe that if he is, Bridget might have turned a blind eye to it. It's a whole lot easier to believe a child is lying."

"Maybe." Hugh sipped his coffee and put the mug down. "On the other hand, it's dangerous to make that assumption."

"Of course it is. Well, when all's said and done, we'll have more evidence than just the girl's say-so."

"And if you don't?"

"Then Al may walk."

"Can you get more evidence?"

Nate settled back in his chair. "I certainly mean to. I've considered Al Lacey a friend all these years, but I saw that little girl in court, and I've talked to her. I believe her, son. I believe her. So I'm going to do my damnedest to hang that son of a bitch."

"Good." Hugh felt relieved. He didn't know a whole lot about what Lorna might have said, but he knew what Anna thought was going on, and he had a strong feeling that after what that woman had been through, she had X-ray vision when it came to a lie about being molested. Anna believed her, and that was good enough for him.

Nate spoke. "So what did this guy say when he called Miss Anna?"

"He said he was going to make her sorry she'd encouraged Lorna to lie."

Nate unleashed a heavy sigh and rubbed his eyes. "Like that, huh? Hell."

"I figure Al Lacey is too much of a coward to actually make good on that threat."

"Maybe. Maybe not. There's a lot on the line here, you know. It might be enough to goad the man into something he wouldn't ordinarily do."

"So how do we protect Anna?"

"Well, I can keep a close eye on her place, but there's ways he can get to her that don't involve physical intimidation."

Hugh arched a brow. "Gossip, you mean?"

"It'd be damn easy to start up gossip about a thirty-something spinster with no known past."

"But everyone has such respect for her!"

Nate shook his head. "Right now they do. But it wouldn't be hard to remind them that they didn't know squat about her until five years ago."

Hugh didn't at all like the sound of this. "That can't be allowed to happen."

"Trying to prevent gossip is like trying to hold back a flood with a broom, and the damage is usually done before you even know it's happening." He rubbed his chin with his hand. "Let me think on it. Meantime, you keep an eye on her, and I'll get my men to drive by regularly to make sure no one's bothering her."

"I'll sure keep my ear to the ground."

"You do that. Let me know if you hear anything at all. Now, what about you, son? How are you doing?"

"I'm doing just fine."

"No more flashbacks?"

"Not a one." Nor did Hugh mind Nate asking. Nate had been part of a Special Forces A Team in Vietnam. If anyone understood what Hugh had been through, it was Nate Tate. Nate had apparently never suffered from any post-traumatic stress syndrome, but that didn't make him insensitive to those who had. Far from it.

"That's great," Nate said. "That's really good news. Billy Joe's doing well, too." Billy Joe Yuma was Nate's son-in-law, a Vietnam vet who was closer to Nate's age than his wife's, but if that had ever caused Nate concern, he had never let anyone see it. "Maybe time really does take care of everything in the end."

If it was possible, the weather seemed to have worsened by the time Hugh left the sheriff's office. He dug his truck out once again, then, taking a chance, he drove out by Marshall's Quick Gas and Grocery. The gas-station-cum-truck-stop was right on the state highway, and miserable though the weather was, it was still open. There were a half-dozen eighteen-wheelers in the parking lot, holed up to ride out the storm.

"Hardly worth the electricity to stay open," Bud Marshall told him. "But I figured, what the hell. I mean, I live right upstairs, and you never know when somebody might get desperate for milk. Besides, those guys parked out there come in from time to time to use the john."

"Well, I'm desperate," Hugh told him. "I never keep much food on hand, but I'm down to next to nothing."

Bud chuckled and shook his head. "'Twasn't nobody expecting this storm. Listen, you want, I can cook you up a burger. I figure the guys in the lot will be coming in looking for some kind of dinner before long, and it wouldn't hurt to heat up the grill."

"Thanks, Bud, but I think I'll settle for a few odds and ends to take home with me. It's getting so bad out there, I don't want to be out any longer than necessary."

"Prob'ly wise. Well, poke around and see what takes your fancy."

He came up with a bag of chips, a loaf of bread, a jar of peanut butter and some cold cuts. He thought about getting some beer, then decided to pass on it. Alcohol had a tendency to lower the walls and let loose things he would rather keep locked up. Best to avoid it entirely.

As he was checking out, Bud said, "You hear about the Lacey girl?"

"I think everyone has."

"Terrible thing. Terrible thing. Can't imagine Al Lacey doing something like that to a child, let alone his own flesh and blood. My wife thinks the girl's lying, but I don't." He lifted his head from his task and looked Hugh straight in the eye. "Lacey used to be our dentist, but I stopped going there three years ago. Won't let my wife or girl go there, either."

"How come?"

"I didn't like the way he was looking at my daughter. I didn't like it at all. So I drive her over to Hansenville to see Charley Dukes."

Hugh nodded. "Think you could talk to Nate Tate about that?"

Bud looked surprised. "Why? Nothing happened."

"It just might help if you talked to him. Nate's gonna need all the help he can get to take this guy off the street."

Bud thought about it. "Don't see what good it'll do, but I reckon it can't cause much harm."

"It might keep Lacey from hurting some other kid."

Just then two of the truckers came through the door on a burst of cold air and swirling snow. Hugh took his change and left, while they joked with Bud about whether he could even thaw a hamburger enough for them to eat.

He figured he would mention his conversation with Bud to Nate before too long—just in case Bud forgot to.

The snow was still blowing and falling. Anna paused before she closed the front drapes against the night, loving the way the blizzard looked. In the past she would have left the curtains open to enjoy it, but since the phone call that afternoon, she felt uneasy. She didn't want anybody to be able to look in her windows and see what she and Lorna were doing.

Once the curtains were closed, she felt able to turn on the living-room lamps. Lorna was still in her room, studying, and the sounds of rock music were still audible through the house. Anna paused in the hallway, listening, and wondering if she should just leave the girl alone or check on her.

Check on her, she decided. It had been hours since Lorna had last emerged, and that didn't seem quite right to her.

She tapped on Lorna's door but got no response. Finally she opened the door a crack and peeked in. Lorna was lying prone on her bed with her face buried in her pillow.

Alarm gripped Anna, and she stepped into the room. "Lorna?"

The girl didn't answer. Anna hit the Off button on the tape player that Nate had brought from the Lacey house with Lorna's other possessions, and hurried to the bed.

"Lorna? Honey, are you all right?" Perching beside the child, she reached out and touched her shoulder. She could feel the tremors running through the girl's frail body. "Oh, Lorna, what's wrong? Tell me, sweetie."

Lorna rolled over, revealing a swollen, tear-streaked face and reddened, puffy eyes. "Nobody loves me, Anna. Nobody!"

"That's not true. *I* love you."

"But my mom doesn't! My dad doesn't! Even Mr. Kreusi hates me! He wouldn't let me come back to school."

Anna hardly knew where to begin. Reaching out, she gripped Lorna's hand and tried to draw her closer. The girl refused to budge and yanked her hand away. "In the first place, Mr. Kreusi doesn't hate you. He had to suspend you because you tried to burn the school down. You know that, Lorna. You know what you did was wrong, and you know you had to be punished for it, just like you're probably going to be punished by the court for doing it. People can't be allowed to start fires and then get away with it."

"But he doesn't believe me, Anna! He doesn't believe me. Nobody believes me. And my mom is saying terrible things about me!"

Anna felt her heart clench. "Who told you that?"

"Mary Jo. When I called her this afternoon. She said everybody's talking about me, and my mom is saying I'm a liar and all kinds of terrible things. Why is she doing that, Anna? Why?''

Anna reached out to her, and this time Lorna came, sitting up and wrapping her arms around Anna as if she were hanging on for dear life.

Anna let her cry her heart out. There didn't seem to be much she could do except hold the child and wait for the storm to pass. But she was angry, furious at Bridget Lacey, and furious at Mary Jo for passing along gossip. Mary Jo had the excuse of youth, but Bridget had no excuse at all except willful stupidity and blindness.

A long time later, Lorna quieted, unable to cry anymore it seemed. She lay back on her pillow and stared blindly at the ceiling, looking for all the world as if something essential had been torn out of her soul. And finally she said one word. ''Why?''

Anna sighed and shook her head, trying to find words that would both explain and comfort Lorna. The task seemed almost impossible.

''I know I did bad things,'' Lorna said dully. ''I know they were bad. But my dad did bad things, too. How come everybody's ganging up on *me?*''

''I don't think they are, honey. I know it feels that way, but I really don't think the whole world is ganging up on you. An awful lot of us are on your side.''

''And Mom? Doesn't she love me even a little bit?'' Lorna's voice cracked, and fresh tears ran down her face.

''Your mother—'' Anna broke off sharply, trying to choose her words very carefully. Finally she gave up trying to be diplomatic. ''Frankly, Lorna, I think your mother's gone a little crazy.''

Lorna's wet blue eyes fixed on her. ''Crazy?''

''Crazy. I think all this has pushed her over the edge. She's trying to make it all go away, but it's not going to go away.''

''How can she think it'll go away if she says terrible things about me?''

''Well, you see, if you're lying, that means everybody can forget about it. People would just shrug their shoulders and

tune. The snow had stopped falling at last, but the wind hadn't let up at all. It rattled the windowpanes and moaned around the corners of the house.

Anna curled up on the sofa with Jazz beside her and tried to read a book, but she couldn't concentrate. The phone was beckoning to her again, urging her to call her stepfather. She didn't usually get the urge this often, and it indicated to her just how much this business with Lorna was disturbing her equilibrium.

Her hard-won equilibrium. That careful balancing act she did that kept her safely on a tightrope over the abyss where her memories dwelt. Lately she felt as if the rope were bucking wildly and she was hanging on with both hands for dear life, knowing that if she slipped and fell into that abyss, her memories would come rushing back and drown her.

What she had wasn't amnesia. No, she knew what was buried in her past, but she'd somehow managed to distance it, until it took an effort to recall actual events. Most of the time, it even felt as if those things had happened to someone else.

But tonight the memories seemed awfully close, and her grip on the tightrope seemed perilously weak. Calling her stepfather would be the stupidest thing she could do. She was in entirely too fragile a state right now.

What was more, she seriously doubted he had dropped dead in the past couple of weeks. What she had to do was get over this ridiculous feeling that she would never be safe until he was dead and buried. After all, she had been safe from him for sixteen years now, ever since she had walked out of that house for the last time at the age of fourteen. He hadn't been able to touch her since, so why the heck couldn't she feel safe?

She sighed, and Jazz lifted her head, looking at her with sad puppy eyes. Anna reached out and scratched the dog's ears, saying, "It's okay, Jazz. It's okay."

Jazz licked her hand, then put her head back down on her paws.

The phone rang, and the sound jarred Anna, causing her for

one horrifying instant to think her stepfather had found her. But he couldn't have. No way. Anna Fleming wasn't even her real name, and there was no way he could know that she had changed it the day she turned eighteen. Nor would he want to find her, she was sure.

But her heart was still hammering as she reached out for the receiver and lifted it. "Hello?" She sounded weak and frightened, even to her own ears.

"Anna?" Hugh's deep, warm voice came over the line. "Anna, is something wrong?"

"No...no, really. I was just...thinking about Lorna." It was a lie, and she felt guilty for it, but she couldn't possibly tell him the truth.

"Oh. Okay. I just had this weird feeling that something was wrong and I needed to call you."

"No, I'm fine, really." But she didn't want him to hang up, and she sought wildly for some subject of conversation. "It stopped snowing."

"So it did." She could hear his smile in his voice. "I'll be over first thing in the morning to dig you out. You and Lorna shouldn't have to do all that alone."

Her old stubborn pride reared its head, making her want to tell him not to come, that she could handle it. But the truth was, she wanted to see Hugh. She wanted very much to see him. So instead of arguing, she said, "Thank you. I'd really appreciate that."

"All I ask in return is another cup of that hot chocolate and a couple of those cookies. It's been a long time since I had anything so good."

A little laugh escaped her. "Are you trying the pity thing?"

"Absolutely. Here I am, a lost little waif with nobody to cook for me and no desire to do it for myself. Well, hell, Anna, I can't see the point of baking cookies just for me. So naturally I'm cadging them from somebody who's already baked them. Do I look stupid?"

She did laugh then, and the sound shivered pleasantly on the line between them. "In return for shoveling me out of this mess, you're entitled to *two* cups of hot chocolate and a half-dozen cookies, plus a breakfast of eggs and ham."

"You're on." He hesitated. "I take it you didn't get any more threatening phone calls."

"No, none." A little shiver of apprehension ran through her. "It's terrible, Hugh. Lorna was in tears tonight because she thinks everybody's against her and her mother doesn't love her anymore."

He swore, a word she wasn't used to hearing anymore, being associated with a church as she was. It was, however, a word she had once used frequently herself, during her street days. It certainly didn't shock her.

"Sorry," he said swiftly. "I shouldn't have said that."

"It's okay. It's a word I've wanted to use myself more than once in the last week."

"Yeah." He sighed; she could hear it clearly. "Look, Anna, I know you've got your hands full, but...maybe if you and Lorna together tried to help me with this youth ranch thing, we could get her mind off her problems. I know that sounds really crass of me, like I'm taking advantage of the two of you, but I'm honestly not. It just suddenly struck me that Lorna needs something constructive to distract her, something important and out of the ordinary. If you've got a better idea, I'll drop it."

Anna hesitated, wondering if he was manipulating her. But no, she'd already told him that she would be happy to offer ideas and discuss the ranch with him, even though she couldn't be part of it. This really wouldn't be anything she hadn't already agreed to, but it *would* include Lorna. And she could see a dozen ways it would benefit the child.

"I think that would be a great idea," she told him. "I really do. How can we start?"

"How about I take the two of you out to see the ranch one of these days soon? You can tell her about it, so she can look forward to it, and this weekend, assuming the roads are good enough and the weather has cleared, we'll go out and look the place over. I really *would* like her input on what she thinks kids her age need and would like."

"I know she'd love to help. Okay. Let's shoot for Saturday."

"Great."

He was silent for a few seconds, and so was she, but this time the silence between them didn't feel strained. It was nice, Anna thought, to be close to him this way. It would be even nicer if he were here, sitting beside her on the couch or across from her in the armchair. Nice if she could look into his craggy, weathered face and see the warmth she always found there. In fact, thinking about it now, she found it surprising how much warmth Hugh Gallagher showed. After all he'd been through, it wouldn't be surprising if he had developed a hard edge.

"I drove out to Marshall's truck stop after I left you," he said. "He was probably the only business in town that was open today. He had a half-dozen big trucks parked in his lot and was pretty much staying open to take care of the drivers. And in case anybody needed milk, he said."

"That was nice of him."

"I think he'd have been utterly bored if he hadn't opened," Hugh said on a chuckle. "For some folks, a snowy day isn't much of a blessing."

"I guess not."

"Anyway, he said something interesting about Al Lacey. He said that he stopped taking his daughter to Lacey for her teeth a couple of years ago because he didn't like the way Al was looking at her."

"Really?"

"Really. I told him he should talk to the sheriff. I'm not sure how much good it can do, but you never know. What I *do* know is that I can't imagine what makes men like that tick."

"Me either." She hesitated. "Are *you* okay, Hugh?"

He was silent for a few seconds, then gave a small chuckle. "Does it show?"

"Does what show?"

"That it's a rough night. And I can't figure out why it should be."

"Maybe it's sitting all alone and listening to the wind moan."

"Could be." He hesitated. "Is it making you feel funky?"

"Just a little."

"Yeah."

She waited, feeling the seconds tick by, wondering if either of them had the gumption to take this conversation any further, or if they were both going to back quickly away from the unaccustomed intimacy. She knew *she* wanted to.

"It sounds a little like an incoming round," he said finally.

"What does?"

"The wind."

She felt her heart go out to him. She had some idea of what it was to wrestle with the past, after all. "I keep wanting to call my stepfather," she admitted.

He laughed briefly. "Aren't we a pair? How old is your stepfather now?"

She had to think about it. That surprised her, since the man had once been the main thing on her mind. "Sixty-four, I guess."

"Well, the old bastard could kick off any day now, then."

"Maybe." She felt awful for discussing such things out loud.

"Then again, seeing what a creep he is, he could live forever. I'm a great believer in that old saying that the good die young. I sure saw enough of 'em do it."

"I'm sorry."

"Hey, you've got nothing to be sorry for, Anna. Nothing at all. That's the risk a man takes when he puts on a uniform."

"It still isn't right."

"No, it isn't. It just *is*. So, did your stepfather go to jail?"

"He got five years' probation."

He swore. "That don't hardly seem right."

"It's actually quite common in cases like this. It's so hard to prove that anything really happened that prosecutors tend to work plea bargains. Plus, nobody wants the child to have to testify in court if it can be avoided."

"I guess I can understand that."

"*I* didn't want to testify," Anna admitted. "I just about panicked at the thought of having to face him and tell what he did to me. It was hard enough telling everyone else I had to tell."

"Lorna will probably feel the same."

"Probably. You know, I've often wondered about that. I can't erase the memory of what he did to me. I have to live with it. So why did it seem so impossible to say it to his face? After all, he already knew it."

"Ah, but you were terrified of him, Anna. Don't blame yourself for that. He'd hurt you and abused you, and had exercised total power and control over you. How could you not be terrified of having to face him? You're...what? Thirty now? You're a full-grown woman who's been standing on her own two feet for a long time. I'll bet you still wouldn't want to face him."

Anna drew a shaky breath, surprised by how well he read her. "No, I wouldn't want to. Not even now."

"And that's understandable. The man hurt you grievously, and it's hardly surprising that you're still afraid of him at a gut level. You can argue with yourself about it all you want, but the fear isn't going to go away. And that's why you wish he'd just drop dead. That's the only way you can be sure he'll never be able to hurt you again. Once burned, twice shy, as they say."

Anna felt her throat tighten. Hugh's amazing understanding made her ache in the strangest way, as if she had suddenly found somebody who really cared about her, somebody she could turn to and trust. She couldn't remember the last time she had felt that way about anyone.

The feeling terrified her. It was full of danger and threat. It could lay her open to terrible wounds and disappointments. She couldn't afford to trust anyone that way. She just couldn't.

"I'm sorry," Hugh said suddenly. "This is probably the last thing you want to be talking about."

"It seems to be all I can think about tonight," she admitted. "But you're right. I don't want to talk about it. I don't want to think about it. Until this thing with Lorna came up, I'd gotten to the point where I didn't really think about it for months at a time. Oh, I don't mean it never crossed my mind, but when it did it was one of those fleeting little things and was gone. It wasn't *possessing* me, if you know what I mean."

"I know exactly what you mean, Anna. I wish I had some kind of remedy to offer, but I don't. I never found a way to keep myself from worrying over things that my mind was determined to worry over. It just goes on until it decides of its own accord to quit bugging you."

"It seems that way."

"I'd suggest getting out and doing something, but that's kind of hopeless right now."

She had to laugh softly. "It sure is. I suppose I could go out and build a snowman in the front yard."

"If the wind didn't blow you away."

He stayed on the phone with her for another hour, talking about the work he was doing at the church, about the youth group's plans for a Christmas play and concert, about anything that occurred to either of them.

When she hung up, Anna felt more relaxed than she had all day. She didn't even think again about calling her stepfather. Instead, she went to bed and slept soundly.

Chapter 9

Saturday dawned bright, clear and warm. The snow was beginning to melt away, leaving the streets and sidewalks slushy and wet. The unexpected warmth was welcome to Anna, who figured it would probably be the last they would see until spring. The weather forecasters were even now talking about another winter storm moving in across the Rockies, and predicting heavy snowfall beginning late on Sunday.

Lorna was excited about going out to Hugh's ranch, and was ready to go a full half hour before he came by to pick them up. Anna was glad to see that she had put aside her sorrow, at least for now. Going back to school had been good for her. She had discovered that her friends were still her friends, and that they were genuinely concerned about her. Anna had worried that their reactions might be very different and that some of their parents might want their daughters to stay away, but that hadn't happened. Nor had John Kreusi done anything to make the girl feel unwelcome.

When Lorna climbed into Hugh's truck to sit between him and Anna, she was chatting cheerfully about everything that came into her head. Hugh smiled at her, then looked over her head at Anna and winked.

"My ranch is out east of here," he told them as they drove out of town. "About twenty miles. The land isn't useful for a ranching operation, but it'll sure provide a lot of room for teaching kids how to ride horses, how to camp out and hike, and maybe even how to raise a few head of livestock."

Lorna looked at him. "You'll teach the girls, too, won't you?"

"Absolutely."

"Good. I get sick of guys acting like they're the only ones who can do anything."

Hugh glanced down at her. "I figured out a long time ago that girls can do anything guys can do if they want to."

"Me too," Lorna agreed, a satisfied smile on her face.

"Except when it comes to upper body strength," Anna said. "Guys will always be stronger in the arms and shoulders than girls."

"In general," he agreed. "But there are exceptions to the rule—which is a good reason not to make it a rule."

Anna decided she liked his attitude.

She didn't know what she had expected to find when they arrived at the ranch—maybe a run-down old house, a couple of sagging outbuildings and endless acres of snow-covered land. Instead she discovered a reasonably neat, large two-story ranch house, a barn in good condition, and what looked like a motel.

"This used to be a dude ranch," Hugh said as they bucked to a halt in the rutted driveway in front of the house. "The last owners had to close it about five years ago because it wasn't making any money, but they did their best to keep it in reasonably good condition so they could get a better price for it. Nobody but me wanted it, though, and after five years they were willing to come way down."

"It looks like you got a good deal," Anna ventured.

He flashed her a smile. "I got an *incredible* deal. Did you ever get the feeling that something was meant to be? That's the feeling I have with this. Like it's really meant to happen."

He looked out at the house and outbuildings, his expression that of a man who saw his dream within his grasp.

He got out of the truck and came around to help Anna and Lorna down. "So," he asked, "do you want to go inside?"

"Of course," Anna said, then looked at Lorna. The girl was turning around slowly where she stood, taking everything in with an almost wistful expression.

"You'll have horses?" she asked.

"Count on it," he answered.

"My dad used to promise that we'd have horses someday, but then he started saying they were too expensive and too much work. He said I wouldn't be good about taking care of them."

"The kids who live here are going to *have* to take care of them," Hugh said. "I'll ride their butts to make sure they do."

Lorna suddenly giggled. "I bet you will."

"Believe it. I'm a great butt rider."

She giggled again, and they all moved toward the house. Anna loved the big, wide porch and had no trouble imagining it dotted with rocking chairs and maybe even a swing. She'd always wanted a front porch like this for long summer evenings. Her imagination filled it with people, with the kind of family she had been deprived of so long ago. Grandparents and parents and grandchildren lazing around in the evening breeze, maybe sipping lemonade or iced tea. It didn't matter to her that the image was clichéd. She needed some of those clichés in her life.

But snow covered the ground and had drifted on the porch, and she couldn't cling to the summery images for long. They stepped through the front door of the house and discovered a huge living room with a big fireplace.

"This was sort of the lodge for the dude ranch," Hugh said. "It'll be a great gathering place for the kids. And through there is a dining room big enough to seat thirty without any trouble. I'm figuring on putting in small tables, with four to a table. Make it cozier."

The walls in the living room were timbered, giving the feeling of a lodge, but the dining room had been wallpapered. The paper was coming loose in the cold and hung in forlorn strips.

"I don't much care for that paper," Hugh said. "It's too busy. I reckon I'll strip the walls and paint 'em white. It'll make the room seem bigger and brighter."

Anna nodded approvingly. Hugh then led them through to a huge kitchen that was equipped with restaurant-style appliances.

"Everything in here works," he said. "It's all ready to heat up and start serving the multitudes. I was concerned at first about the stove—a real restaurant stove can get as hot as six hundred degrees on the outside, but it's not the real thing. It's just an overlarge kitchen range that's insulated, so it'll be as safe as any stove around the kids."

Anna, who never would have thought of such a thing, was impressed that he had.

"The dishwasher is larger than standard, too, but it works pretty much like a home one, so the kids ought to be able to use it without any danger."

"That's good."

He smiled at her. "I figure they need to learn how to cook and clean up after themselves. Necessary life skills. I don't envision having a staff to do it for them. This isn't going to be a country resort."

"They'd have to do the dishes at home," Lorna commented.

"Exactly. And cooking is something everybody needs to know how to do. I've learned that one the hard way."

He showed them the bathrooms, one for ladies and one for gents. Anna thought that was a very useful thing to have in the common area, which would probably get a lot of use in the winter months.

"Now the best part," Hugh said. He led them up a wooden staircase to the upper floor. "The family living quarters."

Anna was delighted. There were three bedrooms, a sitting room, a bathroom and a kitchenette, and all of the rooms had tall windows with views of the surrounding countryside. "I love it up here!"

"It's perfect, isn't it?" he said proudly. "More than I really need just for myself, of course, but if I were to take on a partner who had a family, he or she could use it, and I could sleep in one of the rooms in the guest building."

"Or if you get a family," Anna said.

Hugh looked at her with a crooked smile. "Never going to happen. Nobody wants a formerly crazy vet like me."

Anna felt something inside her almost plummet. "Wendy Tate married Billy Joe Yuma," she reminded him.

"Wendy Tate was too young to know better," he said, then shook his head sharply. "That's not true. Wendy is one in a million, and the two of them are as happy as can be."

"That's right."

His smile grew wistful. "Some dreams aren't worth dreaming. They only make you sad."

"*I* think somebody would want you," Lorna said. "You're a very nice man."

He laughed then, and the shadows disappeared from his eyes. "Time will tell, missy. Time will tell."

They went out to look at the guest rooms next. Each was pretty much an ordinary motel-room arrangement with a full bath.

"I figure I can put four kids to a room in bunk beds," he said. "That means I can take on as many as forty kids—although I'm not planning to do it on such a big scale right off. Starting slow is the best way. Get all the bugs ironed out and figure out if we can handle a larger crowd."

"I agree," Anna said. "It's a lot to take on, even with a handful of kids. What kind of help are you thinking of having?"

"Mainly I want people who can help create a family atmosphere for these kids. I don't want to run a boot-camp type of operation where every minute is regimented. I see it as the kind of place where kids can learn to do new things with supportive teachers who'll take the time to listen to them and help them. I want these kids to learn self-confidence and self-reliance, and how to get along with people. I want them to learn the kind of pride that'll keep them out of trouble."

"Give them what they don't get at home, you mean."

"Exactly. I expect we'll have some behavior problems, so I'm thinking we'll need to have a psychologist on call, but I was kind of hoping for your help. I hear constantly about all the good things you do with the kids in the youth group, Anna. They trust you and like you, and they feel they can turn to you when they have a problem. We need somebody like you."

A bolt of panic shot through her, and she felt her mouth go dry. How could she possibly tell this man that she wouldn't be considered fit for such a role with children? That if he tried to draw her into his plan as a full participant, he was apt to find doors closing in his face at every turn? The only reason she was allowed to work with the youth group was that nobody had inquired that closely into her background. Her arrest record as a juvenile had been sealed, and there was nothing else that might turn up, but surely agencies thinking about sending children to a youth ranch would want to look more closely into the backgrounds of the people running it? And then they would find out. There were ways....

"Anna? Anna, are you all right?"

She blinked and realized she was standing stock-still in the middle of an empty motel room with her hands clenched so tightly into fists that her fingers ached. Through the open door of the room she could see Lorna outside gamboling in the snow. When had she gone outside?

"Anna?"

Moving her head stiffly, she looked at Hugh. Through wooden lips she managed to say, "I'm fine."

"Like hell. You turned white as a sheet a moment ago, and you're standing there looking like a horse that wants to bolt. What did I say?"

"Nothing. Really." She drew a deep breath and lied to Hugh for the second time. "I just felt...a little dizzy, I guess. I'm fine now."

"Are you sure?" His face mirrored concern. "Did you eat breakfast? Maybe I should get you back to town and feed you."

"No, really. I ate. I'm not at all hungry." She managed a smile. "I'm fine now. Honestly."

He looked at her for a moment, as if debating whether to take her at her word, then nodded. "Okay."

But she noticed he took her arm as they walked outside, as if he were afraid she might fall. The gesture touched her.

She insisted they go take a look at the barn. There she found stalls for horses and a loft for hay.

"They kept horses but no other livestock," he explained. "I figure we ought to have a few cows and sheep, though, just so the kids can learn about them and how to take care of them. Besides, they won't feel like they've lived on a ranch otherwise."

"I like cows," Lorna said. Her cheeks were flushed from the cold, and her eyes sparkled as if she were enjoying herself hugely. "Cows are just the sweetest things. A baby cow licked my arm once. I couldn't believe how long and big its tongue was. I like sheep a lot, too. I think that's a good idea."

"I'm glad you approve." Hugh spoke without a hint of patronization. When Lorna offered some more of her opinions, Hugh listened to her as seriously as if she were an expert on the subject.

Anna watched the two of them talking and felt a tug on her heart. The sight of them together filled her with a yearning she couldn't begin to name. Shaking her head, she tried to brush the feeling aside. It did no good to want things she couldn't have.

On the way home, Lorna asked if she could spend the night with Mary Jo. Anna hesitated, still uneasy about the gossip that Mary Jo had passed on to Lorna earlier in the week. Lorna, however, looked as if she wasn't the least bit concerned about such things, and regarded Anna with apparent hope and eagerness.

"When did Mary Jo ask you?"

"This morning, when she called."

"Why didn't you ask me right away?"

"Because I was afraid you'd say no."

Anna wanted to sigh, but she stifled it. "Waiting doesn't usually make it any likelier that I'll say yes."

Lorna smiled sheepishly. "I know. I just had to get up my nerve."

Anna could see Hugh behind Lorna, and saw that he was smiling. He thought it was amusing. Actually, so did she. "Well, all right, as long as she's cleared it with her parents."

"Oh, she did! She said her mom was the one who suggested it."

"Then okay. What time do you have to be there, and when will you be home?"

"She asked if I could come over at four, so I can have dinner with them. And I'll go to church with them in the morning and come home with you afterward, if that's okay."

"That'll be just fine. I need to talk to Mr. and Mrs. Weeks first, though."

"How come?"

"There's just a matter I need to discuss with them, okay?"

Lorna looked doubtful, but nodded. "All right."

Hugh dropped them off and turned down an offer of lunch. Anna watched him drive away and wondered if they had done something to make him want to get away from them. She couldn't imagine what it might have been and tried to tell herself she was being ridiculous, but a subtle sense of anxiety wouldn't leave her. She found herself playing back the morning's events over and over, trying to pick out what might have bothered him.

Maybe he was washing his hands of them because of her refusal to participate in his youth ranch in the way he wanted. But Hugh Gallagher didn't strike her as being that childish.

And maybe nothing at all had happened, she told herself sternly. Maybe he just had something else he needed to do. Or perhaps he felt he had taken enough of *their* time today. Either possibility was as likely as the things she was imagining.

After lunch she shooed Lorna off to her room to pack for her sleepover and took the opportunity to make the call to the

Weeks family. Mary Jo's mother, Mildred, answered the phone.

"Hi, Mildred, this is Anna Fleming."

"Anna! How are you? And how is Lorna?"

"We're both doing fine. Lorna said Mary Jo asked her to come spend the night tonight, and I wanted to make sure that was all right with you."

"Of course it is." Mildred chuckled. "It took me years, but I've finally got Mary Jo trained to ask *me* before she asks her friends. We're looking forward to Lorna's visit."

"Lorna is certainly looking forward to visiting you. But there is a matter I needed to discuss with you. I don't know if you're aware that the court has forbidden Lorna's parents to have any contact at all with her?"

"Yes, I'd heard about that. Don't worry, Anna. Neither Bill nor I will let either one of those people near the child. Good Lord, I can't believe what that woman is saying about her own daughter! If one of my girls came to me with such a story, it'd kill me, but the first thing I'd do is move myself and the girls out, and I wouldn't come back unless I was absolutely sure nothing had happened. And either way, I wouldn't go around town telling everyone that my daughter was a lying slut!"

"Neither would I." Anna had always thought Mildred Weeks was a fine woman, but now she felt a strong burst of warmth toward her. The world needed more mothers like this, she thought. "There's another thing, too. There's an awful lot of nasty gossip going around—"

"Don't I know it! Don't you worry, Anna, Lorna won't hear a word of it here. I already scolded Mary Jo for telling Lorna some of it earlier this week. Mary Jo just thought it was all exciting. She never thought about how it would make Lorna feel. But don't worry. She won't hear another whisper of it from anyone in this family—or from anyone who happens to come around, either, if I have anything to say about it. That poor dear is going through quite enough without people saying ugly things about her."

"Lorna's not lying," Anna felt compelled to say.

"We know she isn't," Mildred said firmly. "We've been uneasy about that man for some time now. It was nearly a year ago when we put our foot down and told Mary Jo she couldn't sleep over there anymore. It wasn't that he did anything terrible, but some of the goings-on just made us real uneasy." She fell silent a moment. "No, even looking back at it, I can't say he did anything *wrong*. It just didn't feel right, if you take my meaning."

"I certainly do."

"And I feel just awful now. I realize Bill and I didn't have anything we could really point a finger to at the time, but oh, how I wish we could've done something to save Lorna from the past year."

"I think a lot of people are feeling that way, Mildred."

"Possibly. Possibly." The woman sighed. "I wish foresight was as good as hindsight."

After she hung up, Anna felt a whole lot better about Lorna spending the night with Mary Jo. She was probably worrying too much, anyway. There was no way she could protect Lorna from the gossip. Not when the girl was back in school with dozens of children who were perfectly capable of keeping her clued in as to what their elders were saying about her. Poor Lorna!

Unable to do anything else useful, Anna went to walk Jazz.

That evening she received another threatening phone call. A man's muffled voice said, "I'm going to make you sorry you made that kid lie." Then, before she could do more than gasp, he hung up.

Anna sat on the couch, staring blindly, holding the receiver tightly in her hand, frozen by fear. She wanted to be angry. She wanted to be furious. She wanted to throw the phone and yell and scream and get even with her tormentor. But she was too afraid to do any of that.

She had too many secrets. Too many dark places in her past. And never, ever, had she been more aware of just how vulnerable she was. All it would take was one person digging deeply enough into her past and she would be ruined in this town.

Finally, with a trembling hand, she put the receiver down. There was no point in calling Nate, she thought. There was absolutely nothing he could do about an anonymous caller who made no threat other than that she would be sorry. She was convinced it had to be Al Lacey—who else would bother?—but she certainly couldn't swear to it. The voice was too muffled. Lacking an actual threat and a confirmation of identity, no one could help her.

Nor were they really likely to think she needed help. No one knew enough about her past to understand how easy it was to terrify her. No one would begin to imagine that what she most feared was the truth. Nor did she think this caller was threatening her physically. Lacey was in enough trouble. He would have to be the worst fool imaginable to get involved in another crime, one that would be a lot easier to prove.

Jazz nudged her leg, begging to be lifted onto the couch with her. She bent and took the puppy into her lap, marveling at how much she had grown in just a couple of weeks. Jazz curled up contentedly and closed her eyes, ready to nap.

Anna envied the dog. It had been a long time since she had last felt this helpless, and it was upsetting to realize that she was a prisoner of her own fear more than anything else. Her past *wasn't* in the past, the way she kept telling herself. Instead, it was very much in the here and now, influencing every decision she made. And she didn't know what to do about it.

Burying her hand in the dog's soft fur, she closed her eyes and tried to find a way out of a mess that was mostly of her own making. Unfortunately, every option that occurred to her had unacceptable risks. Every one of them would put her in exactly the position she was so desperately trying to avoid.

The phone rang again, and she almost didn't answer it. But then a spark of anger flared in her, and she grabbed the receiver, determined to tell her tormentor where to get off.

"Hello?"

There was a silence on the line, then Hugh's voice said, "Anna? Is something wrong?"

And without meaning to, Anna blurted, ''I got another phone call.''

''Threatening you?''

''Telling me I was going to be really sorry I encouraged Lorna to lie.''

Hugh swore. ''That does it,'' he said. ''I'll be over there in ten minutes.''

''But—'' But he'd already disconnected, and she found herself listening to a dial tone.

And suddenly she felt better. For the next couple of hours, at least, she wasn't going to have to sit around and worry about this all by herself.

Hugh swore savagely after he hung up the phone, then went to get dressed. He'd been lounging around in sweatpants and a sweatshirt, feeling kind of blue and lonely, and wishing like hell he'd had the sense to have lunch with Anna and Lorna. Damned if he didn't miss the two of them not five minutes after dropping them off.

Then, sitting here listening to the old building creak and pop in the deepening cold, he'd found himself wondering what Anna was doing to fill the evening hours, and wondering if she was as lonely as he was. If she was at loose ends, too.

One thing had led to another, and finally he'd decided it wouldn't hurt to call, especially since his abrupt departure when he dropped her off had left Anna looking...well, surprised. He would have said hurt, except that he didn't think that highly of himself. No way he imagined he meant enough to that woman to hurt her by leaving abruptly. But he *had* been rude, and he figured he owed her a bit of an apology.

He hadn't had any idea how he was going to explain himself, but he wasn't all that worried about it. The apology was due, and he would make it. Knowing Anna, he thought she wouldn't press him enough to make him admit he'd been running from her like a bat out of hell because he was scared to death of the things she made him want. The dreams she made appear to be just within his grasp.

They weren't within his grasp, of course. No way. She

would never be interested in a man like him, and given her past, it was entirely likely she wasn't ever going to be interested in any man at any time.

But now...now he was fighting mad. Apologies were forgotten. All he wanted to do was strangle the bastard who was frightening her. She didn't deserve this. In all his life, he'd never met a woman he thought was any more basically decent and kind than Anna Fleming. In fact, given the way her stepfather had treated her and the unwillingness of her mother to believe it was happening, it was wonderful that Anna had managed to become such a kindhearted and good woman.

He pulled on jeans and a Shaker sweater, shoved his feet into boots, grabbed his jacket and headed out. He didn't want to think about how frightened she must be, but it was all he could think about anyway. And if he could ever figure out for sure who the sorry so-and-so was who was calling, he would make sure the creep thought twice about doing it again.

Of course, it had to be Al Lacey. Who else could it possibly be? He didn't think anyone else in this town would think Anna was the root of the problem. Only Al Lacey was in a position to see things that way.

Damn!

His truck started easily enough, and soon he was zipping down streets that had frozen over again into ripples and ridges of ice. There had been enough traffic over the evening, though, to keep the meltwater from freezing into a smooth sheet that could be treacherous, so he didn't slow down much.

He reached Anna's in exactly the ten minutes he had promised. He saw her peek out the living-room window as he pulled up, and when he reached the door, he didn't even have to knock. She pulled it open immediately.

He stepped inside without waiting for an invitation and closed the door behind himself. Then, without thinking, he reached for her and drew her into his arms.

Her resistance was no more than a mere hesitation this time before she came willingly into his embrace. God, he thought, how good it felt to hold her! He closed his eyes with the pleasure of it, and lowered his head until his lips touched her silky hair. A warning bell sounded in his mind, but he ignored it. He needed this embrace entirely too much to give it up easily.

But finally even he realized they couldn't stand there that way indefinitely. He needed to let go of her, to talk to her, to ease her fear in whatever way he could. He needed to let her know that she didn't have to be alone.

Chapter 10

Anna laid three aces on the table and looked apologetically at Hugh. "The cards seem to be favoring me tonight." She'd already beaten him on three hands.

He smiled. "Lucky at cards, unlucky in love. I guess that makes me lucky."

"I'm not sure the reverse is true."

His smile broadened. "Are you telling me you don't think I'm lucky in love?"

She felt her cheeks heat. "I don't think I said that."

"No, but I inferred that from what you implied."

She hesitated. Her education hadn't been the best, and while she loved to read, there were still plenty of gaps in her knowledge. Never had she understood the difference between inferring and implying, although she had a sense of it from what he had just said. Trouble was, she didn't know exactly how to answer him. She wanted to keep things light and humorous, but there was no humorous way she could think of to answer him, especially when she had the feeling that she might just have insulted him.

"I'm sorry," he said suddenly. "I'm just teasing. I didn't really misunderstand you."

"Oh."

"Anyway, I've never had any luck at love, so these cards ought to be playing my way. And they're not."

He put his hand down so she could see it. "See? Nothing useful at all. Nothing that's likely to get useful."

"Would you like to play a different game?"

He shook his head, his smile returning. "Actually, I'm enjoying myself. The cards are just an excuse to sit here with you."

Her cheeks flamed. She was sure they were as red as the Christmas napkins in her linen closet. No man had ever said anything that sweet to her, and she didn't have the vaguest idea how to respond to him.

He looked at her as if he were perplexed. Finally, as if he didn't know what else to do, he said, "Would it be possible for me to have a cup of coffee?"

"Decaf?"

"That would be great."

She put her cards down and rose to make the coffee. Conscious of his gaze following her, she felt awkward. Her legs didn't even seem to want to move right, and she twice dropped the coffee filters she took out of the drawer. Finally, with trembling hands, she managed to fill the coffeemaker with water and the basket with the right number of scoops of coffee.

It was surprising, she found herself thinking, how difficult such a simple task could become when you were nervous. And she was definitely beginning to get nervous.

It wasn't that he had really done anything to make her feel that way. She just wasn't used to having a man around like this, and the longer he stayed, the more conscious of it she became.

She stood at the sink, rinsing the coffee scoop and taking as long at it as she could. Then she brought out mugs, milk and sugar, and all the while she was wondering if it would be wiser to ask him to leave.

But she didn't want him to leave. She didn't want to be

alone. Not tonight. Not after that phone call. Not when a sense of unease just wouldn't leave her alone, reminding her that her life wasn't the placid pond she kept trying to turn it into.

Her memories were very near the surface tonight, she realized. Just below the level of consciousness, they were threatening to erupt in a maelstrom of pain and unwanted remembrance. Was just having a man in her house enough to cause that?

"Anna?" Hugh was suddenly behind her, close. Too close. She whirled around and looked up at him, uneasiness filling her almost past bearing. She wanted to run, escape, flee into the icy night and keep going until everything that worried and concerned her was so far away it couldn't touch her ever again.

He reached out and touched her shoulder, then her cheek, with a tenderness that deprived the gesture of any kind of sensuality. The last time anyone had touched her this way was childhood, and the last man to show her genuine tenderness had been her father. Her real father.

"I won't hurt you," he said. "I would never hurt you. If you want, I'll leave."

"No!" The word was out before she even realized she was going to say it.

He cocked his head a little to one side and let his hand fall. "I'm upsetting you."

"It's not...not you," she managed to say.

"So it's men in general?"

She was astonished that he was able to discern her problem so quickly and so easily. Was she transparent? Or was he just unusually sensitive?

"I know fear when I see it," he said. "In my line of work, you learn to recognize it." He sighed and stepped back. "So is it men in general?"

She managed a jerky nod.

He compressed his lips, looking almost sad. "Have you ever had a real boyfriend? A real lover?"

Shame suddenly flooded her, and she lowered her head.

"No, I guess not," he answered for her. He stepped even farther back. "I won't touch you, Miss Anna. I promise."

He turned his back, and she felt she was losing a chance for something precious, but she didn't know how to call him back. She didn't have any idea what it was she wanted from him, but she knew she didn't want the back of his head.

"Hugh..." She managed to speak his name in a hoarse whisper.

He turned and looked at her. "Yes?"

"I...I don't mean to hurt you."

He shook his head sadly. "You didn't hurt me, Anna. I'm hurting *for* you. I think it's just awful that you were wounded so badly by a man you should have been able to trust. Wounded so badly that you get skittish any time I step too close to you emotionally."

"Emotionally?" She didn't understand him.

He nodded. "I don't really scare you physically. I have a feeling you've dealt with that fear, whether you know it or not. You just don't want to be hurt emotionally again. And I can understand that. I'm not a good bet for anybody's trust."

Pain stabbed her heart, but this time it was for him, not her. "Oh, Hugh," she said, forgetting herself in her concern. "Hugh, that's not it at all! It's not *you!*"

He sat down at the table and spread his hands. "Then explain it to me, Anna. If I don't understand, I can't keep from doing things that bother you."

She looked away, staring blindly at the kitchen counter and cabinets, trying to find ways to express what was going on without talking about things she didn't want to talk about. Without raking up things she didn't want to think about.

"I'm...well, since this thing with Lorna started, I'm having trouble with my memories," she said finally. "Things I haven't thought about in a long time are trying to bubble up and make me think about them. It's making me uneasy and edgy."

He nodded reassuringly. She caught the movement from the corner of her eye and found the courage to look at him. "I'm not really comfortable with men, it's true. It usually takes a long time for me to get comfortable with men. I mean, I have to know them for a while before I don't automatically feel threatened every time I see them. I feel comfortable with Reverend Fromberg. I feel comfortable with Nate Tate. I feel comfortable with you."

"Not really."

"Well, more comfortable than I ordinarily would with someone I've just met." She sighed, unable to find the words she wanted in order to explain. "It's so hard...."

"Explaining feelings is always hard. But it's okay. Don't feel like you have to explain anything."

"But I want to," she argued. "Maybe I even need to. I'd like for us to be friends, but that's never going to happen if I keep getting all nervous on you."

"Hey, I've got news for you. We're already friends."

Struck, she thought about that and felt a soft smile gradually dawn on her face as she realized that he was right. They *were* already friends. Maybe not really close friends, but the friendship was definitely there.

"See?" he said as she smiled. "We're friends."

"Yes, I think so, too."

"But I still make you uncertain, don't I? Because you don't know quite what to expect from me."

She nodded slowly, agreeing. "That may be part of it."

"Well..." He paused thoughtfully. "Do you want me to promise that I won't touch you? Would that help?"

As soon as he made the offer, she realized that it wouldn't help, because she did want him to touch her. She actually *wanted* it! The thought astonished her so much that she froze, uncertain what to say or do about this unexpected feeling.

"Okay," he said, "I promise I won't touch you." He gave her a crooked smile. "And I think it's time for me to be going."

He turned and headed for the living room. He was going to get his coat and leave, she realized. Had she offended him somehow? But how? She hadn't said anything.

Except that she had frozen like a deer in headlights when he had mentioned touching her. Maybe he had interpreted her astonishment as fear.

The thought gave her a sharp pang, and she went after him, forgetting herself in her concern for him. Hugh had never been anything but nice to her. He didn't deserve to think she classified him with the men who had hurt her in the past. He didn't deserve her distrust or her fear.

"Hugh..."

He was standing at the coat closet, reaching for his jacket. He looked over his shoulder at her. "Yes?"

"I'm not afraid of you," she said in a rush. "I'm sorry I made you think I was."

He turned from the closet to face her, putting his hands on his hips in a way that made her acutely aware of his masculinity. Her breath nearly stopped in her throat.

"You know, Anna, I might find that a whole lot easier to believe if you didn't keep looking at me as if I were pointing a loaded shotgun at you."

"I don't! I mean...I don't mean to!"

He sighed and turned his head away for a moment. When he looked at her again, some of the exasperation had faded from his face. "I'm sorry. I ought to be more understanding. It's not like I never had a flashback, or never found myself suddenly remembering something unpleasant. But considering how often I seem to remind you of unpleasant things, maybe it would be best if I just keep clear as much as possible."

Her heart sank. She liked Hugh. She liked his easygoing companionship. She was even beginning to like that occasional tingle of sexual awareness he gave her. Considering that she hadn't felt sexually attracted to a man since...well, *ever.* All of her normal development in that regard had been truncated by her stepfather and the men she had sold herself to. For years now she had believed herself utterly *incapable* of feeling such things.

And all of a sudden she didn't want to go back to the numbness that she had once considered a blessing.

She looked at him, twisting her hands together and trying to find some way to tell him these things without dying of embarrassment. Trying to find some way to assure him that she didn't want him to withdraw from her life.

"I'm sorry," she said finally, at a loss. "I like being with you. I wish...I wish I didn't make you feel like you frighten me, because I don't...I don't want you to go away."

Then, embarrassed by having admitted so much, and reluctant to watch him leave, she turned away to go back to the kitchen. There was no way she could ever tell him that the mere sight of him made her want things she had never wanted before. There was no way she could tell him that she had no idea how to deal with the feelings he evoked in her.

"Anna?"

She paused, her back still toward him.

"Come here."

His voice was gentle, so gentle that the sound of it made her throat tighten. So gentle that it never occurred to her not to do as he said.

She turned and walked toward him, feeling her heart thud heavily with each step. Her awareness of everything except her own body and Hugh before her seemed to diminish with every step she took. There was nothing but her heartbeat, her breath, the unexpected but strangely welcome ache between her legs...and Hugh. Only Hugh.

She came to a stop right in front of him. They were close enough now that she could smell him faintly, the delicious aromas of soap and...man. For the first time since her twelfth birthday, the smell of a man didn't sicken her. It drew her, enticing her, and she wondered why.

"Anna..." He murmured her name softly. "Anna, this is killing me...."

She tipped her head a little so she could look up into his face. "What?" Her voice was a choked whisper. There didn't seem to be any air in the room at all.

"I...want to touch you," he said. "It's one of the reasons I think I ought to stay away. I want to touch you, and I'll terrify you if I do. Hell, I'm scared all the time that I'm going to say or do something that will frighten you. It's driving me nuts...."

Tears tightened her throat again, and she closed her eyes, seeking some kind of balance within herself. But there was no balance. She felt awful for making him feel that way, but she didn't know how to stop. Her reactions were so much a part of her that she couldn't even really remember when she *hadn't* been afraid of men. How could she possibly stop responses that were as much a part of her as the way she breathed?

"I'm not afraid of *you,*" she said again. "Not you."

"I'm not really sure that makes any difference."

Her eyes opened, and she looked up at him again, reading the sorrow and longing on his face. He was going to leave, she realized, because he didn't know what to do about this situation. He didn't know how to go on wanting her when she was afraid, and he didn't know how to get past her fear.

But of course *he* couldn't get past it. She had to do that herself, and she didn't have any idea how.

There had been a time when she had been able to reach out and touch men because it hadn't mattered. From within the cocoon of numbness and indifference, she had been able to act boldly. Now that she wanted to reach out and touch, she found herself paralyzed by all the feelings that had once been unable to reach her through her cocoon.

She drew a long shaky breath and sought courage, real courage. Courage such as she had never needed before.

"I want..." Her voice broke, and she had to take another breath before she could continue. "I want...you...to t-touch me."

"Oh, God, Anna!" He turned from her and paced to the far side of the living room. "You don't, not really. You just don't want me to stop being your friend. I won't, I swear. You don't have to say things like that! You don't have to buy my friendship."

She shook her head almost wildly and felt her hair begin to slip free of the pins. "No. No. Really, I... Oh, it's so hard to say! I've never...this is the first time...I've ever felt this way. *Ever!*"

Hugh felt something inside him grow perfectly still. A hush seemed to settle over his mind and heart as her words sank home. He looked at her and saw the truth of what she said written on her face in an expression of yearning.

"Never?" he asked hoarsely, hardly daring to believe what his ears, mind and heart were trying to tell him. Hardly daring to believe the evidence of his own eyes.

"Never," she said, her voice trembling. "I never had a chance. Just about the time I started thinking about boys, my stepfather...well, you know. And since then, I've never wanted anybody to touch me. I even hate it when a doctor has to touch me. But you..." She trailed off, unable to continue.

Hugh swallowed and felt his heart begin to beat heavily. She wanted him to touch her. But now he wondered if he dared. It was dangerous to cross that imaginary line, and he'd promised himself repeatedly that he wouldn't do it with Anna. It would screw up all his hopes that she might be willing to help with the youth ranch, especially if things didn't work out between them.

And they weren't likely to work out, not with her fears always ready to pop up. Not when she was likely to go into a tailspin over nothing at all.

But she deserved the same patience and understanding he had needed from other people when his own fears had swamped him. Not everyone had been understanding, but there were people to whom he owed a deep debt of gratitude he would never be able to repay—except by giving someone else what they had given him.

He tried to tell himself that the youth ranch was more important, but right now nothing seemed as important as the small woman facing him from across the room, awaiting his decision. If he walked out now, he would leave her wounded anew. She had revealed something very intimate, and if he responded wrongly to her trust, she might never be able to trust again.

Faced with her scared yet hopeful expression, he could hardly put the ranch first. Nor did he really want to. Anna had lately become his major preoccupation, and he had the feeling that if he didn't settle his relationship with her somehow, he was never going to have any peace of mind again.

But all those thoughts seemed to be drifting away on a tide

of more important things, like his growing need to hold her close.

He crossed the distance between them and opened his arms, inviting her in. Everything else would just have to wait.

She looked at him for a moment, not moving, and he began to wonder if he had misunderstood everything up until now. Maybe she hadn't really said she wanted him to touch her. Maybe he was losing his mind once again, slipping into some place that had no relationship to reality....

But then she stepped forward, into his arms, and he felt wonderment as her arms wrapped around his waist. Then he closed his own arms around her and held her snugly against him.

Oh, God, it had never felt so right. A pang of fear pierced him, but he pushed it aside. He'd worried and wondered and puzzled enough things for one night. Right now all he wanted to do was give himself up to the absolutely joyous feeling of being held by a woman. By a woman he had been wanting to hold for what seemed like the longest time.

Lowering his head, he pressed his face to her silky brown hair and breathed deeply of her fragrance. Anna Fleming was in his arms, and nothing had ever seemed so right.

Anna listened to the steady beat of Hugh's heart beneath her ear, felt the softness of his sweater against her cheek, but mostly felt the solidness of the man who held her. She was overwhelmed by a feeling of safety that she had thought she had lost forever until just a few hours ago, when Hugh had held her for the first time.

A man's arms could make her feel safe. She absorbed the feeling with every pore, storing it up against future nights when there would be no one to make her feel this way. She clung to the feeling, trying to memorize it so she could take it out on cold nights and close her eyes and remember in every detail what these moments had felt like.

But eventually it was not enough to feel safe. Eventually her body, young and healthy, began to remind her of other needs, needs she had never allowed herself to experience before. Needs that had been locked away in a dungeon so deep she had long since forgotten them.

She wanted more, and like a flower seeking the sun, she turned her face up. Her eyes were closed, so she couldn't see his face, but she heard his sharp intake of breath.

"Anna?" he asked on a whisper.

Then, before she could think what to say or do, his lips touched hers, gently. Oh, so very gently. At first she wasn't sure she felt the caress, but as her lips began to tingle she became aware of the heat of his mouth brushing ever so lightly against hers, as if he were afraid a stronger touch might shatter her into a thousand pieces.

"Hugh..." she heard herself murmur.

Maybe she meant it as an invitation. Maybe not. He took it as one anyway, and bowed his head lower until his mouth pressed firmly against hers. For a few seconds he just nestled there, leaving her to wonder if he would ever, ever, really kiss her. Because she wanted him to kiss her. The yearning was growing in her until she could think of nothing else except what it would be like to be kissed by a man she wanted to kiss her.

Then his lips moved, caressing hers gently. The ache between her thighs began to deepen, and she felt herself press closer to him, as if she wanted to melt right into him. His arms tightened around her, but the feeling didn't frighten her. It seemed right. So very right. She wanted him to hold her tighter still, to kiss her even more deeply.

As if he read her mind, his tongue began to tease along the seam of her lips, begging entry. Shivers of pleasure poured through her, and for an instant, just an instant, she thought of the other times she had kissed men this way and how she had never felt anything at all. But Hugh's kiss was special, the key to so many locked places inside her.

She let her head fall back farther so that she could give him what he asked. When his tongue slipped into her mouth and began to play teasingly with hers, a deep fire began to burn in her. More. She wanted more.

His hands moved against her back, stroking her gently, and

it was as if that touch sensitized the rest of her body. She was suddenly achingly aware of her breasts pressed hard against his chest, of the bulge of his masculinity pressed hard against her belly.

For an instant, memories out of the past rose sharply, filling her with dread, but then they drifted away, carried on a stronger tide of the need he was waking in her.

Hugh lifted his head. Anna's eyes fluttered open, and she looked up at him, dismayed he had stopped kissing her. She didn't want him to stop. She wanted him to follow this miraculous journey to its end.

"Are you okay?" he asked huskily. "I felt you stiffen...."

"I'm okay," she managed to say, wondering why her voice sounded so thick. "I just had a memory...but it's gone now. Really."

He smiled, a sleepy, happy smile. "Yeah?"

"Yeah."

He hugged her tight, so tightly that her ribs felt the pressure, then loosened his hold just a little. "Can we move this to the couch? I don't know about you, but my legs are ready to give out."

Another spear of fear stabbed her, but she ignored it. A nod. She managed a nod.

He began to walk backward to the couch, drawing her with him. "I'd carry you, except I don't want you to feel you're not in control."

She was touched beyond words. And when he sat on the couch, he drew her onto his lap so that she straddled him, facing him.

"See?" he said. "You can get away at any time. I promise. Just say no, and I'll stop immediately, okay?"

She managed another nod and then sank against him with a sigh as he drew her close for another kiss. The fire already ignited grew even hotter, filling her with yearnings that didn't have names, needs and hungers she had never before known.

Gently, gently, she felt herself rocking against him. Part of her wanted to be embarrassed, but another part of her recognized that she couldn't stop. She needed him, needed to feel him between her legs, needed the pressure and release and rhythm of the movements of her hips.

Hugh's hips began to move, too, rising to meet hers in the most delicious way. When his hands slid down her back to grasp her hips, she was glad to feel them take charge, moving her even more deeply against him.

His mouth wandered from hers, following the contours of her cheeks, the hills and valleys of her chin and throat. The heat of his lips against the hollow of her throat made her gasp and arch against him in a way that filled her with new delight. He growled a sound of approval and licked her there with his tongue, fueling her passion.

She gasped and pressed harder against him. The ache between her legs was growing stronger, compelling her past all reason. She was a slave to it now, driven by needs as old as time, needs she had never before experienced.

Fear twinged sharply, disturbing her preoccupation. Not fear that Hugh might hurt her, but fear that she might not find what her body was so desperately seeking. For an instant she heard herself, heard the ragged pants of her breathing, the soft mewling sounds she was making, but before she could draw back in fear and embarrassment, Hugh spoke roughly.

"It's okay, Anna," he said raggedly. "It's okay.... Just let it...let it...."

Somehow she knew what he was trying to say, and the embarrassment faded away as she realized he was every bit as caught up in passion as she was.

There had been a time when she had thought passion to be an ugly, animalistic thing, but her body was teaching her otherwise now. It was showing her how wonderful she was able to feel, how strong the hunger was, how much she needed another human being to make her feel whole.

Higher and higher she climbed, afraid she might not be able to climb high enough, afraid she might fall, afraid she might suddenly freeze within reach of the pinnacle and never get there at all.

"Easy, sweetie," Hugh whispered. "Easy. There's plenty of time...."

She wanted to cry out, to wail that she couldn't, that she didn't know how to get there...and then his hands slipped from her hips to cup her breasts. Even through the layers of her sweater and bra she could feel the heat of his hands. He began to lightly rub his palms over the nubs of her swollen nipples. Electric sparks shot through her from her breasts to her womb and she felt everything inside her, everything, clench tightly.

And in one explosive instant, she reached the peak and tumbled over into completion.

Hugh felt her crest, and he gathered her trembling body close, holding her tightly while the aftershocks ripped through her. His own body was aching fiercely for the satisfaction he had just given her, but he ignored it.

Now was not the time, he told himself. It was plain as the warts on a toad that no one had ever given Anna anything sexually without demanding something in return—if anyone had ever given her anything at all—and he wanted to be different. He wanted her to know that it was possible for a man to *give* to her. He wanted her to know it was possible to be with a man who didn't use her to satisfy his own selfish needs.

But it was hard to resist the urge when she was so close. He could feel the heat of her through his jeans, and it would have been easy, so easy, to just press himself to her and find release. And it was hard, so hard, to be noble about this.

The thought made him smile wryly against her hair. It was such an odd word to apply to himself, *noble.* It didn't fit at all. No, he didn't want to be noble, he wanted to be *different.* He wanted to be the first man in her life who had given without taking. And he wanted her to feel safe with him.

Her tremors stopped finally, and she relaxed against him, making a soft sound of contentment when he ran his hand down her back. She was happy, and the realization filled him with joy and pride. It was such an easy thing to do for her—and such a sad thing that no one else in her life had done so.

Presently she lifted her head and looked shyly at him. "Did you...?" She trailed off, her cheeks turning red.

He shook his head and smiled. "Don't worry about it. This was for you."

"That's not fair."

He chuckled. "Making love isn't about being fair. It's about bringing pleasure to someone. I feel real good about what just happened, so let's leave it at that, okay?"

"But you said—"

"I needed to touch you. I did. And it was even nicer than I thought it would be." Afraid she might continue to press him when his willpower was at a phenomenally low ebb, he took her by the waist and swung her off his lap, setting her on the couch beside him.

"Well, will you look at that?" he said, touching the tip of her nose with his finger. "I fell down on the job."

"What?"

"I didn't even get your glasses off."

She laughed then, an easy, warm, delicious sound unlike any other laugh he had heard from her. It was also a sexy sound, and he found himself wanting to scoop her up and carry her away to bed with him so he could make love to her until they were both too weak to move.

Another time, he promised himself, even though he knew he wasn't going to let it happen. Even though he knew this was one woman he couldn't afford to get involved with.

He had to find a way to leave now, before he forgot his common sense and lost the last dregs of his self-control. But somehow he had to manage it without leaving her to wonder if she had done something wrong.

Damn it, he should have known better than to allow this to happen in the first place. Anna wasn't like other women. She didn't have enough self-esteem to deal with his departure right after the intimacy they had just shared. She would wonder what she had done to offend him or disappoint him.

So he had to hang around a while longer and ignore his own hunger as best he could. He had to sit within arm's reach of temptation and pretend he wasn't tempted at all. He needed his head examined.

"What I would really like right now," he said finally, "is another cup of coffee."

She hopped up off the couch as if she had been propelled by a spring. "I'll get it for you."

But he didn't let her bring it to him; he followed her into the kitchen. He feared that if he stayed on that couch, his mind was never going to stop suggesting ways to take advantage of it and her. After the intense moments just past, he had no trouble at all imagining what it would be like to make love completely to Anna Fleming, and he liked the images entirely too much for his own good.

They sat at the table again. Hugh absently picked up the cards they'd left scattered earlier and put them back in the box. Every time he glanced at Anna, he found her watching him with an expression between wonder and confusion. He didn't know which worried him more. The wonder, he decided. He didn't want her to fixate on him just because he was the first man in her life ever to give her an orgasm.

"Thank you," she said suddenly.

"For what?"

"For..." She paused, and color tinted her cheeks again. "I didn't know it could be like that, Hugh. I didn't know I could feel like that."

Oh, hell, he thought. Oh, hell. She was going to talk about it. He wanted to run before he could get sucked in any deeper. He already cared entirely too much about this woman, and listening to her say what he had already guessed was only going to make him care more.

"Almost everybody can feel like that," he heard himself say gruffly. "I didn't do anything special."

A shadow passed across her face. "Yes, you did," she argued quietly. "You most definitely *did* do something special. All the other men who've ever touched me did it for themselves. You did it for *me*."

"I did it for both of us," he said flatly. "You weren't the only one who enjoyed it."

She smiled shyly. "I hope not."

"Of course not." He took a swig of his coffee and tried to

think of a way to end this conversation. He wasn't at all comfortable with what he'd started here, and now that his head was a little clearer, he was wondering why he hadn't managed to keep this relationship businesslike, the way he had originally intended. Anna Fleming had gone to his head in a dangerous way, and now she was turning him into a total idiot who couldn't even figure himself out.

"I need to be going," he said abruptly.

She looked surprised, then disappointed.

"It's late," he said. "You have to be in church early in the morning, and you need your sleep." *And I need some space to straighten out my own head.* He rose from the table and watched as Anna rose with him. Something in her expression made him say, "Anna, I just need some space to think. I didn't expect to take our relationship in this direction."

She nodded her understanding, but her expression looked wooden in a way that told him he was hurting her, whether he intended to do so or not. And all of a sudden he could see that whatever he did now was going to hurt her. Stay or go, the price was wounding her. Hell's bells!

He went to get his jacket, aware that she trailed after him. He had to find something to say to her that would make it all right, but he was damned if he could think of a thing. He pulled his jacket on and zipped it up, pausing to look at her one more time before he left.

"I'm sorry," he said finally, because there didn't seem to be any other words to say to her. "I'm sorry." Then he bent and brushed a light kiss on her lips.

"I'll call you." Then he stepped out into the frigid night, wondering if he was destined to hurt everyone he ever came in contact with.

Sometimes it sure as hell seemed like it.

Chapter 11

Anna woke in the morning feeling emotionally bruised. She didn't want to go to church. She didn't even want to get out of bed, but finally she padded into the kitchen and started a fresh pot of coffee. The pack of cards still lay on the table where Hugh had left them, and his coffee cup sat by the sink, waiting to be washed.

He hadn't meant to hurt her. At some deep level she knew that, but she felt hurt anyway. He had managed to get past some of her strongest barriers and awaken her to feelings she had never had before, and then he had taken flight as if it had all been a big mistake.

Which it had been, she admitted honestly. He wasn't wrong about that. He wanted her help with his ranch and nothing else. And she didn't want to get involved with either him or his ranch, because her past would eventually catch up with her and destroy the life she had built for herself.

Not that it was much of a life, she thought as she sat at her kitchen table and sipped coffee. She was barely making enough money to get by, she didn't have any real friends because she was afraid to let anyone get too close. Even her work with the church youth group, satisfying as it was, didn't give her any real ties to this community. She could pack up and move on at any time, if she had to.

Except for Lorna. Suddenly she thought of Lorna, and the idea of leaving that child behind hurt. Seriously hurt. As it was, she didn't know how she was going to handle it when the court ordered the girl to be put in a regular foster home, but at least if she stayed here she could keep in touch with Lorna.

Who did she think she was kidding? She didn't want to leave Conard City. For the first time in her life she had things she was truly afraid of losing. She didn't want to leave the church, or the youth group, or her job. Because even though she had tried so hard not to make any ties here, she had made them anyway. And if her past came out, she was going to lose everything that mattered to her: her job, Hugh, the respect of her employer…and most of all, Lorna.

She could have cried, except that she had long ago learned crying didn't help anything. She had cried when her stepfather raped her, but he hadn't stopped. She had cried when her real father had left, but he hadn't come back. She had cried when she had realized that she was either going to have to starve or sell her body to survive, but that hadn't changed the situation any. And she had cried after she'd slept with those men for money, but the hurt hadn't been mended.

So was she going to sit here and cry over something that hadn't happened yet? Hugh was right. Their relationship shouldn't take this direction. Absolutely not. It was too dangerous for her. She ought to be grateful to him for having the wisdom to see the problems, instead of moping because he hadn't wanted something more from her.

Her past hadn't been uncovered, nor was there any reason to think it would be, as long as she didn't get involved too deeply in Hugh's youth ranch project. As long as she stayed clear of that, no one would go digging around in her past.

That meant she couldn't keep Lorna, but surely she could live with having Lorna nearby. She would just be a sort of aunt to the girl, rather than a foster mother.

She could live with that. Yes, she could. It would hurt, but she was used to that kind of pain. Her whole life had been filled with it.

The phone rang, and she jumped. She almost decided not to answer it, but then she remembered Lorna was with Mary Jo Weeks. What if something had happened?

Tensing in expectation that it would be Al Lacey with yet another threat, she picked up the receiver.

"Anna?" It was Lorna, her voice full of warmth and laughter. "Anna, would it be all right if we meet you after the eleven-o'clock service instead of the nine-o'clock? We're just having so much fun that Mrs. Weeks said it would be okay with her if it's okay with you."

"That'll be fine, honey. I'll see you then."

Anna hung up the phone, feeling at once relieved and disappointed. She was missing Lorna, but on the other hand, this would give her time to get her own head together before she had to face the child.

She was walking down the hallway to her bedroom to get dressed when she heard a knock at the front door. She froze, wondering who it could possibly be, fearing that it might be Al Lacey come to create some new unpleasantness. But that was ridiculous, she told herself. There was no reason to believe the man would do anything at all except make nasty phone calls.

She went to peek out the front window and felt her heart leap when she saw Hugh standing out there on her front step. Without even thinking about the fact that she was still in her robe, she hurried to open the door.

"This is ridiculous," he said, and stepped inside. Never taking his eyes from her, he kicked the door closed. "I've been up all night thinking about you."

Something inside her quivered, and she felt suddenly breathless. "Good morning to you, too," she managed to say.

"Don't get difficult on me, Anna. This is difficult enough."

"What is?"

He glared. "I don't want to get involved with you. It'll mess up my plans to get your help with the ranch."

"I can't help you with the ranch. I told you that."

"Well, I didn't believe you. I still don't believe you. But you know what? I don't give a damn. I may be losing my mind, but nothing seems to matter except that I want you. I'm going out of my mind with wanting you."

A shiver passed through her, a shiver of delight and fear. On the one hand, she was thrilled that he wanted her enough to put everything else aside. On the other, she was scared to death of what that might mean. Despite what had happened last night, she still dreaded sex. The men she had been with before—only a few, she reminded herself honestly—had left her feeling raw and dirty and so very cold. She didn't ever want to feel that way again.

Hugh had given her hope last night, hope that it didn't always have to be a dirty, disgusting act. That it might be something in which she could find joy and delight. Going any further with him would be taking the risk that that frail hope would shatter. What if he left her feeling the way the others had? What if he left her feeling that she was nothing but a used husk?

"You're scared," he said.

She nodded jerkily. "I've had... My experiences have been...bad."

He stepped closer. "But last night wasn't bad, was it?"

She shook her head.

"It can all be that way, Anna. All of it. Give me a chance to show you."

Torn between desire and fear, she looked away, trying to make up her mind one way or the other. Remembering how bruised she had felt this morning, she wondered if she would feel bruised in a couple of hours when he left. It was such a risk!

"I'm sorry," he said abruptly. "I shouldn't have come."

He turned and reached for the doorknob, and Anna suddenly knew that the only thing worse than taking this risk would be not taking it.

"Hugh! Wait."

He paused, then turned slowly to face her. In his eyes she

could see his yearning. "It's crazy," he said. "It's really crazy. I figured out a long time ago that I'd be smart to stay away from women. I mean...look at me. A down-at-the-heels handyman with a bad past and overinflated dreams of building a youth ranch. I freaked out, Anna. For all everybody in this town is acting like it never happened, I know it did, and so does everyone else. So what woman in her right mind would want anything to do with me?"

"Hugh..." Anna reached out to him, forgetting all her own fears as sympathy and concern for him rose in her. She wasn't the only one with a past or problems, and it was high time she started remembering that.

He shook his head. "Let me finish. I figured it would be crazy to get involved. And it is. But...well, ever since the night of the wedding, I've been thinking about you more and more."

Anna listened, uncertain what to make of this, fearing the worst and hoping for the best.

He sighed heavily. "I see secrets in your eyes, Anna Fleming. I see pain and fear, and shadows from the past. I guess maybe you can understand that the past haunts me, too."

She nodded. That was indeed something she could connect with.

"The thing about the past," he continued, "is that it has only as much power as you give it. You have to face it straight on. Quit hiding from it. Accept it."

She caught her breath and held it, trying to understand what he meant. Did he mean she should confront her own past? She couldn't do that. It would ruin her!

"I've been hiding," he went on. "Plain and simple. I've turned my back on where I've been and how I came to be here, and I've been acting like a damn turtle with my head stuck in my shell, avoiding anything that might make me face all that.

"But I'm facing it anyway, sweetie. I'm facing it because I can't get you out of my mind. I'm facing it because I want you so damn much I can't stay in hiding anymore. I've got to accept who I am and what I've done, or I'll never be able to ask anybody else to accept me."

She nodded, understanding, but terrified of where this was leading. Had he somehow found out about her past?

"I was a soldier," he said. "I hurt people. Some of the people I hurt thought I was a friend. But I wasn't. I was an enemy soldier behind enemy lines who was pretending to be one of them. And because of me, some of them died. I have to live with that. Tell me, Anna, can a woman want somebody like me?"

Her heart went out to him, and she instinctively held out her hands. "Of course a woman could want you, Hugh! Of course she could."

He gave her a crooked smile. "What about the woman who's standing in front of me?"

"You don't know me...."

"Then tell me, Anna. Tell me what it is that puts those shadows in your eyes."

"I can't. I can't!"

"Did you kill anybody? Maim anybody?"

"No!"

"Are the cops looking for you?"

"No."

"Then you don't have any secrets worth hiding at all." He took one of her hands and squeezed it gently.

He didn't understand, she thought. He didn't understand at all.

"I want to make love to you, Anna. Will you let me?"

After what he had just told her, she couldn't possibly say no. She couldn't hurt him that way. And it suddenly struck her that she had once given herself for money. How could it possibly be as bad to give herself to a friend out of compassion?

"Hugh..." She whispered his name and stepped toward him.

He lowered his voice. "When do you have to be at church?"

"At eleven."

"Not enough time, but it'll have to do." Holding her hand, he tugged her gently down the hallway toward her bedroom. "You try so hard to hide yourself," he said quietly as he led the way. "You pin up your hair, and wear glasses and those shapeless dresses. But you know what, Anna? I've never seen a more beautiful woman, especially now, with your hair down."

Her bed was still rumpled from her difficult night. He pulled back the covers, then faced her. "Take off your robe for me?"

She couldn't do it. Men had made her undress for them before. Her stepfather had demanded it. She couldn't do it now. It was too much like before. Was she out of her mind? She couldn't possibly do this...and yet she couldn't possibly stop.

"Can I help?" he asked finally.

She nodded shakily.

He reached for the belt of her terry-cloth robe and untied it. With gentle hands, he pushed it from her shoulders and let it fall to the floor. She shivered, even though she wore a warm flannel nightgown.

"I like this," he said, gently touching her sleeve. "Soft, warm and cuddly."

Then, as if he sensed she was verging on flight or collapse, he guided her to the bed and helped her lie down.

Standing beside the bed, he reached for his own clothing. His jacket flew across the room to land on a chair. His shirt followed, revealing his muscled chest and broad shoulders. The pale light of the winter day that filtered through the drawn curtains was just enough to let her see how powerful he was. How beautiful he was.

He reached for the buckle of his belt and dropped his jeans, revealing olive drab boxer shorts. He sat on the bed beside her, yanked off his boots and kicked his jeans away. Then, still wearing his shorts, he stretched out beside her.

Her heart was hammering so hard, she felt as if she couldn't get enough air. Turning her head, she looked at him.

He propped himself up on his elbow and smiled down at

her. ''This is your show, lady,'' he said softly. ''If I do anything you don't like, anything that frightens you, just say so.''

She managed another nod.

''God,'' he said, ''you look so frightened.'' Reaching out, he gently stroked her cheek with a fingertip. ''Don't be afraid. I swear I won't hurt you.''

She didn't see how this could do anything *except* hurt her, but she didn't say so. Hugh wanted this so much that he'd come back here this morning and laid himself bare to her. How could she possibly deny him?

Bending, he kissed her, and almost from the instant his mouth met hers, she felt something inside her softening and opening to him. Part of her wanted to keep her distance, to remain cold and unmoved as she had once done to protect herself. But somehow she knew that wasn't going to be possible this time. Hugh had already gotten within her defenses, and it was too late to protect herself. What happened now was going to affect her as strongly as anything in her life ever had.

He sprinkled soft kisses on her face, then trailed his mouth down her throat. Before she even knew he was doing it, the buttons on the neck of her gown fell open, and his mouth began trailing hot kisses over her chest. No one had ever kissed her this way before, as if he was trying to give rather than take, and she felt herself grow even softer.

He didn't ask anything of her. He allowed her to lie there, and he asked not a thing as his hands began to roam her gentle curves through the flannel.

A slow heat began to build in her as he explored her. Gentle tongues of flame seemed to leap from his hands everywhere he touched her. Even the caress of the flannel against her skin began to arouse her, sensitizing nerve endings she had never before been aware of.

Across her breasts and down to her belly his hand roamed. She had been touched in these places before, but never like this. Never with such dedication to pleasing her, never with concern that she like what was being done to her.

But Hugh cared. She could feel it in every kiss and caress, and it began to thaw something long frozen inside her. She felt her arms move of their own accord, felt her hands grip his shoulders, felt that wonderful deep pulsing begin again between her legs.

"You're so sweet," he whispered to her, and dropped a gentle, questing kiss on her mouth. "Open for me, Anna. Let me in."

Her mouth opened to receive him, and at the same instant his hand slipped up under her gown, turning the gentle glow of passion into a conflagration that burned through her and burned away every preconception about this act that she'd ever had.

Nothing and no one had ever made her feel this way before.

"Want me, Anna," he whispered raggedly. "Oh, sweetheart, want me, too!"

"I want you," she said huskily, hardly recognizing her own voice. "Oh, Hugh, I want you, too."

"Thank heaven," he whispered, and buried his face in the side of her neck. His hand, rough and callused from hard labor, found her naked breast and closed on it. A ribbon of sheer delight ran from her breast to her core, causing her womb to clench in reaction, and for the first time in her life she felt herself grow damp with passion.

"So sweet," he murmured again.

Somehow her nightgown was up around her shoulders and his mouth had closed on her breast, sucking gently at first, then more strongly, as her hips began a helpless undulation in response. When his hand trailed down to her dewy center, she clamped her thighs around it, holding him there, wanting him never to stop touching her there, wanting answers to all the mysteries.

Her own hands began to wander restlessly over his back and shoulders, trying to draw him closer. She needed him now, she realized dizzily. She needed his weight on her and his heat within her. His mouth and hand would never be enough to assuage the roaring hunger he had built in her.

"Hugh…oh, please…"

"In a minute…just a minute…."

His finger slipped between her dewy folds and gave her a

touch so exquisite that it was almost painful. She cried out, and he swallowed the sound with another kiss. Relentlessly he stroked her, teaching her that pleasure and pain were indistinguishable, carrying her higher and higher with each movement of his hand.

And then he took his hand away. She made a sound of protest, but before it fully left her lips, he was back, moving over her, between her legs. Instinctively she lifted herself to him and felt him slide home.

Nothing had ever felt so right.

With each thrust, he answered the need deep inside her, taking her higher and higher on a tide she was helpless to resist. Then, just when she thought she could take no more, he lowered his head and took her breast in his mouth, sending yet another blinding shaft of pleasure zinging to her core.

She shattered then, into a thousand flaming pieces of pleasure. Moments later, she felt the shudder rip through him, heard him groan, and knew he had joined her.

He coaxed her into the shower with him. "Trust me," he said, "you don't want to go to church smelling like a woman who's just been loved."

She blushed and tried to draw the covers higher, but he tugged them insistently away and let his eyes feast on her.

"You're gorgeous," he said, and smiled right into her eyes. "And now I've seen it all, so you don't have to be shy anymore."

When he tugged her hand, she rose and went with him to the bathroom. She had been naked with men before, but only this time seemed to matter. Her attitude toward her body had changed, she realized suddenly. It was no longer an object that had once been used against her will. Now it was an integral part of her, not simply a possession she felt detached from. That detachment had protected her in the past, and now she worried that its absence had left her vulnerable.

But that didn't seem to matter, at least not right now as Hugh stood with her in the tub and soaped her gently while hot water sprayed on them. His touches were gentle and arousing, and when she realized that her body was awakening once again, color stained her cheeks.

He saw the blush and correctly interpreted it. "It's okay," he said gently. "It's all right." His soapy hand slipped between her legs and caressed her gently. "It's supposed to feel like this."

She found herself clinging desperately to his shoulders, afraid that at any moment her legs were going to give out. And suddenly, twisting out of the depths of her mind came an image of herself and what she was doing. She was behaving like a wanton, something she had long ago sworn she would never do.

"I can't," she gasped. "I can't!"

"It's okay...."

"No!" She shoved him away and grabbed the shower curtain, yanking it open. Nearly stumbling, she climbed out of the tub, grabbed a towel and ran for her bedroom. Once there, she closed the door and leaned against it, shaking and weeping all at once.

How could she have done this to herself again? How could she carry on like this when she had sworn she would never again let a man touch her that way? Oh, God, was she losing her mind?

A gentle rap on the door caught her attention and caused her heart to leap into her throat. She didn't want to face him. She couldn't face him. Not now!

"Anna? Anna, did I hurt you?"

"No...no..."

He was silent for a moment. "I guess I made a mistake," he said finally. "I'm sorry. I'll leave now."

Part of her desperately wanted him to stay, but the part of her that was terrified of what she was becoming kept her silent.

"Anna? I'm going now. But...maybe it's high time you faced your past, because you're sure as hell not going to have a future until you do. I'll see you around."

Her past. Why did he keep referring to her past? Oh, God, what if he knew about it? What if he had found out? What if that was why he had wanted a fling with her, because he figured she was cheap?

The thought filled her with even more shame, and finally she collapsed on her bed, weeping silently for things lost and things that could never be.

Hugh left Anna's house feeling bruised and angry, though he wasn't quite sure why he felt angry. Maybe because he had let himself down. He'd promised himself that he wouldn't get involved with a woman, and then he'd made the supremely stupid move of getting involved with a woman he needed to have a business relationship with. For all Anna protested that she wouldn't help him with his ranch, he had persisted in believing that he would find the right key to unlock her resistance. Now he had gone and made it all but impossible by getting sexually involved with her. He couldn't imagine any way on earth that she would now consent to a business relationship with him.

That made him furious at himself.

Then there was Anna and what had happened between them. He had honestly thought he'd carried her past her very natural reluctance to let a man make love to her. Instead, he apparently hadn't done anything of the sort. As far as he could tell, he had simply added to her injuries.

And it didn't matter a drop of water in the Sahara that he hadn't meant to hurt her at all.

Nor did he feel qualified to figure out her emotional state or to try to help her with it. Apparently matters were worse than he'd suspected, and simply enjoying making love wasn't going to get her past her problem.

So, he told himself, the only thing he could do now was stay clear. In time she would realize that he wasn't going to make a move on her, and then maybe they could get back to discussing a business relationship. He needed her for the ranch. People who could work well with children, who could inspire in them the kind of affection and trust Anna did in them didn't exactly grow on trees around here, and in dealing with a troubled child her ability was worth far more than a slew of professional degrees. She just naturally loved kids, and they just naturally loved her back. He needed her to be the foster mother to all the children he hoped to help. Professional expertise he could hire, but a mom was something else altogether.

But he'd gone and done all the wrong things, and had probably blown it for good.

Cursing his stupidity and his sex drive, he drove back to his apartment. If there was any mending that could be done, only time could do it. He had to keep clear of her and bide his time. There weren't any other options.

Not now. He'd blown all the other ones.

Chapter 12

A week later, Anna and Lorna went to court together to hear Judge Williams announce that with the prosecutor's agreement, she was going to withhold adjudication on the arson charge. If Lorna completed a year's worth of the psychological treatment she had already begun, then the charge would be dismissed. If she failed to complete treatment, the matter would be reopened.

Then the judge turned to another matter. "Miss Lacey, your father has decided to plead to the charges against him in exchange for receiving probation rather than a jail sentence. He would be required to move to another city and to stay away from you, and social services will investigate his fitness to parent your sister. However, I'm not going to agree to this plea bargain if you aren't happy with it. As I see it, taking the deal will prevent you from having to testify in open court against your father. But if you want him to go to jail, you're going to have to testify. No one can make that decision for you. Do you understand?"

Lorna nodded. Anna looked at her, feeling anger and dismay on the child's behalf. It seemed so unfair that a girl of thirteen should have to make decisions like this.

"I guess what it comes down to," the judge went on, "is how badly you want your father to go to jail right now. If that's important to you, then you'll have to testify. On the other hand, taking the plea will require him to move a long way away from you and forbid him from ever seeing you again. I can give you a few days to think this over, but I'll need your answer by Monday. All right?"

Lorna nodded again. "Yes, ma'am."

"And now we come to the question of a permanent foster home for you."

"I want to stay with Miss Anna, Your Honor."

Anna felt a bubble of panic begin to rise in the pit of her stomach. How was she going to handle this? She would love to have Lorna live with her, but there was no way she could take the risk.

The judge looked at her. "Miss Fleming, how do you feel about that?"

"I...um..." She looked at Lorna and wondered how she could possibly say no, even though there wasn't a chance in hell that she would get permanent custody of Anna.

"I could just give you guardianship," the judge said, "but I'd prefer it if you would apply to become a permanent foster parent. By doing so, the state will be able to pay you something toward Miss Lacey's upkeep. In my experience, church secretaries rarely get paid enough to support themselves, let alone another person. Now, I'm planning to require Dr. Lacey pay child support, but given that you have no official standing unless you become an approved foster parent, I'm not sure that he couldn't make things difficult for you somewhere down the road. If this is something you want to do, if you do indeed wish to keep Miss Lacey permanently, then you'll have to apply to become approved. And I'll need your answer on that Monday, as well."

"Yes, Your Honor."

Two minutes later, she and Lorna stepped out of the courthouse into a bright, cold afternoon. Sun glared off the snow that covered the square, and Anna squinted.

"Anna?"

"Yes?" she turned to look at Lorna.

"Don't you want to keep me?" The child's lower lip quivered.

"Yes, of course I do! I'm just not sure it's possible. Look, could we talk about this at home?"

"No! I don't want to talk about it at home! You don't want me. Nobody wants me."

"Lorna..." But the girl was already turning and running. Anna started to go after her, but she slipped on a patch of ice and fell into a snowbank. Before she could regain her feet, Lorna had disappeared around the corner of a building and vanished from sight.

Shivering, shaking from the emotions that buffeted her, Anna stood on the icy walk for a long time, wondering what the hell she was going to do now.

"I'll have my men keep an eye out for her," Nate Tate told her when she called him an hour later and told him what had happened. "She's just upset, sweet pea. She'll come home."

"I hope so. I can't imagine where she might have gone, Nate. All her friends are in school for another hour and a half."

"She's probably just walking around in the cold, feeling sorry for herself." He sighed. "I don't mean to sound harsh here, sweet pea, but kids that age are a royal pain in the butt. Everything is so damn cataclysmic to them. Now, I'm not saying that little girl hasn't been through an awful lot, and she's got as much right to drown in self-pity as anybody, but all she's doing right now is getting colder and lonelier. Eventually she'll turn up. They almost always do."

But Anna, who had once run away, knew exactly how far a child that age could go, knew exactly what could happen to kids who didn't come home.

She didn't share any of that with Nate, though. It would open too many doors that she wanted to keep closed.

Then she had to call Dan and tell him that she wouldn't be back to work that afternoon, because Lorna had run away.

"No, of course you have to stay at home in case she shows up," he said. "I know exactly how you feel. My Ginny ran away last year."

"Really? I didn't know that."

"Of course not. I didn't tell anybody. Thank God she came home before I finally called the sheriff. But I was about out of my mind with worry."

"Why did she run away?"

"Because I grounded her for a week for being out past her curfew." He sighed. "Teenagers are the devil to raise. I'll be glad when mine are safely grown up. Call me if you hear anything, and I'll do likewise."

Anna found it impossible to hold still, so she paced her house from one end to the other. At first Jazz trotted after her, right at her heels, but finally the puppy grew weary and curled up on Lorna's bed and fell asleep.

She wasn't used to the house being this quiet anymore, Anna suddenly realized. These days, whenever she was home, Lorna was usually here, too, and there was music in the background, or the sounds of her talking on the phone with one of her friends, or the sounds of her friends who had come to visit. Now there were no sounds at all except the whoosh of the central heat and the whine of the refrigerator compressor. And right now the only sound on earth Anna wanted to hear was the sound of Lorna's voice.

She had the worst urge to call Hugh and tell him what had happened, but she didn't dare. Since they had made love, he'd stayed away from her. On the rare occasions when they happened to run into one another, he always gave her a pleasant greeting, but he didn't linger to talk.

He must know about her past, she decided. He must have heard about it from somewhere—maybe from Al Lacey, who had made those threats. Her heart slammed as she considered the possibility.

Her juvenile records had been sealed, but sealing them didn't mean they were totally inaccessible. Someone with money—and Al Lacey certainly had money—could probably hire someone who knew how to get hold of those things. What if he had? What if it was already being whispered around town that she had been arrested for prostitution? What if Hugh had heard about it, and that was why he had dropped her so suddenly and so completely? What if that was why he no longer wanted her help with his ranch?

Her heart climbed into her throat again and lodged there, threatening to choke her as she faced all the possibilities. But no, she told herself, if gossip was going around the community about her, she certainly would have caught wind of it. At the very least, some people would be treating her differently, and she had seen none of that.

But the fact that the story wasn't in common circulation didn't mean Hugh hadn't heard it somehow. The more she thought about it, the more convinced she was that he *did* know, and that was why he was avoiding her. In fact, that was probably why he had come on to her in the first place. Because he knew she was cheap.

But what did it matter what he thought? It was nothing but what she would have expected from someone who learned what she had done. They would all turn their backs on her, all these nice people who were so kind to her now. None of them would want to admit that they knew her.

But none of that really seemed to matter right now. The only thing that mattered to her was Lorna, and whether the girl was all right. Closing her eyes, Anna prayed that the phone would ring and someone would tell her where Lorna was. It didn't matter if it was a deputy sheriff, a schoolteacher, or the parent of one of her friends. Just someone, anyone, with the news that Lorna was all right.

A half hour after school let out, Anna started calling Lorna's friends. None of them had seen her since earlier in the day. Anna's worry mounted with every passing minute, until she felt as if she were going to crawl right out of her skin.

The early-winter night fell and brought with it a whole new surge of anxiety. In the dark Lorna would be harder to find.

In the dark there was a lot more danger to a young girl on her own.

She fed Jazz her evening meal, then stepped out back with the puppy, leaving the door open so she would hear the phone ring. No one called. By nine she began to fear the worst. Lorna had hitched a ride with someone and was miles away. Lorna had been kidnapped. Lorna was lying dead in a ditch somewhere....

Just after nine, someone rapped loudly at the door. The knock wasn't Lorna's gentle tap, and fear clutched at Anna. Her heart in her throat, she ran to answer it.

Lorna was standing there, with Hugh right behind her. The child's expression was sullen. Hugh looked frazzled.

"I believe you were looking for someone," Hugh said. "She's here, but she doesn't want to be here, so...if you don't mind, Miss Anna, I'll just step inside to keep an eye on her until the two of you settle the problem."

Anna hardly heard him. Before he had even finished speaking, she stepped forward and threw her arms around Lorna, hugging her as tightly as she could. "I was so worried," she said shakily. "I was so afraid something bad had happened to you...."

Lorna refused to hug her back. She stood stiff and unresponsive. When Anna finally let go of her, she walked inside like a condemned prisoner.

Anna looked after her, then looked up at Hugh. She hardly noticed the frigid air that was making her shiver. "Inside," he said. "It's cold out here. You'll get frostbite."

She turned and went into the living room. Lorna stood there with her shoulders hunched and her head bowed. Her expression was downright mutinous. Figuring she wouldn't learn anything there, Anna looked at Hugh. "Where did you find her?"

"She came to me, actually. I had no idea she'd run away. Along about eight-thirty, there she was, knocking on my door. She wanted to know if she could come live at the ranch with me."

Anna nodded and drew a deep breath, trying to calm the storm of emotions that was buffeting her, so she could think.

"For some damn reason," Hugh continued, "Lorna thinks you don't want her. Me, I don't exactly think that's true, but maybe I'm wrong. Anyway, I got her to agree to come here and talk to you about it."

"She doesn't want me," Lorna said stonily. "Every time I ask her, she has an excuse."

Hugh didn't say anything. Anna felt her heart squeeze and begin to ache anew. She didn't see any good way out of this, for either her or the child. What purpose would it serve to open her past to scrutiny when it would only disqualify her anyway?

But that seemed like a lame excuse now. By refusing to explain the reasons for her hesitation, maybe she was hurting Lorna even more than she would be hurt if Anna couldn't be approved as her foster parent. Maybe, for Lorna's sake, she had to explain her hesitation. She didn't have to go into detail, after all. The mere existence of a police record ought to be enough to make Lorna understand the problem.

"I *do* want you," Anna said.

"Yeah. Right. Like my parents want me." Lorna's voice cracked. "You heard the judge. He's willing to go away and never see me again. And you know what? So's my mom. They didn't even try to fight it."

Anna caught her breath as understanding hit her. Lorna didn't see how the offered plea bargain would protect her. She saw it as her parents giving her up without even a fight.

"Lorna—"

The girl shook her head sharply. "The counselor said my dad doesn't really love me. If he really loved me, he wouldn't have hurt me like this. She said he would have put me first, before his urges. So he doesn't really love me."

Feeling helpless, Anna could only listen.

"So okay," Lorna said with a little shrug of her shoulder. She still wouldn't look at them. "I can handle that. He's sick, you know? That's what everyone says, that he has to be really sick to do what he did to me. And maybe sick people can't really love. But what about my mom? Why doesn't *she* love me? What's wrong with me?"

"Honey, there's nothing wrong with you at all," Anna said fiercely. "Absolutely nothing."

"Then why don't you want me?"

The question cut Anna to her soul. Tears burned in her eyes, and her throat tightened as she faced just how seriously she had hurt this child with her hesitations. "Lorna, I *do* want you. I love you very much. The problem isn't you at all. It's *me.* They'll never let me be your foster mother. Not even if I beg and plead."

For the first time, Lorna looked at her. "Why not?"

"Remember when I told you what a mistake it is to run away when you're only fourteen? How there's no way to live on the streets when you're too young to even get a job?"

Lorna nodded.

"Well...I did some things that were wrong so I could get by. I stole food...and other things. And I have a police record. They'll never let me be your foster mother when I have a police record."

Hugh cleared his throat. "I guess I'll be going now. You two have a lot to talk about." Without pausing, he opened the door and left.

Lorna and Anna looked at one another across the gulf, and at the same instant closed the distance between them. This time, when Anna hugged Lorna, the girl hugged her back. And both of them burst into tears.

After she called the sheriff's office and Dan to tell them Lorna had come home, Anna cooked them a simple dinner of hamburgers and French fries. For the moment, Lorna seemed content to let things rest where they were. But after dinner, when they were washing the dishes, she brought the subject up again.

"I don't want to go live with strangers, Anna."

"Maybe they wouldn't be strangers."

"They probably will be. I might not even be able to stay here in Conard City."

"Who told you that?"

"The psychologist. She said that sometimes, because there aren't any places available in a town, kids get sent to other towns. I don't want to leave all my friends."

"I can certainly understand that." In fact, it seemed unbearably cruel to uproot the child that way after all that had happened.

"She tried to tell me it could be a good thing to go somewhere nobody would know what had happened to me, but I like it better here. My friends know what happened, and they don't hate me. Some of the grown-ups probably do, but I don't care about them."

Anna nodded as she finished drying a bowl and put it away. That was the last of the dishes, so she joined Lorna at the table.

"I don't think it's fair," Lorna said. "People keep telling me I didn't do anything wrong, but I keep getting punished anyway."

"I don't think you're being punished, honey."

"It feels like I am." Lorna found a crumb on the table and pushed it around with her forefinger. "Sometimes it's just plain awful being a kid."

"Yes, it is."

Lorna gave her a wan smile. "I still want you to be my foster mother. Are you really sure they wouldn't let you?"

"Pretty sure."

"So I'm supposed to go live with somebody who doesn't know me and doesn't care about me. Somebody who is maybe doing it because they want the money."

"I don't think anybody becomes a foster parent because they want the money," Anna said, stifling a qualm. "I don't think it's very much money, anyway. I think most people do it because they like children and want to have children in the house."

"Maybe. But that doesn't mean they'll like *me*. Or even really care about me. Why should they? I'll be a stranger."

"But that would change, honey. Anybody who gets to know you will love you."

Lorna shook her head. "Maybe not. But you already love me, so why should I have to give you up? It's not right!"

It didn't seem right to Anna, either, but she didn't know what to say to Lorna. If she agreed, she might be encouraging the girl to nurture false hopes, and that would only hurt more in the long run.

On the other hand, maybe she was just being too cowardly.

As if she had read her mind, Lorna looked at her and said, "How can you know they won't let you if you don't try?"

Anna drew a long breath, facing the stark reality of her situation. She had always been a runner, someone who fled when things got tough. Maybe that was what she was doing now. And maybe she owed it to herself and Lorna to quit running.

"I'll think about it," she finally said to Lorna. "I need to think about it, all right? Give me a few days. Not because I don't want to keep you, Lorna, but because I'm going to be opening up a real can of worms here. Regardless of the decision the authorities make about you, it's going to change my life forever."

Lorna nodded, her eyes suddenly shining with hope. "Okay," she said. "The judge said until Monday. I can wait that long."

Anna couldn't sleep that night. The past was a bear growling at the door of her mind, demanding to be let in. Long after Lorna had fallen asleep, she paced the house, listening to the night wind moan around the corners and wondering if she could live with a big mistake. Because whether she applied to be Lorna's permanent guardian or refused to do so, she was going to have to live with consequences of major proportions.

The famous rock and a hard place, she thought wearily at one point. Either one was apt to injure her seriously.

But not applying to be Lorna's guardian was also apt to injure Lorna. The weight of that rested heavily on her heart.

Finally, weary of pacing, she sat on the couch with Jazz, cuddling the puppy close in her lap.

Seeing Hugh tonight had added to her miseries, she realized.

She was missing him with an ache that went to her very soul, and seeing him again had only made her more aware of it. But the quick way he had left when she mentioned she had a police record had only convinced her that he already knew all the details. Otherwise he surely would have been curious enough to stay, wanting to know more, wouldn't he?

At some point she dozed off without even being aware of it. She heard her stepfather's voice as he came into the room in the middle of the night, calling her name softly, telling her that he wanted to play their "little game." He'd always tried to make it seem like a game, but she had never believed it was.

And suddenly she was a child again, lying beneath her blankets with her eyes squeezed shut, trying to convince him that she was asleep, too heavily asleep to be awakened by his whispers and his touches. She could feel him sitting on her bed, could feel the blankets being pulled away, could feel her heart hammering wildly as she tried to control her breathing so he wouldn't guess she was awake and feeling as if she was going to suffocate because her fear made her need air and more air....

Anna jerked awake, bathed in a cold sweat of terror, the events as vivid in her mind as if they had happened just yesterday. Jazz sensed her fear and whimpered.

With a trembling hand, she petted the dog, then lifted her to the floor. Jazz stretched and yawned, then headed for the kitchen to find water.

Anna stayed where she was, staring blindly at her familiar living room, trying to shake the terror that sleep had brought her. He couldn't hurt her anymore, she told herself. The man couldn't touch her or hurt her ever again.

But he was still controlling her life. Even at a distance and over all these years, he was still affecting every decision she made. His control was an evil thing, causing her to make choices she would not have otherwise made.

And so it had been since the first time he had come to her room. Except for him, she would be a very different person, living a very different life. Once she had had dreams of becoming a doctor. Once she had even wanted to be an astronaut.

And all of that had been lost to her fear. Fear of him. Fear of the things she had done while trying to escape him. Fear of what other people would think of her.

He had given her a legacy of fear, and there didn't seem to be any way to get rid of it.

You have to face your past or you'll never have a future. Hugh's words came back to her, a mere whisper among all the frantic thoughts scrambling around in her brain. He was right, she realized. Absolutely right. She could live the rest of her life in hiding, or she could face her past and refuse to let it control her ever again.

So easy to say. So hard to do. She'd made a practice of hiding for so long that she honestly didn't know if she could find the courage to do what Hugh had suggested and what Lorna needed.

And if she did, would she really be free if her entire life was destroyed and she needed to start over again?

There didn't seem to be any answers, and Monday loomed all too close.

Chapter 13

"Hugh is still coming for Thanksgiving dinner, isn't he?" Lorna asked.

It was Wednesday morning, just five days before the judge expected Anna's answer, just two days since Lorna had run away. Two of the longest days of Anna's life. In the past she'd always believed herself to be decisive, but all of a sudden she had turned into a dithering idiot. Should she or shouldn't she?

Just this morning she had finally decided what to do, and now Thanksgiving was staring her in the face. She had a sudden urge to scream wildly.

"I don't know," she finally managed to say, hoping she sounded more pleasant than she felt. The lack of sleep the past two nights was taking a serious toll.

"He doesn't come over anymore," Lorna remarked. "Doesn't he like us?"

"I'm sure he likes us just fine," Anna said. Right now she would like to have a close, personal conversation with the person who had invented Thanksgiving. How in the world was she going to manage to make a festive day for Lorna when she felt as if the whole world was coming apart at the seams? "He's just been very busy."

"Then he'll be coming tomorrow for dinner?"

"I'll call him and ask," Anna said, wanting an end to this conversation *now.* In fact, given the mood she was in, she would like to serve Hugh Gallagher the worst Thanksgiving feast he'd ever eaten. She couldn't believe the way he had used her and then vanished from her life. No, she admitted miserably, she *could* understand it perfectly well. It was what everyone else was going to do when they learned the *real* story of Anna Fleming. Yup, she was going to come out of this with nothing at all except another miserable memory.

"Well, I hope he comes," Lorna said as she picked up her schoolbooks. "He said he would."

Which probably meant that he would, Anna thought gloomily. Whatever else he might be, he was a man who did what he promised. Except that he had promised not to hurt her, hadn't he? Yet he had hurt her worse than she had been hurt in a long, long time.

"Remember," Lorna said, "I get off early today."

"At one, right?"

"Right."

"Why don't you just come to the office, then? Dan said he'll let me off early, too, and we can go shopping for a turkey."

"Great!"

Anna watched as Lorna left on her way up to the corner to meet a friend to walk to school with. Then she turned her attention to finishing her own preparations. Thanksgiving was so late this year that she was already panicking about Christmas. So much to do at the church and with the youth group, and so little time. And the shopping. This year she had to shop for Lorna, and she was already beginning to wonder what she would be able to manage financially.

Lorna, on the other hand, seemed to have stopped worrying about everything. Apparently she was convinced she was going to live with Anna. Anna wished she was half so convinced herself.

The only thing she knew for sure was that this morning she had decided to take the risk. She would face the demons and apply to become Lorna's foster mother. But to get to that point, she had to screw up her courage and talk to the only people she knew who could give her a reference, and tell them the entire story. Now she was dithering about when and how to bring up the subject.

But first she decided to call Hugh and get that out of the way. Besides, if she waited to call him, he would be off on some job, and she wouldn't know what size turkey to buy for tomorrow.

How had she gotten herself into this mess?

Hugh answered his phone on the first ring. Apparently he was up and about and ready to start the day. Anna wished she felt as cheerful as he sounded.

"Hi," she said, feeling as if she were going to choke. "It's Anna. Lorna and I are wondering if you're still coming for Thanksgiving dinner tomorrow?"

She knew she wasn't imagining his hesitation, but finally he said, "Sure. Absolutely. What time?"

"Say two?"

"I'll be there with bells on. Thanks, Anna."

When she hung up, she was shaking. How could it be so difficult to make a simple phone call? She looked down at her hands and marveled at the way they were trembling. The same way they trembled when she called her stepfather.

She closed her eyes, drawing a deep breath to calm herself. She was just overtired, she decided. Overtired and overworried. Naturally she was shaking. All she needed was a good nap.

The phone rang, and she reached for it, half hoping it was Hugh calling back with an excuse. What she heard made her scalp prickle.

"Anna?"

It was a woman's voice, and even after sixteen years Anna still recognized it. Her throat locked, and her hand froze on the receiver. She couldn't have moved a muscle to save her life.

"Anna, it's your mother." Rose's voice sounded taut, stretched almost to breaking. Even over the hundreds of miles, Anna could hear her rapid breathing.

"How did you find me?" Her own voice sounded attenuated, strained by the effort of passing through her constricted throat.

"Someone...someone called me. Anna—"

"Who called you?" Anna squeezed her eyes shut, wanting more than anything in the world to slam the phone down, but utterly unable to.

"A private investigator."

Her heart slammed so hard it hurt. Her lips felt wooden, and her mouth was suddenly as parched as the desert. "What did he want?"

"He wanted to know about...what happened with Van."

Van was her stepfather. The man who had inhabited her nightmares for so long. And suddenly Anna was angry. She had no doubt who was behind the investigator. "So what did you tell him? That I was a lying little slut?"

"Anna! Oh, Anna, no..." Her mother's voice broke on a sob. "Anna, baby...oh, God! I told him it was none of his damn business, and if he wanted to know, he ought to ask you. But I managed to get out of him where you live, and I...Anna, I *needed* to talk to you!"

Anna's fingers were aching from the way she was gripping the phone, and she was pressing it so hard to her ear that it hurt. She ought to hang up right now, she told herself, but somehow she couldn't. "So talk," she heard herself say woodenly.

"I called because...because... Anna, I was wrong. I was never more wrong in my life. I should have believed you when you first tried to tell me what was going on. I'm so sorry...so sorry.... I was your mother. I should have protected you...." Her voice broke into sobs.

Anna listened to the woman cry, feeling so detached that she knew it was unnatural. This ought to be hurting, or making her angry, or something. Anything except leaving her so far removed that she felt less involvement than she would have felt listening to a stranger on the street.

"When did you reach this startling conclusion?" she finally asked.

Rose's sobs had lessened, and she managed to answer brokenly. "About five years after you...ran away, I found the photographs."

The photographs. Anna felt her heart sink to her toes. Detachment was deserting her, being replaced by stark fear. The photographs. For all these years she had tried not to think of the pictures Van had taken of her. Of them. Pictures that were somewhere out there like a ticking time bomb, waiting to fall into the wrong hands and ruin the rest of her life. "What did you do with them?" Nothing, probably. Her mother had always been good at doing nothing.

"I...used them to make Van give me a quick, clean divorce. And then I burned them. All of them. Anna, I'm so sorry I didn't believe you...."

More sobs. This time Anna heard them differently. Much as she didn't want it to, her mother's grief was reaching her, however dimly.

"I've been trying to find you ever since," Rose went on, her voice shaking. "I've looked everywhere.... I didn't know you'd changed your name."

"So what do you want from me?"

"Nothing! Nothing. Really. I just...I just wanted you to know that I know. And I was really worried about this private investigator calling. Anna, somebody must want to hurt you."

So Al Lacey was trying to carry out his threat. Anna almost wanted to laugh, because she had already made up her mind to tell the truth to the only people she really cared about. There was nothing Lacey could do to her now that she wasn't going to do to herself. "It doesn't matter," she told her mother, then wondered why she even cared enough to put the woman's mind at rest. "Nobody can hurt me anymore."

A bald lie, but she said it anyway, hoping that saying it could make it true. And she wondered why she kept clinging to the phone, why she didn't just say goodbye and hang up.

Surely she didn't want contact with this woman who had turned a blind eye to what was going on all those years ago?

"I realize," Rose said after a moment, her voice still unsteady, "that you've probably convinced yourself of that. I hope it's true. But I've lived long enough to know that there are always ways somebody can hurt someone. Always..." Her voice trailed off.

Anna didn't know what to say. After all these years, this woman was a stranger to her, a stranger whose memory was shrouded in bitterness.

"Well," said Rose finally, "let me give you my phone number. Just in case anyone tries to say you lied about what happened. You can count on me to stand beside you."

Anna wrote the number down, sure she would never use it, then said goodbye to the woman who had been her mother. After all these years, she couldn't even feel vindicated. It was too late for that. Her mother hadn't believed her when it had really mattered. What difference did it make now?

But even as she thought that, her throat began to ache and tears began to prickle in her eyes. She was just feeling raw, she told herself as she wiped her eyes with the back of her hand. Too much had been going on lately. Her emotions were too near the surface, and her defenses were down.

The best way to deal with this would be to go to work and do what she had to do. Keeping busy had always been her salvation.

The church office was surprisingly quiet that morning, given that it was the day before a holiday. The preparations for the church's Thanksgiving dinner were going on in the church basement, but apparently no one felt the need for any help from either the minister or his secretary.

There was no time like the present, Anna told herself. Taking advantage of the lull, she mustered her courage and asked Dan if he could spare a few minutes to talk with her.

He put his work aside with a smile and invited her to sit. "What's on your mind?"

"Lorna has asked me to become her permanent foster mother."

"I think that's a splendid idea! The child is obviously very happy living with you. The turnaround has been apparent to everyone."

"Most of that probably has to do with being away from her father."

"To be sure. But it wouldn't be as marked if she weren't happy living with *you*, Anna." He paused, studying her thoughtfully. "I take it there's a problem of some kind. Don't you want to take her?"

"I do. I want to very much. But you're right, there's a problem."

"And that is?"

Anna clenched her hands into tight fists and wondered if she was going to be able to force the words out. There were things she hated to even think about, and talking about them was so much more difficult. She couldn't even bring herself to look at Dan.

"It's all right," she heard him say gently. "I've been a minister for twenty years, Anna. I don't think there's much I haven't heard."

She didn't find that reassuring. Somehow she didn't think women around here ever confessed to prostitution. Her heart was galloping, and her throat felt tight with unshed tears. It was going to be even more difficult than she had imagined. But finally, keeping her gaze fixed on the rug, she managed to start speaking.

"When I was twelve, my stepfather raped me."

"I gathered something like that from things you've said."

She nodded, but she still couldn't look at him. "My mother didn't believe me when I tried to tell her. All in all, it went on for nearly two years before I got up the nerve to run away."

"I'm so sorry," he said softly. "So very, very sorry, Anna. I can't begin to imagine what that must have been like for you."

"Well, it gets worse," she said, grabbing the arms of her chair and hanging on for dear life. She had to force herself to take several deep breaths so she could continue. How could she expect anybody to understand that she wasn't an innocent victim, that she had done terrible things in the name of survival and had only herself to blame? Nobody could excuse that, could they?

"How much worse?" he asked finally.

"I was fourteen. I couldn't find work. At least, not honest work."

"Ah." His tone held comprehension.

"I stole. I got away with it, too. I stole food and clothes, but I couldn't get enough. I couldn't afford a place to live, and it was getting cold, so I…so I…" She trailed off, nearly panting from the force of the emotions that gripped her.

Then, as if from a distance, she heard Dan say gently, "So you prostituted yourself."

Stunned, she looked at him at last and found nothing but kindness on his face.

"It's an old story, Anna. And not at all uncommon for girls in your position. Why shouldn't you sell what had been taken from you by force so many times? The way your stepfather treated you taught you that such things weren't precious or special. He taught you to devalue yourself. By selling what he had taken, you even managed to regain a modicum of control over your body. It's all very complicated, of course, and I'm sure I'm making a hash out of it, but believe me, you aren't unique. What makes you special is that you didn't make prostitution a way of life."

At that a bitter little laugh escaped her. "That was pure luck."

"How so?"

"The third man I propositioned was an undercover police officer. He arrested me, and I was placed in juvenile detention. Eventually they charged my stepfather and put me in foster care. I don't know what would have happened otherwise."

"Nor is it even worth thinking about. *This* is what happened to you, and if you don't mind, I'm going to say a little prayer of thanks for that police officer."

Anna shook her head, fighting back more tears. "I don't

mind. I'm grateful, too. I've been grateful it happened that way. Except that..." She looked away again. "Except that I have a police record. It's sealed, of course, but it's still there. It'll probably disqualify me from being a foster parent."

"I can't say for certain, but I'd be very surprised if it did. After all, you're living an exemplary life now, and have been for some time. The whole reason juvenile records are sealed is because we, as a society, understand that children make mistakes that shouldn't shadow their entire lives."

"Maybe." She managed a wan smile. "Regardless, I'm going to try. I'd like to use you as one of my references, but I wanted you to know about this so you wouldn't be acting blindly, and so you wouldn't be embarrassed if it all comes out."

Dan smiled gently. "Anna, I would never be embarrassed by my association with you. Never. And I'll be proud and delighted to be a reference for you. Nor should you worry that this will all come out publicly. I believe these investigations are private."

Warmth and relief started to flood Anna, but before she permitted them to take hold, she had to deal with the rest of it. "It may still come out. Al Lacey made some threats. And this morning I had a call from my...mother." She almost choked on the word. "She found me because a private investigator has been digging into my background. He called her to ask about what happened between me and my stepfather."

For the first time Dan looked shocked. "No," he said in a tone of disbelief.

Anna nodded. "It's true."

"I don't disbelieve you, Anna. I'm just appalled that Al would be doing something like this. Good heavens, hasn't the man already done enough damage?"

"Apparently not." Her hands were shaking now, as much with reaction as anything.

"But what could he possibly hope to gain?" Dan shook his head and frowned thoughtfully. "Unless he hopes to discredit you so he can argue that you exerted undue influence on Lorna, maybe even put her up to fabricating the story."

"But he's already agreed to a plea bargain."

"Has he? Then I guess he couldn't find anything useful to use against you." He gave her a half smile. "Foiled."

She wanted to smile back, but her mouth was trembling too hard. Reaction was setting in, and she feared she was going to embarrass herself by crying.

"It's all right, Anna, really," Dan said. "I'll be glad to be a reference for you. And don't worry about Al. If he tries anything, I'll deal with him. As for being a foster parent...go for it. I'll be behind you a hundred percent."

"Thank you. I was thinking about asking Sheriff Tate to be a reference, too. Do you think he'd mind?"

"I'm sure he'll feel the same way about it that I do. But why don't you let me talk to him? I can explain everything you've told me and save you the difficulty of having to repeat it. Would that help?"

Anna was more grateful to him than she could even say. When she returned to her desk, she sat for a long time trying to calm herself and get past the shakiness all the tension and fear had left her with.

Just as she was beginning to calm down and relax, Nate Tate entered the building and hung his Stetson on the coat tree. He gave her a warm smile and said that Dan wanted to see him.

And all at once Anna was nervous all over again. She managed to smile and tell him to go on in, but when the door closed behind him, it was all she could do not to scream from the tension. Oh, God, now she had to wait to see how this came out. She didn't think she could stand it.

Trying to look calm, trying to ignore her racing heart, she turned on her computer and began to type the church bulletin for Sunday. She had to keep busy, and at least doing the bulletin would occupy her mind, because, except for a few notes, Dan pretty much left it up to her to decide on layout and content. It was a task that usually gave her pleasure.

Today she could barely concentrate on it, much as she wanted to. From Dan's office she could hear the faint sounds of the men's voices as they discussed her, and she wished she knew what they were saying. It seemed to take forever, but in reality it was no more than fifteen minutes before Nate emerged.

When he did, he came over to Anna's desk and sat in the chair facing hers. "I will," he said, "be proud to be a reference for you. What's more, I have no doubt Marge would be glad to do the same, if you want her to."

Anna felt tears welling in her eyes again. "Thank you."

Nate smiled and shook his head. "Nothing to thank me for. I know the woman you are now. I've seen the work you do with children. What's past is past. Besides, I don't see that you did anything so terribly wrong in the circumstances."

Anna shook her head. "I still feel awful about it. It *was* wrong."

"In one sense. But people will do far worse things to survive, sweet pea. I've seen it. In my opinion, you don't have a damn thing to be ashamed of or to apologize for. Both Dan and I are agreed on one thing—we can't imagine anyone who would be better suited to helping Lorna through the days and months ahead."

"Thank you." She wished she could say more, could find better words to express her gratitude and relief, but there didn't seem to be any. Nate's expression, however, suggested that he knew exactly how she was feeling.

"Now," he continued, "as for Al Lacey...I think I may have a private word with him. I've got a real strong distaste for people who try to obscure their own problems by messing up other people's lives. Not that it really surprises me—that tends to be the way most criminals think. What amazes me is that in all these years I never guessed what a creep this guy is." He shook his head. "And here I thought I had a good nose for people."

"It would be nice if bad people looked like bad people," Anna remarked.

Nate flashed a sudden grin. "It'd sure make my life a whole lot easier, but it ain't gonna happen, sweet pea. Well, you go ahead and use me and Marge for references. Wouldn't surprise me if half the church or more was willing to stand up for you.

Folks around here like you, Anna. They like you and respect you, and I can't imagine there are too many who would ever allow an unkind word to be spoken about you."

He rose, grabbing his Stetson and heading for the door. "Say, are you going to be helping Hugh Gallagher with his youth ranch? I know he was hoping you would."

Anna hardly knew how to respond to that. Hugh had hardly spoken a word to her since the night he'd brought Lorna home. "I don't think he's interested anymore," she said finally. "I've got too many problems in my background."

He leaned toward her, looking down at her with eyes that saw too much. "Hugh doesn't strike me as a man to make too much out of somebody's past. What's more, sweet pea, your past is only as big an obstacle as you make it."

Then he was gone, leaving behind a gust of cold air and a silent office.

Hugh Gallagher joined Billy Joe Yuma that morning to take Thanksgiving dinner up to the vets in the mountains. Billy Joe's wife, Wendy—who was also Nate Tate's daughter—had gotten her mother and her sisters and a couple of friends to bake Thanksgiving turkeys early. Everything was being carried on ice in coolers and would have to be heated up once it was delivered, but Hugh figured those guys in the hills were going to be delighted with turkeys, stuffing, cranberry sauce, vegetables...the kind of a meal they couldn't make over a campfire. Or wouldn't bother to.

"Wendy's talking about doing hams for Christmas," Billy Joe remarked.

"Sounds like a good idea." Hugh stared out at the wintry countryside as they drove higher up the pine-forested slopes of the mountains. "You know, I've been thinking. Maybe I ought to kill the idea of the youth ranch. I could just run a halfway house for guys like those in the mountains."

"You could." Billy Joe glanced at him. "I thought the youth ranch was a really great idea, though. Nate's sure been looking forward to it as a way to deal with troubled kids around here."

"I know, but...well, I don't have the best background for dealing with kids. Not after...you know."

"I know. I don't have the best background for flying an emergency medical helicopter, but here I am. When Nate hired me, he was taking a hell of a chance that I wouldn't just suddenly go on Saigon time again."

"Yeah..." Hugh didn't know quite how to express his disquiet. All the time he'd been thinking about this ranch idea, he'd known his past was going to be an issue and that somehow he was going to surmount it. But now, since his rupture with Anna, he didn't feel positive about anything anymore. Everything looked insurmountable.

"What's wrong, Cowboy?" Yuma asked.

"Nothing, really. Just a general sort of feeling." Which wasn't exactly true. Anna Fleming had been the first real obstacle he'd encountered in his plan, and here he was getting all down about it, as if everything was hopeless. Damn, he wasn't going to get anywhere with anything if that was all it took to knock him off his pins.

"Life is getting you down, huh?" Yuma said. The car slipped a little, then regained traction, as they came around a snowy curve on the seldom-used road.

"I reckon." He shook his head, trying to get rid of the morose thoughts that were plaguing him. "It's the holiday season, I guess."

"Yeah. It's hard when you don't have a family."

The remark was a shrewd one, and it made Hugh uncomfortable. "I'm having Thanksgiving dinner with Anna Fleming and Lorna tomorrow."

Yuma glanced at him. "Is that a problem?"

"No. Why would it be?"

"You tell me. You don't sound real happy about it."

"I'm looking forward to it, actually," Hugh lied. The truth was, he couldn't imagine anything more uncomfortable than facing a silent Anna across a Thanksgiving turkey. He couldn't imagine why she'd renewed the invitation, and he couldn't understand why he'd felt compelled to accept it.

"Wendy like to have driven me crazy a couple of times when we were courting," Yuma remarked.

"I'm not courting Anna."

"Oh." Yuma glanced his way. "Sorry. It was something about the way you said her name. Guess I misread it. Anyway, Wendy was a handful. That woman chased me until I damn near panicked, then she went away and came back acting like she didn't care a fig for me. I thought I was relieved."

"You weren't?"

Yuma hesitated. "You know, I really can't say. I just know that it wasn't long before I was tied up in knots all over again. I'll tell you one thing, though, Cowboy. With a woman, it never pays to be *too* damn honorable."

Hugh stared at him. "There's no such thing."

"The hell there isn't. Wasn't it you who put your mind to making me so damn jealous that I clean forgot I was trying to avoid Wendy for her own damn good? Seems to me you had a few words of your own to say on that score. Something about getting my head out of my nether regions, if I remember correctly."

Hugh had to laugh in spite of himself. He clearly remembered hanging around Wendy Tate like a fly around honey for the few days it took to make Yuma jealous enough to cut the crap and ask the woman to marry him. But it had been as obvious as the nose on his face that Wendy and Billy Joe were deeply in love.

This thing with Anna wasn't obvious at all. Right now he just wished it would go away, because it was making a mess of all his good intentions.

"The point I'm trying to make here," Yuma went on, "is that a woman appreciates an honorable man as long as his scruples don't get in the way of loving her. That's one time she'll be just as happy to see him forget all those noble ideas. Trust me."

"Well, I'm not in love with her."

Yuma didn't reply, which was almost as good as saying he didn't believe it.

Hugh returned his attention to the countryside, noting that

they were within ten minutes of their destination. It would be good to get out and hike through the snowy woods. It would clear his head and ease the sense of doom that seemed to be pervading his days.

No, he told himself, he wasn't in love with Anna. He was attracted to her, but that was all. As far as he could tell, she had too many problems to deal with, and until she dealt with them, a man would be wiser to keep clear.

Here there be dragons, the old maps had said. A wise man didn't venture into dragon-infested waters.

And right now he damn well didn't want to think about Columbus.

Chapter 14

It was embarrassing, but Anna had to admit to Lorna that she didn't have the foggiest idea how to cook a turkey.

On Thanksgiving morning they'd both risen early to stuff the bird and put it into the oven. Anna had dealt with one problem by buying prepackaged stuffing, but for the rest of it, she was winging it.

"I never had to cook one before," she told Lorna. "I've always been alone, or eating at the church. My job was to bring pies." She had pies, two of them that she'd made yesterday evening. The bird was altogether a different matter.

"I never cooked one, either," Lorna admitted. "Do you have a cookbook?"

She did have one, an all-purpose cookbook that she hardly ever used because she rarely felt like cooking anything fancy just for herself. The directions for cooking and stuffing the turkey were explicit, so they set to work, opening the bag the turkey came in, only to discover that there were directions in there, too. That caused them both to laugh and set the tone for the rest of the morning.

By the time Hugh arrived, everything was just about ready.

Lorna had set the table with a snowy white paper tablecloth they had bought at the store yesterday, and paper napkins. Anna didn't have any fancy dishes, but her plain blue ironstone ones didn't look bad. A bowl of jellied cranberry sauce made a sparkling ruby centerpiece. Beside it sat a freshly tossed salad. The mashed potatoes were keeping warm on the stove, and the turkey was sitting on the counter, waiting the required thirty minutes before carving.

Anna and Lorna were feeling pretty proud of themselves, and the look on Hugh's face when he stepped into the kitchen was purely appreciative.

"Boy," he said, "everything smells so good!"

"I hope you're hungry," Lorna said. "I talked Anna into buying a really big turkey."

Hugh waggled his eyebrows at her. "I didn't eat at all today so I could save room for this feast."

Anna, who'd been expecting to feel awkward, found herself relaxing. Apparently whatever was troubling Hugh was something he'd left behind so it wouldn't disturb the day. That was fine with her—at least for now—so she pasted on a smile and made up her mind to enjoy herself.

Anna asked Hugh to carve the turkey. He seemed glad to have something useful to do and joked with Lorna as she stood holding the platter for him to place slices of breast meat on.

"Hey," he asked, "does anybody like the dark meat?"

"Not me," Lorna and Anna piped in unison.

"Good, that means more for me." He promptly cut a thigh for himself.

They said grace, then sat together at the table to eat. Anna found herself thinking how nice this was. It had been years since she'd last had a Thanksgiving meal in a family setting, and she guessed the same was true for Hugh.

It would, she thought, be so easy to get used to this, to sitting around a table with Hugh and Lorna, to watching them laugh and tease one another. Even as she thought it, her heart ached with yearning. Someday, somehow, she wanted to have a family again. A real family.

But that could never be. Stifling a sigh, she made an effort to join the lighthearted conversation between Hugh and Lorna. The two of them, she thought, had somehow reached an amazing level of comfort together, a kind of comfort she wished she could share.

But there was no way she could be comfortable today, anyway. Not with the court appearance looming over her head. Not with the prospect of having her life turned inside out in public over Lorna.

But maybe none of that would happen, she told herself. Maybe the investigation would go smoothly; maybe she would even get guardianship of Lorna. Dear God, how she hoped so, because even after this short time, she knew that losing Lorna would leave a gaping hole in her life and her heart.

Hugh insisted on doing the dishes himself, since they had done all the cooking. Afterward they played cards and then a game of Monopoly that ran on until Lorna's bedtime.

The realization of the time hit Anna hard. Suddenly she couldn't avoid thinking about the court appearance Monday. The feeling wasn't a whole lot different from the stage fright she had experienced as a youngster before a school play. Butterflies settled in her stomach, and the court appearance loomed threateningly.

Which was ridiculous, she thought. Her mind was already made up. All she had to do Monday was tell the judge she was going to apply to become Lorna's permanent guardian. The approval process would drag on for months, probably, during which time she would still have Lorna. There was nothing to be nervous about right now.

Except Al Lacey and what he intended to do with whatever his private detective had managed to find out. Telling herself it didn't matter, especially now that she'd talked to Dan and Nate, wasn't the same as believing it.

"Is something wrong?" Hugh asked. He had made no move to leave after Lorna had said good-night and gone to bed. Anna wondered why he was lingering, after avoiding her for so long.

"Nothing," she answered. "Really. For some stupid reason I'm nervous about the hearing Monday. That's all."

He nodded and twisted on his chair so he could reach the coffeepot. He refilled both their mugs, then put the pot back. "So, are you going to apply to keep Lorna?"

Anna nodded, wondering how much he knew or guessed about all this. It was possible she was already the subject of widespread gossip and just didn't know it.

"Well, I can sympathize," he said presently. "Yesterday I was saying to Billy Joe Yuma that maybe I ought to just give up this whole idea of a youth ranch."

"But why?"

He gave her a rueful smile. "Because I all but get cold sweats when I imagine how people are going to react to the idea of putting troubled children in the hands of a guy who was a homeless, insane drifter for a couple of years. That doesn't look real good on a résumé."

"But it's such a wonderful idea! And you won't be doing it alone. I mean, with all the people you'll need to hire, it's not as if they'd be placing these kids in the hands of one person. Besides, whatever happened before, it's not true of you now."

He looked straight at her. "The same could be said of you, Anna."

She felt punched. He *did* know, she thought wildly. And that *was* why he had stopped asking her to help with his ranch. Why he had stopped coming by to see her. Why all his friendship had so completely dried up.

"You don't know," she heard herself say woodenly, believing that he really did.

"So tell me," he suggested.

Tell him? She stared at him in astonishment. "Tell you what?" she heard herself ask. "You already know!"

Now it was his turn to look surprised. "Are we crossing wires here? You told me I didn't know. You're right, I don't know what it is you're so worried about, except that you apparently have some kind of juvenile record. So what's the big deal, Anna? Our whole relationship has been like dealing with quicksand. I never know where it's safe to put my foot, and you won't tell me. I know something has got you seriously worried, but I sure as hell don't know what it is. So don't sit here and tell me I don't know and then get in high dudgeon when I ask you to tell me, because I'm supposed to already know!"

"How can I believe that, when you've been avoiding me like the plague?"

His mouth opened as if he wanted to say something, then closed. He shook his head. "Whoa. Can we backtrack here?"

Anna, who hadn't had enough sleep in several nights now and was looking forward to another sleepless night, was in the mood for a fight. She recognized it and considered apologizing and backing off. But then it occurred to her that among the reasons she wasn't sleeping was this man and the way he had been treating her for the past several weeks. Why not get it all out in the open so she knew where she stood? Why not clear the air?

"Sure," she said, feeling her chin thrust forward. "Backtrack."

"All right." He leaned forward, resting his elbows on the table.

He was wearing a nice shirt today, but he had rolled up the cuffs. Almost as if her eyes were magnetized, Anna found herself looking at his forearms and admiring their strength. Looking at his shoulders and admiring their breadth. He was a powerful man, but his strength had never hurt her physically. That somehow seemed very important to her.

"Backtracking," he said, "I *have* been avoiding you."

"I knew it."

He sighed. "Anna, please, just let me finish before you try to start a fight, okay? I *have* been avoiding you. But not for whatever reasons you're apparently imagining. After we... made love, and you ran out of the shower and locked the bedroom door on me...well, I decided I'd made a mistake. I'd obviously done something that had upset you—although I still don't know what. And that's the problem here. How can I avoid hurting you or upsetting you if I don't know where the mines are buried?"

She started to open her mouth, but he held up his hand.

"Please. Let me finish. Then you can have your say. So I knew I'd hurt you, and I got the distinct feeling that you didn't want me around anymore." He gave a humorless half smile. "When a woman you've just made love to locks you out of the bedroom and won't talk to you, you kind of figure you've made a really big hash of things. So I left.

"And after I left, I figured I'd do best to stay away for a while. Whatever was bothering you, you needed time to calm down. I figured that later we could maybe be friends again. And I figured that trying to make us lovers was something I'd be wisest to avoid from here on out, since it apparently upset you so much."

Anna wasn't ready to buy it. It sounded awfully thin to her. "I'm supposed to believe you want us to be friends after the way you've been avoiding me?"

"Look," he said, "I'm not perfect. I'm going to admit I was weighing this whole youth ranch thing into the matter, too. I figured that I'd offended you somehow, and if I kept offending you, you sure as hell weren't going to want to help with the ranch. I thought we'd get back on a business footing a whole lot sooner if I just stayed clear so you realized I wasn't going to pounce on you every time you turned around. Now, I'll be the first to admit that sounds pretty ridiculous, but at the time I was thinking it, it actually made sense."

"So you just want us to have a business relationship?" Anna couldn't express why that disappointed her so much, when the last thing on earth she wanted was a personal relationship with a man. But she expected him to dismiss even that possibility now, anyway, since he clearly didn't want any kind of relationship with her. Why else would he have avoided her? She couldn't believe it was because he honestly thought that would help get things back on a business footing between them.

"Given what was going on, Anna, that seemed like the wisest course. I mean, you made it pretty apparent you didn't want anything else. Hell, you ran away from me and wouldn't even talk to me."

Anna suddenly felt uncomfortable, as she admitted her own

fault in all of this. What she had steadfastly refused to admit over the past weeks was that she had shut Hugh out in a way that would probably make anybody reluctant to talk to her again. Except wouldn't most people have demanded an explanation, rather than just telling her that she needed to deal with her past? She kept getting hung up on that.

"Anna," Hugh said finally, drawing her out of her thoughts, "I don't know what it is you're so afraid of, or what I did to offend you, and I'm worried about doing it all over again, because I don't know what I'm dealing with here. And that, I guess, is the real reason I've been staying away. Never mind what I've been telling myself. The truth is, I'm scared to death I'm going to step on a land mine. That doesn't make it very easy to relax and trust somebody."

The first trickle of belief began to run through her. He wasn't lying, she thought. He really didn't know the whole story.

"Talk to me, Anna. Tell me what it is. That way I'll know where the mines are, and maybe we can get back to being friends."

Why not? she found herself thinking. Why not. She'd already told Nate and Dan and survived. Why not tell Hugh what he was so eager to know? He talked as if there was some little obstacle they could just ignore once she explained it, but she knew better. Once he knew the truth, there would be no further possibility of "friendship."

"You know my stepfather molested me," she said finally. "Oh, why not be blunt about it. He *raped* me. Repeatedly. With force. With threat of force. With threats of harm against my mother and my friends if I didn't do exactly what he told me to do and if I didn't keep my mouth shut. I used to pretend to be asleep when he came into my room at night, hoping he'd go away. But he'd just go ahead and do what he wanted anyway. It didn't matter. The only thing that mattered was that I didn't fight him too hard or make too much noise, because then he'd hit me and threaten to do something really awful, like telling my friends about me, to shut me up."

She couldn't look at Hugh, but she could feel him looking

at her. It was like laying her soul bare, and her stomach roiled uneasily. But now that they'd started, the words just kept coming, as if the spillway had opened on a dam, and nothing was going to stop the flow now.

"I tried to tell my mother, but she didn't believe me. She accused me of lying because I hated my stepfather. When she didn't believe me, I didn't think anyone would."

"I can understand that."

Anna nodded, fixing her gaze on her clasped hands. What she needed to do was get through this without breaking down or throwing up. She wondered with a strange detachment if she was going to be able to do it. She hadn't told anyone about it with this kind of detail since she'd received counseling after the police picked her up.

"It went on for nearly two years," she said tonelessly. "At one point I took a hammer and put it under my bed, figuring I'd pull it out and threaten him the next time he came. Or maybe I'd beat him over the head with it when he was all limp and weak afterward." Something in her voice betrayed bitterness and disgust now, but she didn't try to rein it in. She was lost in her memories, seeing them almost as if they had happened to someone else.

She fell silent then, remembering how she had waited night after night, looking for the right moment...a moment that never seemed to come. "I would have killed him," she told Hugh. "I really think I would have killed him. But I never got the chance. He found the hammer, and he told me if I ever tried anything like that again he was going to use it on me."

Hugh swore softly.

"Finally...finally I got to where I didn't feel much about it one way or the other anymore. It was like it was someone else he was touching and using. I'd go away in my head, you know? I'd make up stories, or imagine I was in some beautiful place all by myself. I got really good at it."

Her eyes were starting to burn, but she ignored them, the way she ignored her tightening throat.

"I'm not sure exactly when I decided I wasn't going to take it anymore. I'm not even sure why I suddenly decided to run away. I mean...it just happened. Like it had been building without me being aware of it until...boom! There it was. I was going to run away.

"I didn't have any money to speak of, but I stole some from my mother, packed a couple of things in my schoolbag and left for school one morning. Only I never went to school. I got on a bus and went to New York."

"Why New York?"

Startled, for she had almost forgotten he was there, she looked at him. "Because it seemed far enough away and big enough that he could never find me there."

Hugh nodded. He started to reach out, as if he wanted to touch her hand, but he drew back at the last moment. "That was a brave thing to do."

"It was a stupid thing to do," she said flatly. "In retrospect, I had a lot of better options. I just didn't think anybody would believe me. I was sure everyone would think just what my mother had, that I made it up because I hated my stepfather. So I ran away, figuring I could pretend to be older and get a job or something."

"I'll bet it wasn't that easy."

"Of course it wasn't. Back then, kids didn't have to have social security numbers for the IRS, so I didn't have a social security card or any way to get one. Not that anybody would have believed I was sixteen. I was fourteen, and I looked twelve. Nobody ever bought my story about being older. Not once."

She looked down at her hands again. "Sometimes a business owner would feel sorry for me and give me a few bucks. It wasn't long before it was obvious I was a runaway. I mean, I didn't have any place to stay where I could clean up, not on a regular basis. Sometimes I'd meet older kids who would let me crash with them for a few nights, but I couldn't stay permanently, because I couldn't help with the expenses. So I started stealing food and clothes when I could, and washing up in public rest rooms. But then it started to get cold." Her voice grew unsteady.

Once again Hugh reached out toward her, but she pulled

her hand away. She couldn't bear anyone to touch her right now. Not anyone.

"I decided there was one job I could do where nobody would ask me for a social security card. One job where my age was an advantage. Besides, Van had taken it any time he wanted. Why shouldn't I get money for it?"

"Oh, Anna," Hugh said quietly, sadly.

"It felt worse, though," Anna said. There was a pressure growing in her chest, making it difficult to breathe and talk, but she forced the words out anyway. She didn't know if she was doing it because she wanted to punish him for asking, or because she finally, at last, just needed to tell someone about what all this had done to her.

"It was worse," she said again, "because this time I was choosing to do it. They didn't rape me or force me. They paid me. And I hated myself for it. I really did. I felt even worse than Van had made me feel. I figured I didn't deserve to live at all anymore, and one of these guys was going to kill me. I told myself it was going to be a good thing, that I deserved to die."

She drew a deep breath. "It was the worst thing I've ever done. Worse even than stealing. It seems stupid, but that's how I feel about it. Anyway, I was lucky. The third guy I propositioned was an undercover cop. He arrested me."

"And that's what you're worried about? A juvenile record for prostitution?"

She nodded and reluctantly dragged her gaze to his face. He didn't look disgusted or even very surprised. "I'm applying to become Lorna's guardian, but I don't think I'll be approved. And with a background like mine, I wouldn't be an asset for your youth ranch, either. I know you were thinking I could balance out your problem, but I just have a bigger one, Hugh. A much bigger one. Nobody will want a former prostitute looking after kids."

"And what about what happened between us?" he asked. "Why did you run from me like that?"

"Because..." It was suddenly almost impossible to speak. All her clinical detachment evaporated in an instant, and pain pierced her. "Because I felt...cheap. Like I was...doing it all over again."

He nodded slowly. "What we did wasn't cheap, Anna. It was beautiful. The most wonderfully intimate and affirming thing two people can do together if they care about one another. I wasn't using you. Believe me, I wasn't."

She was breathing rapidly now, trying to hold back tears once again. "Really?"

His expression grew sad. "Really, Anna. Really." He rose and came around the table. Taking her hands, he drew her to her feet. "I swear I wasn't using you. I wanted you, yes, but I thought you wanted me, too. I wanted us to be together and share that wonderful experience. And if it seems that I cast you aside afterward, because I've been avoiding you, I'm really, really sorry. I wasn't casting you aside, I was trying to do the only thing I could think of to avoid making the situation worse. I guess I made some stupid choices."

Before she could decide how to respond, he continued. "Thanks for telling me what the problem was. I appreciate it. Don't worry about it anymore, Anna. From here on out, you can set the limits between us. I'd like to spend more time with you, but I'm not going to push you. And if you want me to go away, I'll go. All you have to do is say so."

"Don't go." She could hardly believe she was saying it, but she was. She was actually asking a man to stay. Her heart hammered wildly, and she felt as if she were climbing out of some long, dark tunnel.

He searched her face, then wrapped his arms around her, hugging her close with a tenderness that made her throat ache anew. "It's okay," he said. "It's okay. You'll see. To hell with the rest of the world, sweetie. It doesn't matter a damn what any of them think of you. All that matters is what you think of yourself. And as far as I can see, you've got a whole hell of a lot to be proud of."

She turned her face up to him, filled with a sudden fierceness. "And so have you, Cowboy. So have you."

He smiled then. "So okay. We'll face 'em all down." He squeezed her gently, then brushed the lightest of kisses on her lips. "Meantime, I'm going to skedaddle. You look exhausted. In fact, you've looked exhausted all day."

"I haven't been sleeping well."

"I can tell. You go to bed now. I'll come over tomorrow evening, if that's okay, and we can talk more then."

Her heart gave a strange little leap when she realized that Lorna was planning to spend tomorrow night with Mary Jo again. But she was also too tired and feeling too emotionally wrung out right now to think about what that might mean. She walked Hugh to the door, accepted another light kiss and said good-night.

Then she stood at the living-room window and watched him walk to his truck and climb in. For the first time in what seemed like forever, she actually felt that things were starting to get better.

And that night, for the first time in days, she slept soundly and well.

It wasn't until the next morning that it struck her that once he'd heard her story, he'd been in an awfully big hurry to leave.

Chapter 15

Monday morning, while Anna was getting dressed for court, the phone rang in the living room. She heard Lorna call out, "I'll get it, Anna!"

Her first thought was that it must be Hugh, and her heart leapt with an eagerness that was almost frightening. This time, instead of telling herself that Hugh had left early the last few nights because he was disgusted, she was trying to believe that he had left for the very reasons he had cited. She had a tendency, she was beginning to realize, to interpret people's actions in the worst possible ways—a tendency to assume that they were acting out of disgust for her. It was becoming increasingly clear that that just wasn't the case. Just look at Nate and Dan. There was no reason to assume Hugh couldn't be just as generous.

So she found herself hoping it was him, but when Lorna didn't come back to get her, it became apparent it must have been one of her friends. She felt deflated, then scolded herself with a reminder that he had said he would be coming by tonight.

She chose her prettiest dress to wear that morning, a navy

blue A-line with a white collar and long sleeves. Looking at herself in the mirror, she wondered if it wasn't high time she bought a few things that were less conservative. The church-secretary image was fine for work, but surely she could be a little brighter on her own time?

When she came out of her bedroom, Lorna was sitting on the couch in the living room, wearing a violet dress and white stockings. Her long blond hair was caught in a butterfly clip on the back of her head.

"Don't you look lovely," Anna said approvingly.

"Thank you."

Lorna sounded subdued, and Anna felt a spark of worry. "What's wrong, honey?"

Lorna shook her head.

"Are you nervous about today?"

"I guess."

Anna stared at her in perplexity. Lorna hadn't been nervous about going to court before. "Are you worried about making a decision about the plea bargain?"

"No." The girl shook her head. "I'm fine, Anna. I'm just tired this morning."

It was possible, Anna thought. "Who was on the phone?"

"Wrong number."

She couldn't have said why, but in that instant Anna knew that Lorna was lying. But why? She considered pressing the issue, then decided to wait and see what might develop. She all too clearly remembered herself at that age, and how stubborn and angry she could get when an adult pried into private things.

The meeting this morning was being held in the judge's chambers rather than the courtroom. Anna expected to get there and find just the judge and a court reporter present. Instead, to her dismay, Al and Bridget Lacey and his attorney were waiting in the anteroom.

"No, don't go in there," the bailiff said. "You two ladies are to go directly in to the judge." He guided them through the door across the hall into the conference room where they had met Judge Williams to take Lorna's statement weeks ago.

But as fast as the bailiff moved, it wasn't too quickly for Anna to see the significant look that Lacey sent his daughter. Lorna seemed to shrivel.

"That was inexcusable," Anna told the bailiff as soon as the door closed behind them. "Do you know what that man has done to this child? He's not supposed to be anywhere near her!"

"I'm sorry, ma'am," the bailiff said. "He wasn't supposed to be here this early. His hearing isn't until nine-thirty."

Anna was furious and wanted to shake somebody, but she couldn't do any more. Lorna sat at the long table, looking frightened and shrunken, as if she wanted to curl up on herself. Anna would have blamed it entirely on the encounter with her father, except that it had started before they'd left home. What in the world was wrong?

The judge entered the room, along with the court reporter, and greeted them warmly. "This should only take a few minutes," she said. They waited while the stenographer typed in the information about the hearing and its purpose, then Judge Williams turned to Anna and Lorna.

"Miss Fleming, have you decided whether to apply for permanent guardianship of Miss Lacey?"

"Yes, Your Honor, I have. I'm going to apply."

"Excellent. I want you to know that both Reverend Fromberg and Sheriff Tate have spoken to me personally about your application. I'm aware that there may be...some difficulties, although I doubt it. So I want you to know that I'm going to keep a personal eye on your application to ensure that it's handled properly and processed as quickly as possible. In the opinion of people I respect—and in my own opinion, for that matter—there is no guardian better suited to this case. In the interim, your guardianship is reaffirmed indefinitely."

"Thank you, Your Honor." Anna felt her heart swell with the first stirrings of hope. Maybe it all *would* work out so that she could keep Lorna.

"Now, Miss Lacey. I explained to you on Monday that a plea bargain has been offered in the case against your father for sexually abusing you. The terms are that he has to move away, that he can't have contact with you again, and that he'll be on probation for the next five years. Neither can he have contact with any minor child, including your sister. I've decided to increase that probation to ten years. I'm also going to require him to attend a program for sexual offenders. How do you feel about this? Should the court accept or refuse this bargain, keeping in mind that if it is refused, the case will have to go to trial?"

Lorna didn't answer. The judge waited a few moments, then said, "Miss Lacey?"

"I...don't know."

Judge Williams sat back in her chair and looked kindly at Lorna. "I understand this must be difficult for you. Are there any questions I can answer that might help you make a decision?"

"W-what will happen if...I say I lied?"

Anna felt her heart slam. No! There was no way this child had lied about this. No way! She opened her mouth, but the judge waved her to silence.

Francine Williams' voice was gentle. "Did you lie, Miss Lacey?"

Lorna's head was bowed, and her hands were twisting on her lap. "What if I say I did?"

"It's a crime to lie to the court, Miss Lacey. But the important thing right now is that you tell me the truth, whatever it is."

Lorna nodded.

"Did you lie, Miss Lacey?"

Lorna lifted her face, and her cheeks were streaked with tears. "My mom called me this morning. She said...she said if I tell you I lied, I can come back to live with them, and I can have a horse of my very own. She said my daddy would never touch me again, that he promised. But if I don't tell you I lied, she said I'll never see my sister again. Not ever."

The room fell silent as Judge Williams pondered. Anna's hands formed fists, and it was all she could do not to say anything. Every cell in her body wanted to shriek with shock, anger and disbelief that anyone, most especially a mother, would put a child in this position.

"Miss Lacey," the judge said finally, "it appears you have a difficult decision to make here. From what you just told me, it's apparent that you did *not* lie on your deposition when you made your statement to me under oath. I can't prevent you from recanting your earlier statement, if that's what you decide to do. But I want you to think very carefully about what it means if you do. Not only will your father not be punished for a very serious crime, but you will be branded a liar in front of the whole world. You might be charged with perjury.

"Now, regardless of what you decide to do here today, you are going to have to do it under oath. That means that you *must* tell the truth or commit the crime of perjury. Do you understand?"

Lorna nodded, fresh tears running down her cheeks. The judge administered the oath, and Lorna swore to tell the truth.

"Miss Lacey," Francine Williams said, "did you lie to this court when you made your earlier sworn statement that your father sexually abused you?"

Lorna gave a great hiccuping sob. "N-no..."

Anna felt a huge surge of relief flow through her, and she reached out to put her hand reassuringly on Lorna's arm. At that moment, she thought, she could cheerfully have killed Bridget Lacey.

"Did your mother call you this morning and try to persuade you to say you lied when you testified that your father had sexually abused you?"

"Y-yes."

"Do you still say that your father sexually abused you?"

"Yes." The girl's voice was growing steadier with each response, and her tears were easing. "He hurt me just like I said. But I don't want to lose my sister...."

"I can't make any promises on that score, Miss Lacey. Your sister's custody is not an issue before this court, and the court can only deal with matters in its jurisdiction. The only thing I *can* do, and something that I am going to do, is forbid your father to have any contact with any minor children during the term of his probation. Do you know what that means?''

Lorna shook her head.

''It means that for the next ten years, your father cannot see your sister. At all. What I cannot do is remove your sister from your mother's care. Her parental rights can't be terminated unless she does something to warrant termination. This winds up meaning that your father can't live with the family anymore.''

Lorna nodded.

''If your father does, for *any* reason, have contact with your sister—or any other minor child—he'll go to prison for the rest of his sentence.

''Now, I told you that social services will be investigating the family situation. If they should decide that your mother can't be trusted to keep your father away from your sister, they'll probably ask the court to remove your sister from the home. The same will apply if they feel your sister is at any risk of being abused at any time, even after your father's sentence is completed. Do you understand?''

Lorna nodded, looking miserable.

''As for you being able to see your sister—well, I'll speak to social services about it. I don't see why something can't be worked out. I'll definitely do what I can to ensure it.''

The judge asked a few more questions, then returned to the issue of the plea bargain. Lorna agreed to accept it rather than testify.

Judge Williams ended the hearing, but indicated that they should remain where they were. ''I have some business I want to take care of before the two of you leave here. I'll have the bailiff bring in some hot cocoa or coffee for you, if you'll be kind enough to wait for a little while.''

Anna was in no hurry to go out into the hall again, where they might run into Al Lacey. She nodded agreement to the judge, then scooted her chair over closer to Lorna so she could hug the girl.

''You did a brave thing, Lorna.''

Lorna turned and threw her arms around Anna's neck, crying onto her shoulder. "I'm so scared, Anna," she said brokenly. "So scared. He hurt me, but he's still my dad!"

"I know that, honey. I know that."

"Why couldn't he be like everybody else's dad?"

"I don't know." Questions like that never had any answers, she thought wearily. All she could do was hold Lorna and ache for her, and ache for all the other little children who were betrayed by the people they should have been most able to trust.

"Do you think I'll ever see my sister again?"

"If there's any way possible, we'll find it. I promise."

Lorna nodded and straightened, wiping at her eyes with the back of her hand. Anna searched her purse and found some clean tissues, which she handed to the child. Lorna murmured a thank-you and dabbed at her eyes.

"I'm sorry," she said, when her sniffling had quieted. "I was just so scared. At first I thought I had to do it, because she's my mother. But I was scared about going back there to live, because I don't think my dad would keep his promise. And I was scared about not seeing my sister again if I didn't.... I was so confused."

Anna hesitated, then went ahead and said, "Your mother was wrong to ask you to lie."

Lorna nodded. "I know she was. I mean, she always taught me not to lie, not even about little things. I couldn't believe she wanted me to lie now."

"She's trying to make this all go away, Lorna. It was wrong of her to ask that, but that's why she did it. She wants it all to just go away."

"So do I!" A fresh tear ran down Lorna's face. "I want it all to go away! I want it all to never have happened. But it *did* happen, and nothing anybody says or does is going to make it go away, Anna. How can it go away, when I can't forget it?"

There was no answer to that, either, and it struck Anna as a very sad thing that a child should be asking such questions. "Time helps, Lorna. That's all I can tell you. Time makes it easier. You don't think about it as often. It will always hurt, but it will get so you don't think about it for long periods of time.''

Unless something happened to reawaken it all. Anna looked past Lorna, thinking about how much time she had spent in the past month thinking about those very things, as if her childhood, once remote, was suddenly as close as yesterday. It would all fade again with time, but she supposed that every so often it was going to come back to her and start her hurting all over again. She hated to think that Lorna was probably going to endure the same process for the rest of her life, too.

The judge returned a few minutes later. ''You won't have to worry about this happening again,'' she told Anna and Lorna. ''I've taken some steps to ensure that it doesn't. You can leave now...and don't worry, no one is out there to bother you.''

Lorna left at six to spend the night with Mary Jo, and Hugh arrived at seven. When Anna opened the door to let him in, she was surprised to see it was snowing again.

''We're supposed to get a couple of inches tonight,'' he said.

''That's not so bad.''

''As long as the wind doesn't kick up and build huge drifts everywhere.'' He hung his jacket on the peg by the door and kicked his boots off, leaving them to dry on the braid rug in front of the door. ''Is Lorna here?''

''She went to spend the night with a friend. They've been planning it for days.'' She didn't want him to think she had arranged it because he was planning to visit tonight.

He hesitated. ''Did you hear what happened to Bridget Lacey?''

''No. What?'' She was shocked to realize that she half hoped the woman had driven her car off a cliff.

''She was arrested this morning for witness tampering.'' He arched a brow at Anna. ''You wouldn't know anything about that, would you?''

''My God.'' Anna sat abruptly on the couch. ''I had no idea the judge did that.''

"What happened?"

"She called Lorna this morning just before we went to court and tried to induce her to say she'd been lying about her father molesting her."

Hugh shook his head in disgust. "You really have to wonder what's wrong with some people's brains, don't you? I can't believe anyone would be so stupid—or so cruel. That woman isn't fit to be a mother."

"No, I don't think she is." Anna shook her head. "I'm certainly not going to make any more excuses for her. And Lorna's worried sick about her little sister."

"Of course she is! I can't believe they'll let that little girl stay with that family. Neither parent is fit."

"But what will they do with her if they take her away? Lorna will be heartbroken if she can't see her sister again."

"Maybe *you* ought to think about taking the little one, too."

Anna barely let herself consider the possibility, even though it appealed to her. "I'd love to, but I can't. Hugh, I have to *work*. And I can't afford day care."

"I didn't think of that. Are you going to call Lorna and tell her about her mother?"

"Absolutely not! If I call her now, it'll ruin her time with Mary Jo. She'll feel responsible and worry about it. No, tomorrow's soon enough to tell her about this." Soon enough, but no time would be good enough. Poor Lorna, this was going to upset her even more.

Hugh leaned over and touched her shoulder gently. "How about a change of subject?"

Anna summoned a smile, trying to put her concerns aside for now. "Sure. To what?"

"Oh, something like, what happened to all that leftover turkey?"

She had to laugh. They went into the kitchen and pulled the turkey from the fridge.

"Now, you let *me* make the sandwiches," Hugh said. "My culinary skills may be limited, but when it comes to making a sandwich, I have no equal."

He proceeded to construct sandwiches that would have done

any deli proud. "I take it you and Lorna had a rough morning?"

"Just a bit."

"I'm real sorry about that. In my so humble opinion, I think the two of you have been through quite enough."

"I couldn't agree more. Where do I lodge a complaint?"

"Beats me. If you find out, let me know, will you?"

He carried the sandwiches to the table and sat next to her. She pulled napkins from the caddy, handing one to him and spreading hers in her lap. It was nice, she thought, to be having an impromptu meal with him. It was all too easy to imagine a future where the two of them did this regularly, sitting together at the end of a long day.

The yearning made her uneasy, because it reflected a major shift in her attitude. For so long she had believed that solitude was safety, that her life was far better for living it alone. Over the past few weeks, however, she had found herself wishing for things she knew she would never have, and every one of those wishes seemed to revolve around Hugh Gallagher.

As usual, part of her mind tried to warn her that that way lay grief, but this time, for the first time, she argued back. She was entitled to want such things. She was entitled to wish for a normal life, with a husband and children. She had done nothing so wrong that she should have to spend the rest of her life paying for it with loneliness. Even if life never granted her these simple but important blessings, she had a right to wish for them.

With that small but important argument, with that small but important shift in her belief about herself, she felt a sense of freedom begin to blossom. There was, she realized, nothing intrinsically wrong with her. She had done some bad things, and some bad things had been done to her, but they didn't make her a bad person.

"Anna?" Hugh was looking at her, concern creasing his brow. "Is something wrong?"

She shook her head. "No, I'm fine. Really, I'm *fine*." She said it with a smile.

He smiled back. "What brought that on?"

"I just realized I'm not a bad person."

"Of course you're not!" He put his sandwich down and reached for her hand, clasping it gently. "I've never known anyone who was further from a bad person than you."

"But the things I did—"

"You did from necessity," he interrupted her. "I've seen people do a lot worse. The point, Anna, is that you didn't do anything to hurt someone else. The only person you hurt was yourself. Most of us can't say that."

"But I stole."

"To survive. It may be against the law, but I don't see it as a moral crime. Not when it's a matter of survival."

"That's debatable," she said, but a soft smile curved her lips. She liked having him champion her this way. She liked knowing that he didn't think she was a shamefully bad person.

"Don't try to debate it with me," he said. "You'll lose. You aren't a bad person, and you never were. Period."

"Neither are you."

"No, I'm not. I've done some bad things, but I probably saved a lot of lives by doing them. I'll never know, and I'm tired of beating myself up over it. All any of us can do is the best we can at the time. That's what you did. That's what I did. And trust me, a bad person wouldn't still be beating herself up over things she did when she was fourteen."

She nodded, feeling his words fill her heart with a soothing balm.

He picked up his sandwich again. "There, now that we've settled that..."

She laughed again, loving the easy way he lightened the moments when they became too intense. Loving the way he looked at her over the top of his sandwich, a smile glinting in his eyes. An impulse to touch him swept over her, and before she could prevent it, she had reached out and laid her hand on his arm.

He put his sandwich down again. "Aw, Anna, I'm going to have to kiss you."

"I wish you would."

The smile in his eyes was suddenly something much hotter.

Her breath stuck in her throat, and she couldn't tear her gaze from his.

"Be sure, Anna," he said quietly. "Be very, very sure, because I am gonna be one mad dude if you regret this."

Even now, he made her want to smile. "I'm sure," she managed to say, and was absolutely positive that she had never been surer of anything in her life.

He rose from the table and reached for her, drawing her up against his hard chest, cradling her as close as he could possibly get her. His kiss tasted like turkey sandwich at first, but before long she could taste the heady flavor of him.

"Anna," he whispered raggedly. "Oh, Anna...you've been driving me nuts for weeks. I dream about you every night. I wake up every morning wishing I could see you. You haunt me...."

His words reached to her soul, plucking new feelings forth, feelings of warmth and softness and trust, feelings of beauty. Oh, how beautiful he made her feel, and never, not once in her life, had she felt beautiful.

He plucked her glasses from her nose and set them on the table, then swept her up in his arms, carrying her toward the bedroom.

"Stop me now, Anna. If you're going to want to stop me, stop me now."

She didn't want to stop him. She wanted him never to stop. She could feel his muscles trembling with eagerness, and his eagerness fueled her own. "Don't stop," she said throatily. "Please don't stop...."

He set her on her feet beside the bed and gripped her shoulders, looking down into her eyes. "This can't be a mistake. I swore I was never going to do this again. Don't let this be a mistake."

If she had ever felt fear, she couldn't remember it now. If she had ever been reluctant, she was incapable of it now. She needed his hands on her flesh, his mouth on her skin, his body against hers and inside her. It seemed to have come out of nowhere, this sweeping, undeniable fire of need, but she knew it had been building since the very first time she had set eyes on him.

Always, always, she had been drawn to Hugh Gallagher, even in the months before they first spoke in the church basement. From the moment she had first spied him on the street, she had felt drawn. Only now did she realize that she had been waiting for him her whole life long.

Never had anything been so right.

He pulled her sweater over her head, then paused, admiring her small, firm breasts in their lacy cups.

"So pretty," he whispered, and ran his finger along the edge of the lace. Shivers trickled through her, and her breath began to come in small, soft gasps.

He reached behind her and released the clasp of her bra, freeing her breasts. She looked down as he drew the material away and set her free. And this time she *felt* free. She *was* free. This was Hugh, and that made everything special.

Lifting her head, she looked up at him and laughed with delight. He smiled back at her and reached for the snap of her jeans. "You don't need these, darlin'," he said. "Trust me, I'll keep you warm."

She *did* trust him. That was what was so wonderful. She trusted him so much that she was able to shed all the inhibitions and fears that had kept her away from him. He gave her a safe place to be herself. A safe place to just *be.*

When he lifted her and laid her down on the bed, she felt as light as a feather falling.

Hugh stood over her, stripping away his clothes, devouring her with his eyes. "I'm scared," he said suddenly. "I'm scared you're going to run from me...."

Anna shook her head and reached out to clasp his hand and draw him down to her. "Not this time," she said. She felt as powerful as the earth mother, and as old and wise as time. She *knew.*

His hot flesh covered hers, shielding her from everything else in the world, closing her into the haven described by his arms. Inch by inch, he trailed molten fire over her skin with the touch of his lips and hands. She thought she had awakened the first time they had made love, but it had been nothing like this. This time she felt as if she were a pure, burning flame of passion, free of all constraints. Free of all her past.

Her own hands roamed him, learning contours she had been almost too shy to touch before and discovering what a sheer delight it was to touch him. Never had she imagined how good the sensation of warm, dry sky beneath her palm could feel. Or how very sexy a man's angles and planes could be.

He seemed to enjoy her touches, making sounds that reminded her of a large, purring cat. Encouraged, she grew more daring even as his touches swept her higher on the roaring flames of passion.

His mouth found her breasts, bringing them to aching life until she arched, begging for harder touches. She felt as if her whole body were blossoming, reaching for her lover's touch in the same way a flower reached for the sun.

A deep, hard ache built in her, driving her onward, causing her to arch up against him with her hips, seeking more of him, and more.

Then, in an instant, he was sheathed inside her, filling her and completing her. A momentary satisfaction caused her to gasp; she had never felt anything so perfect, so right, so satisfying…and then hunger goaded her again, causing her to lift against him time and again, taking him deeper and deeper with each thrust. More…more…more…

He caught her hips with his hands, bringing her even closer, and that simple movement catapulted her over the cliff edge into completion.

Only dimly, as she drifted slowly back to earth, was she aware that he followed her.

"That sandwich is stale," Anna said.

They stood together in the kitchen, she in her flannel nightgown, he in his jeans.

"I hate to waste it."

"By now it's probably growing a million little salmonella bacteria."

He grimaced at her, a laugh in his eyes. "Okay, okay. Damn, you sure know how to spoil a man's appetite."

"I'll make you a fresh sandwich."

He caught her around the waist as she started to pass him on the way to the refrigerator. "No," he said. "I don't want you to wait on me."

"Don't be silly." But her breath caught as she looked up into his eyes and saw the banked fires there.

"I'm not being silly," he said. "I want our relationship to get off on the right foot. I'm a grown man, Anna. If I get hungry, I can make myself something. You don't have to take care of me."

"Oh, a liberated male." She knew she must be grinning like an idiot, but she didn't care. She was as close to delirious as she had ever been. "Fine. I don't have any problem with that. But what if I *want* to do it?"

A smile crinkled the corners of his eyes. "Oh, well, that's different."

"I had a feeling it might be."

But he helped anyway. They made fresh turkey sandwiches, laughing and talking all the while. After they ate, they went to sit in the living room, curling up together on the couch and talking in the aimless but intent fashion of people who are just learning to know one another.

"Have you ever been married?" Anna asked him.

"No. I never met anybody I felt I could spend the rest of my life with." He shifted a little, tucking her closer under his arm and running a finger along her forearm. "I kept waiting for the magic."

"Magic?"

"Yeah. You know. That feeling that *this is the one.* I came close a couple of times, years ago, but...I don't know. Something always made me back off. I can't see getting married unless I feel with my whole heart and soul that this is the right person."

"I never even came close before."

"It's kinda hard to do unless you date."

She gave a little laugh. "Just a little."

"So will you date me?"

"Date you?"

"We'll go places and do things together and see where it all goes." He looked down at her, a smile deep in his eyes. "I'm feeling lucky. How about you?"

She *was,* she realized. She was feeling very lucky. "I don't think I could be any luckier than I feel right now."

"Trust me. You could be a whole lot luckier." He started to bend his head to kiss her, but just before their lips met, the phone rang.

"I'd better get that," Anna said. "It might be Lorna."

It wasn't Lorna. It was an all-too-familiar male voice saying, "I'm going to make you sorry you got involved in all of this."

Something inside Anna snapped. She heard it in the back of her head like a breaking twig. Fear was the furthest thing from her mind as anger surged in her.

"Listen, you disgusting, slimy toad, you don't frighten me! What are you going to do? Tell everyone in town that I was raped by my stepfather? Well, go ahead! I don't care if the whole damn world knows about it! Now go crawl back under your rock and don't ever let me see you or hear from you again. Get out of my life, and get out of your daughter's life before one of us decides to give you what you really deserve!"

She slammed the phone down so hard she thought she might have broken it, but she didn't care. Tremors of rage ran through her, making her shake violently.

"I'm going to kill him," she said. "I'm going to find a way to kill that bastard!"

Hugh came over to her and wrapped his arms around her, holding her tightly, as if he could protect her. "Want me to go knock his block off?"

"No!" Anna lifted her head and looked at him. "*I* want to knock his block off."

Hugh shook his head. "Sorry, sweetheart, but I don't think you're quite big enough to succeed. You're a tiny little woman, and he's kind of a big guy. But you sure told him off good."

"I could throttle him and his wife both. I could wring their disgusting necks!"

"I can sure see why you want to."

"Do you know what else he did?"

"No. What?"

"My mother called me a couple of days ago. My *mother.* I haven't spoken to her since I ran away from home! But she got my phone number from a private detective who was looking into my background. There's no doubt in my mind that Al Lacey hired him."

"Probably." Concern was evident in his face as he looked sadly down at her. "I'm so sorry, Anna. What did your mother tell him?"

"Nothing, apparently. She called to warn me about it, and to tell me she was sorry for not believing me when I told her Van was raping me."

"She did? When did she reach that conclusion?"

"About five years after I left." Anna shuddered and wished she could burrow right into him and hide from everything.

"What changed her mind?"

Much as she hated to even remember those pictures, she found she didn't mind telling Hugh. Telling Hugh things was surprisingly easy. "She found the photographs he took."

"He took *photographs?*" He was plainly appalled. "My God! What happened to them?"

"She burned them. After she used them to get a divorce."

He nodded. "Well, thank God for that. You don't need to be worrying if those pictures might turn up sometime. Damn it, I can't believe what a jackass that man must have been. A disgusting creep, yeah. I already knew that. His kind don't deserve to live. But how stupid do you have to be to take pictures of your crime?"

Anna had never quite seen it that way before, and somehow, surprisingly, it made her feel good. She *liked* the idea that her stepfather was a stupid jerk, stupid enough to collect evidence against himself. "He *was* stupid," she agreed.

"An IQ of two." He shook his head. "Damn, it's hard to

believe. But what about your mother? How do you feel about that? About her?"

Anna leaned against him, listening to the steady sound of his heartbeat, loving the way it felt to be able to lean against him this way. Loving the freedom she had found in his arms. "I don't know, Hugh. I've been angry at her for a long, long time. And I haven't seen her in over sixteen years. I don't know that I really feel anything one way or another anymore."

"But she's your mother."

"Yes. I don't know. I don't feel ready to make any kind of decision about whether to ever talk to her again or just forget she even called."

"It'll take time."

"Yes, it will."

He tipped her face up and kissed her gently on the mouth. "We have plenty of time, sweetheart. Plenty of time for getting to know each other. Plenty of time to decide things. But I'm going to leave right now."

"Why?"

"Because you're about to come under scrutiny as a potential foster parent. I don't think it would look too good if your neighbors report that you've had a man as an overnight guest."

She couldn't argue the justice of it, but she was starting to feel wounded again. Was this all he had wanted? Just to get laid?

But he was already turning away, heading for the bedroom and his clothes. Anna looked at the clock and was astounded to see it was only ten-thirty. She felt as if her entire life had changed, and it was only ten-thirty.

But nothing had changed, she told herself. Nothing at all. Hugh had gotten what he wanted, and now he was leaving again.

Before he left, he came to give her a tight hug and a lingering kiss. "I'll call in the morning," he said. "Just to see how you're doing."

"Sure." She didn't think he would. She had told him about the pictures, and he was hightailing it out of here as quickly as he could go. It must be that he didn't think the pictures had been destroyed. Yes, that was probably it. He was afraid they might turn up sometime and adversely impact his ranch.

This time she didn't stand at the window to watch him leave. And she never expected to hear from him again.

Chapter 16

When he left Anna's house, Hugh went hunting. It was late on a Monday evening, and except for the roadhouses and bars, Conard County was pretty well settled in for a long winter's nap. Snow continued to fall steadily, but not heavily, and the roads wouldn't become impassible for hours yet, so he didn't even hesitate about driving out to Al Lacey's house.

He supposed he could get in trouble with the law for what he was about to do, but he was damned if he cared. That creep was going to stop tormenting Anna, and that was all there was to it. Besides, he wasn't going to beat the man, merely have a cautionary word with him.

But he had to do something about it. It had been bothering him all along, but he hadn't felt as if he had a right to do anything about it. It was Anna's business, after all, and unless she asked someone to intervene, nobody really should. But things were different now. He and Anna had a relationship, and he was feeling entirely too possessive to let this continue.

It struck him, when he was halfway out to Lacey's place, that he'd probably been too abrupt in his departure from Anna's. Hell, from the minute he'd realized who that call was from, he could think of only one thing: confronting Al Lacey. Now Anna was probably wondering if something she had told him had sent him into flight.

That woman's self-esteem was way too low, and if he spent the rest of his life doing it, he was going to find some way to give her back the confidence she was entitled to. She was a lovely, sweet, intelligent young woman, who shouldn't spend the rest of her life feeling so damn undeserving.

Of course, from his perspective, it could be difficult to deal with her defensiveness and her readiness to assume the worst, but she was worth it. Hell, she was worth a whole lot more than a little trouble like that.

But he sure wished he'd thought to make a more reasonable departure. Well, he would have to mend that fence in the morning, because right now, he was going to fix a wagon.

It was a quarter after eleven when he reached the Lacey house, but there were enough lights on downstairs to indicate that Al wasn't tucked into bed yet. Not that it would have mattered. As angry as he was right now, Hugh would have rousted the jerk from sleep and not turned a hair.

Al Lacey opened the door to Hugh's knock. He looked haggard and angry.

"I want you to stop making threatening phone calls to Anna," Hugh said without preamble.

"I'm not making any phone calls to anybody!"

Hugh took a step forward and jabbed his index finger into Lacey's chest. "It's like this, Lacey. I know you're making those calls. And if she gets another one, ever, I'm going to hunt you down and make you sorry you were ever born. And if I hear one whisper of gossip about that little lady, I'm going to hold you personally responsible. If you think you've got troubles now, just try me. Are we clear?"

The two men glared at one another for several seconds, but then Lacey's gaze flickered. "What the hell do I care? I'm leaving town, anyway."

"The sooner the better," Hugh said.

He heard the door slam behind him as he walked to his car. His knuckles were itching for the feeling of landing a solid punch, and just a few weeks ago, he might have done it. But not now. Now he didn't want to do anything that might upset Anna, or take her from him.

He drove home through the falling snow, trying to figure out what to tell her in the morning to smooth her feathers, because he didn't for an instant doubt he'd messed up again.

He had to learn to take his leave better, he thought. He had to learn to start explaining to her. He couldn't keep on carrying on as if he was the only person in the world, because now Anna was a part of his world, too. And next time he got a burr to do something, he promised himself, he was going to explain it to her before he went charging off.

He just hoped that by morning she hadn't decided she hated him.

Anna was roused from a sound sleep by the ringing of the phone. The sun still hadn't come up, and she could hear the wind howling outside her window. She grabbed her robe from the foot of the bed and jammed her feet into slippers, then hurried out to the kitchen to answer the phone.

It was Lorna. "Anna? My dad called a little while ago. He told Mrs. Weeks that my mom is in jail and it's all my fault."

"Lorna..." Anna hardly knew what to say, except that she would like to kill Al Lacey.

"It's okay, Anna," Lorna said. "Mrs. Weeks told me it's not my fault, because I didn't make my mom do things that were wrong, just like I didn't make my dad do things. She said none of it is my fault."

"Honey, it isn't. Trust me on this. It's no more your fault than it would be your fault if one of them decided to rob a bank."

Lorna gave a little laugh. "That's exactly what Mrs. Weeks said. Anyway, I'm calling because...well, we're snowed in."

"Oh, no!"

Lorna laughed again. "Yup. Mr. Weeks said he doesn't think he'll be able to get me home before late this afternoon, and I didn't want you to worry."

"Thank you. But about your mom—"

"It's okay, Anna. Really. It's like Mrs. Weeks said. I'm the kid and they're the parents. They're supposed to know better, and if they do things that are wrong, it's not my job to protect *them.* They're supposed to protect *me.*"

"That's absolutely right."

"So I'm okay with it. Really. I'm just worried about my sister, but you said we'd find a way to work that out, so all I'm going to do is pray really hard that God takes care of her. He will, won't He, Anna?"

Anna's own opinion was that God didn't much bother with individual worries—if He did, would parents molest their children?—but she didn't have the heart to disillusion Lorna. "Pray hard, honey," she said. "Pray really hard. God will find a way."

Lorna sighed. "I'll be grown up before long, so maybe I can do something about Mindy myself."

"That's possible, too. We're certainly going to look into ways to make sure you can still see her."

"Okay. Well, I gotta go eat breakfast now. I'm sorry I woke you up, but I didn't want you to start worrying or anything. And I was wondering..."

Anna waited, wondering why Lorna was hesitating. Finally she prompted her. "Wondering what, Lorna?"

"I was wondering...can I call you Mom?"

Anna felt as if she were walking on air. She hardly cared that the blizzard of the decade was blowing around her house and drifting snow into banks ten feet tall that were going to challenge even the snowplows. Lorna wanted to call her Mom! She hugged the joy close and ran the conversation through her mind over and over again.

She was pacing the kitchen, drinking her second cup of coffee and thinking that life just couldn't get any better, when she heard a knock on her front door. She couldn't imagine who would be out on a morning like this and decided it must be a stranded motorist who wanted to use the phone.

Humming under her breath, she went to answer the door

and was astonished to see Hugh standing there, bundled against the bitter day.

"How in the world did you get through this storm?" she asked, stepping back to let him in. All her upset of last night was forgotten in her joy this morning. She was simply glad to see Hugh and wanted to share her good news.

"I walked," he said.

She closed the door, feeling a gust of wind and icy snow blow up under her nightgown as she did so. "Why in the world did you do that? You could have just called."

"Calling wouldn't work," he said simply. "I had to see you."

She stepped back away from the flying snow as he pulled off his hat, his scarf, his jacket and his boots. His jeans were caked with snow and ice, and he looked down at them.

"Is Lorna here?"

"She's snowed in at the Weeks' house until this afternoon, probably. I just talked to her."

"Well, to hell with it, then," he said, and stripped off his frozen jeans. "Where can I hang these?"

"How about throwing them in the dryer?"

"You have a dryer?"

"The church set me up really nicely. All the amenities, and my rent is sinfully low."

"Can't complain about that."

She showed him where the dryer was and watched him throw his wet clothes into it. He was, she thought, really quite cute standing there in his flannel shirt, briefs and socks. His legs were gorgeous, and she could get quite used to the sight of him running around this way.

When he finished starting the dryer, he turned to her and asked, "Are you mad at me?"

"I'm not mad at anybody in the whole world this morning."

He raised an eyebrow. "What happened? You sound ready to burst with good news."

"I am." She savored his attention for a moment, while she poured him a cup of coffee and handed it to him.

He accepted it gratefully. "So, are you going to tell me, or do I need to beg?"

She laughed then. "I had the nicest conversation with Lorna this morning. She asked if she could call me Mom."

For an instant she feared he wouldn't understand, but then his whole face softened, and he smiled. "Oh, Anna, that's wonderful. That's truly wonderful. I'm so happy for you."

"I'm dancing on air. I don't think anything in the whole world could make me any happier."

"Really? So you're not mad at me about the way I left last night?"

She sat at the table and reached for her own coffee cup. "Well, I was a little upset last night. It seemed like you couldn't get out of here fast enough."

"I couldn't." He pulled a chair out, turned it around and straddled it. "But it wasn't because of you, sweetheart. I realized after I left that you probably thought so, but it wasn't because of you."

"Then what was it?"

"I hightailed it out of here because I couldn't wait to have a couple of very pointed words with Al Lacey."

Her mouth formed an *O* of surprise, and her eyes widened. "Did you? Did you really?"

"Let's just say that I left him with the impression that if he doesn't leave you alone, or if he ever spreads any gossip about you, I'm probably going to rend him limb from limb."

Were it possible, her eyes grew even bigger. For an instant he wondered if he'd made a serious mistake. It wasn't beyond the bounds of possibility that she might resent him for interfering, or that she might object to him making threats of violence. He had known women who would feel that way.

Just as he thought his stomach was going to sink all the way to his boots, Anna laughed. She clapped her hands in delight and laughed, a lovely cascade of sound that made him grin in response.

"Thank you," she said. "Oh, Hugh, thank you! You can't know how good it feels to have somebody stand up for me like that! I've been all alone for so long. This is just wonderful."

"Well..." He hesitated and cleared his throat, and finally decided there would never be a better time. "Well...if you like...I'd be happy to stand up for you for the rest of our lives."

As his words penetrated, her smile began to fade. He nearly panicked, thinking he'd gone and said it exactly the wrong way. Or maybe he was mistaken, and she didn't care two figs about him. Maybe...

"Hugh?" She said his name in a husky whisper. "Hugh?"

"I realize," he said hastily, "that there are a hundred reasons why no woman wants a guy like me. You don't have to tell me. But I've kinda...well..." He swore and drew a deep breath before continuing. "It's the magic, Anna. I've been feeling it with you almost since the first words we spoke to each other. I've been telling myself that I was imagining it. I've been telling myself that it would wear off. But I'm not imagining it, and it's not wearing off."

She blinked and continued to look at him as if he were speaking a foreign language. It occurred to him that he wasn't using the right words.

"It's getting stronger, Anna. I'm crazy head over heels in love with you—which is probably why I've been acting like a jerk these last couple of weeks. Damn, I'm scared! All I know is that when I'm with you, I feel like I've come home for the first time in my life. Like I've come home for good. Will you at least give me a chance?"

Her face was softening, but he still couldn't tell what she was thinking. Never had he imagined it could be so difficult to tell a woman he loved her. This was worse than going solo into enemy territory. It was easier to face a firefight.

She spoke. "A chance for what?"

"A chance to prove I can be a good husband. A chance to...well...convince you to fall in love with me."

A tear sparkled on her eyelash, and he really panicked. She hated him. She never wanted to see him again. She was just trying to find a kind way to tell him to get lost.

But then she spoke. "I love you, too, Hugh."

For an instant her words didn't penetrate. When they did, he couldn't believe them. "You do?"

"I do. I love you so much I'm terrified by it. And when I'm with you I feel…safe. Safe for the first time in my life. Safe to be me, exactly as I am. I love you, too."

"So…" He stood up, nearly knocking the chair over in his eagerness. He came around the table, and when she rose, he wrapped her snugly in his arms. "So you'll marry me?"

"But what about your ranch? What if my background keeps you from having the youth ranch?"

"Sweetheart, the way I figure it, neither you nor I has anything to apologize for, and neither one of us is going to creep around any longer as if we do. To hell with the rest of the world. If I can't have a youth ranch, I'll find something else to do. But we're not hiding any longer. Will you marry me?"

"Yes. Yes! Oh, yes!"

He kissed her long and hard, and stopped only when they both needed breath. In two minutes, tops, he was going to have her in bed with him again, but first he had to deal with something very important. "What about Lorna? I guess I should ask her, too. If she doesn't want me as part of the family, maybe we'd better hold off until I can convince her."

Anna pointed to the telephone. "Call her right now—555-1545."

His mouth felt dry, and he realized he was really concerned about this. With a slightly unsteady finger he punched in the number, identified himself and asked to speak to Lorna. Moments later he heard her cheerful voice.

"Uh, Lorna? I just wanted to know how you feel about…well, I just asked Anna to marry me. Are you okay with that?"

A moment later he turned and handed the phone to Anna. "She wants to talk to you."

"Me? What did she say?"

He shrugged, feeling that sinking sensation come back. "All she said was she wants to talk to you."

Anna took the phone. A moment later she hung it up.

"Well?" Hugh demanded impatiently.

Anna smiled. "She said, 'Go for it.' She wants to call you Dad."

Epilogue

"Mommy! Mommy, Daddy's coming home!" Seven-year-old Mindy danced into the room, her blond pigtails flying. "I saw him on the hill!"

Anna put aside the skirt she was hemming for Lorna and went to the window to look out. From her second-story eyrie she could see the distant hill and the unmistakable mounted figures of Hugh and the six boys he had taken out with him for an overnight camping trip. "He sure is, sweetie. Where's Lorna?"

"Helping Miss Mildred with the birthday cake for Daddy."

Miss Mildred was the cook they had hired to help out with the meal preparations when Anna had become too pregnant to keep up her old pace. She looked down now at her rounded belly and smiled. Could life be any more perfect? she wondered.

Three years ago, shortly after she had been cleared as Lorna's permanent foster parent, the girls' mother had decided to give up Mindy, too. Apparently the constant visits of the child welfare authorities had been more than Bridget wanted to put up with. Mindy had been promptly placed in Hugh and Anna's care with her sister.

A little over two years ago they had received their first batch of troubled boys at the ranch. That program had gone so well that they were now receiving youths on a regular basis, and next Saturday they would be receiving their first group of girls. Along with the program's success had come a group of new employees to help with the care and supervision of all the children.

These days Anna wasn't able to contribute as much as she had in the past, but she was still keeping her fingers in the pie as much as possible. And she still loved living in the second-floor apartment, although when the baby arrived, they might start feeling a little crowded. Hugh was talking about building an addition.

But right now she had to go down to greet the returning group, the way a mother should. Because that was how she looked at all these children. They weren't temporary guests or transients in her life, but children she loved dearly. Hugh seemed to feel the same way, and when the kids eventually left, they kept in touch. Some of them even came back for holidays.

She passed the kitchen and called out a greeting to Mildred and Lorna, who looked as if they were having a wonderful time. She and Mindy reached the stable yard just about the same time the group of riders did.

"Hi, guys!" Anna called out. "Did you have a good trip?"

A chorus of happy yeses answered her, and soon she was awash in tales of wolves on Thunder Mountain, and coyotes, and how good the fish they had caught this morning had tasted for breakfast.

Hugh waited until all the boys had finished talking and had taken their mounts into the stable. Then he scooped up Mindy with one arm and hugged his wife with the other. "How are my favorite ladies doing?"

"Fine," Mindy answered for both of them. "We're making a surprise for you."

"Mindy, hush," Anna said gently. "You don't want to give it away."

Hugh grinned down at her. "It couldn't have anything to do with the date, could it?"

"Don't be difficult," Anna said. "Pretend you didn't guess. It's a surprise."

Lorna came out onto the porch and called a greeting to Hugh. "Mindy, come in here for a second, will you? I need you to do something for me."

Hugh set the little girl down and watched her tear across the yard and disappear into the house. And suddenly he and Anna were all alone, surrounded by the Wyoming summer afternoon.

"How's my sweetheart?" he asked softly.

"Just wonderful. How are you, darling?"

"Never been better. And never been happier to come home."

"It does feel good, doesn't it?" she asked, smiling up at him.

"Sweetheart, there's no better feeling in the world than when a cowboy comes home."

He bent to kiss her, and she lifted her arms to wrap them around his neck and hold him close. Inside her, a gentle, warm peace settled.

When Cowboy came home, she came home, too.

* * * * *

Available September 1998
from Silhouette Books...

World's Most
Eligible Bachelors

THE CATCH
OF CONARD COUNTY
by Rachel Lee

Rancher Jeff Cumberland: long, lean, sexy as sin. He's eluded every marriage-minded female in the county. Until a mysterious woman breezes into town and brings her fierce passion to his bed. Will this steamy Conard County courtship take September's hottest bachelor off of the singles market?

Each month, Silhouette Books brings you an irresistible bachelor in these all-new, original stories. Find out how the sexiest, most sought-after men are finally caught...

Available at your favorite retail outlet.

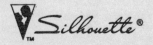

Silhouette® ™

Look us up on-line at: http://www.romance.net PSWMEB1

Take 2 bestselling love stories FREE

Plus get a FREE surprise gift!

Special Limited-Time Offer

Mail to Silhouette Reader Service™

3010 Walden Avenue
P.O. Box 1867
Buffalo, N.Y. 14240-1867

YES! Please send me 2 free Silhouette Intimate Moments® novels and my free surprise gift. Then send me 6 brand-new novels every month, which I will receive months before they appear in bookstores. Bill me at the low price of $3.57 each plus 25¢ delivery and applicable sales tax, if any.* That's the complete price, and a saving of over 10% off the cover prices—quite a bargain! I understand that accepting the books and gift places me under no obligation ever to buy any books. I can always return a shipment and cancel at any time. Even if I never buy another book from Silhouette, the 2 free books and the surprise gift are mine to keep forever.

245 SEN CH7Y

Name (PLEASE PRINT)

Address Apt. No.

City State Zip

This offer is limited to one order per household and not valid to present Silhouette Intimate Moments® subscribers. *Terms and prices are subject to change without notice. Sales tax applicable in N.Y.

UIM-98 ©1990 Harlequin Enterprises Limited

SILHOUETTE·INTIMATE·MOMENTS®

TRINITY STREET WEST

**where danger lies around every corner—
and the biggest danger of all
is falling in love.**

Meet the men and women of Trinity Street West
in this exciting miniseries by award-winner

Justine Davis

continuing in August 1998 with

BADGE OF HONOR

(Intimate Moments #871)

Working with Sergeant Kit Walker to expose a dirty cop had Miguel de los Reyes's all-business mind wandering in rather…passionate directions. But he was the chief of police. Falling for a subordinate—no matter how sexy she might be—was out of the question. Not only could it jeopardize the case, but it just might break his hardened heart.

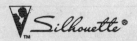

Silhouette®

Available at your favorite retail outlet.

Look us up on-line at: http://www.romance.net SIMTSWEST